TOM BENN's first novel, *The Doll Princess*, was shortlisted for the Dylan Thomas Prize and the Portico Prize, and longlisted for the CWA's John Creasey Dagger. Benn's creative non-fiction has appeared in the *Paris Review*, and he won the BFI's iWrite scheme for emerging screenwriters. His first film, *Real Gods Require Blood*, premiered in competition at the Cannes Film Festival and was nominated for Best Short Film at the BFI London Film Festival. Originally from Stockport, he teaches on the UEA Crime Fiction Creative Writing MA and lives in Norwich.

@Tom_Benn

OXBLOOD

or

Our Ladies of
the Good Death

TOM BENN

BLOOMSBURY PUBLISHING
LONDON · OXFORD · NEW YORK · NEW DELHI · SYDNEY

BLOOMSBURY PUBLISHING
Bloomsbury Publishing Plc
50 Bedford Square, London, WC1B 3DP, UK
29 Earlsfort Terrace, Dublin 2, Ireland

BLOOMSBURY, BLOOMSBURY PUBLISHING and the Diana logo are
trademarks of Bloomsbury Publishing Plc

First published in Great Britain 2022
This edition published 2023

A catalogue record for this book is available from the British Library

ISBN: PB: 978-1-5266-3951-6; EBOOK: 978-1-5266-3949-3;
EPDF: 978-1-5266-5136-5

2 4 6 8 10 9 7 5 3 1

Typeset by Integra Software Services Pvt. Ltd.
Printed and bound in Great Britain by CPI Group (UK) Ltd, Croydon CR0 4YY

To find out more about our authors and books visit www.bloomsbury.com
and sign up for our newsletters

AUTHOR'S NOTE

Oxblood takes place in a Manchester, England, of the 1960s, 1970s and 1980s. I have tried not to engage in the moralising or the sanitising of this history. I wished to grant fictional and forgotten lives freedom to speak wrong, think wrong, act wrong, love wrong and live true. I hoped to resist the softening, denying or excusing of once-pervasive casual bigotries that make a normative present feel better about its past self. Who benefits most from the erasure of language or attitudes in these historical contexts? Who is most comforted, most absolved, by their dishonest omissions? *Oxblood* may be set in the past, but it is not purely about the past. It was written in and for the present, by a Mancunian mongrel whose white father and black mother remind him that this is not ancient but living history. It is how we got here. It is why we are still here. It can show us how we might get somewhere else, as long as we are honest about it, and refuse to forget. But that's enough historical moralising and sanitising from me.

I'm bad and I'm going to hell, and I don't care. I'd rather be in hell than anywhere where you are.

Miss Quentin in The Sound and the Fury

(For graves have learned that woman-head,
To be to more than one a bed)

John Donne, 'The Relic'

An' de old woman gib her a ball of cotton, an' tell her to t'row it back of her, but not to look back, whatever she hear.

Pamela Colman Smith, Annancy Stories

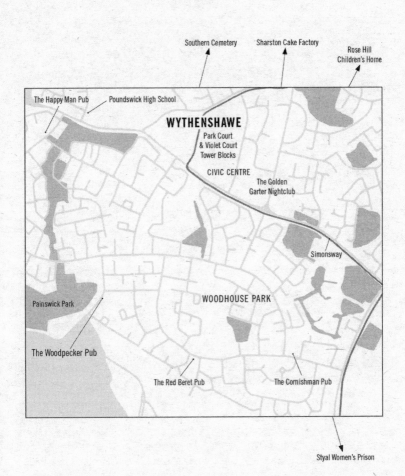

Southern Cemetery

Sharston Cake Factory

Rose Hill
Children's Home

The Happy Man Pub

Poundswick High School

WYTHENSHAWE

Park Court
& Violet Court
Tower Blocks

CIVIC CENTRE

The Golden
Garter Nightclub

Simonsway

Painswick Park

WOODHOUSE PARK

The Woodpecker Pub

The Red Beret Pub

The Cornishman Pub

Styal Women's Prison

The old woman: Oh, Mother. . .
The young nurse: Is she here?
The old woman: No, love. She's long gone. But I need her.

BUT THAT SPRING SHE was fourteen and would do anything. She would take off her knickers and gift them to him there if he asked her. She slipped out of the now to imagine this and her smile went, her whole face slack as he talked at her muted. His talk blew cool and stale. It rushed up her neck and reached her nose. The smell of menthol cigs brought back her hearing. He was laughing so she laughed along. This was upstairs towards the back of the bus that leaned out of town on a blood-hot Sunday in March of '84, at teatime, quarter full, a weird red sky at Jan's window, clouds like babies' fingers. Below, as the bus wound her home, were cars and streets and shuttered shops and pavements of lugging, stooping, strutting funny-peculiar people – things that meant summat to Jan, but she wasn't sure what, even though she was mithered enough to recognise when she felt it. Yet whenever she turned to see town from a bus window her gaze would drift up. She chased between buildings, checked if the sky had a colour.

And then he'd got on alone two stops after them and she had looked out at town and looked up and down and seen nowt and looked harder when he sat opposite her, and then in front, making her feel all things at once since he was black and beautiful, since he turned and spoke to her. He was old: seventeenish. He lived in Longsight so was getting off again soon.

Ten stops about. Jan counted them.

She watched him talk and shook her head. She answered back, sweating. Her eyes wouldn't roll at his teases – of the ones she heard she'd heard before – and were tearing up. His features went runny. Her feet kicked for him whenever she made him laugh. White thighs glued to the prickly fur of the bus seat; her left hip jabbed Alice's right. Tiny Alice, trying hard: kohled, earringed, sitting bolt straight next to her, for once not drowsy but shy and wary, even with head hair as short as the bus seats'. He ignored Alice, for now, whose chest was bigger but disguised thank fuck by a stripy lad's shirt lifted from a box of swag outside a shut Oxfam, two Sundays gone. Jan's red Benetton pinched from the same box. It was clinging to her front now with sweat and tugging. Her white shorts were once Alice's. They'd finished long on Alice's legs – legs now bruised into the aisle by Jan's. In Alice's mouldy bedroom Jan had made her cut the white shorts. Although Alice's mam was unshockable and a decent seamstress she'd been out for the night and Jan had mithered till Alice cut them herself. She cut them so fast and high she snipped the pockets and wouldn't wear them again. But they fitted Jan just right.

Stop three:

By now Jan could only breathe short. The bus hissed and voices ran upstairs. He looked round at who'd got on and she re-posed and pulled her Benetton tight to offer herself as he faced back.

'D'yever go Caribbean Club?' he said.

'Yeah. Course.'

'Fridays are dead good. Have I seen yous there?'

'Might have.' She split her white thighs and put her hands in the hot space. Then she straightened her arms, shifting most of her weight and rocked forward. He was already leaning over his seat and his menthol cig-smell rushed her again. She tasted it. She wanted to lick the day's grease from his face. The bus bounced past Ardwick Green, accelerated in fits; she toppled back into her seat; he finished whatever he was saying and watched her, watching how things settled.

In this Jan showed him that these pale Wythenshawe girls had bloomed early, and that this was accidental only in Alice, who was still indifferent to her own power and not quite afraid of it or able to direct it, which neutered her to some lads, Jan had noticed, and for others doubled Alice's power over her own. So Jan grinned at him still and grinned in pain.

'How old a'you two, then?'

Alice looked at Jan. Jan refused to look at Alice.

'Have a guess,' Jan said.

'. . .Seventeen?'

Her ribs swelled apart with pleasure. Things inside her unhitched. Jan breathed just fine.

Jan could have him.

Jan would have him.

Stop two:

'This is me next. You and all.'

She drummed his seat with more kicks.

'. . .Jan?' Alice whispered close.

What?

'How you gunna get back? When your mam rings us, what am I saying?'

But the bus hissed and he stood and she stood and she knocked past Alice's bruised legs, grinning back: 'See yous tomorrow then, yeah? Ta-ra.'

CAROL DODDS SHUT HER front door finally and thought about all her dead men. This was as square Nedra Dodds, her maminlaw, waddled out to the gate in chocolate suede hat and ginger anorak to fetch her grandson – Carol's eldest at twenty-two – from Strangeways.

The dead Dodds men –

Carol endured.

(Living dead, she was.)

But her lovely gentle daft bow-legged Vern. Soft-skinned Vern. His hands like daughters' hands. Vern Jenkins, who had predeceased the Dodds men having been murdered by them and buried by them, and yet still visited her house regularly of a night. Vern dead –

had defeated Carol.

This was May Day morning '85, midweek, in Woodhouse Park, Wythie, a beautiful black baby upstairs, undeclared, quiet as a secret, dreaming in her son's vacant room, having stolen it early because he couldn't wait till December so came two month too soon and lived.

Meanwhile, Carol's lad, freed today from his first stretch and finally a Dodds man. Right from being born he was sweet, soft; he'd resisted them, his late fathers living through him, but for only long enough to learn there was no good to be done or honest work to be had or prospect to be lost, round here or in town. A proud rum bugger now. Of luckless blood and lazy charm. Another Dodds man now with the Devil in him as planned.

And soon to discover he was roomless, an uncle.

5

But Nedra wasn't gone yet. Through the warped diamond Carol watched her without watching. Then Carol went into the front room and got a better look before her maminlaw vanished behind five-foot privets and made for Civic Centre to bus it into town for the first time in a year. Nedra's cooking was wrapped and dished on the kitchen and coffee tables and cooling on counters. More scran in the fridge. She'd been baking since ten to six. Carol had lain awake listening to stuff happen underneath her: the kitchen drawer squeaks and the tearing of Cook's matches and the whisk rattle.

Carol endured. Ever since her maminlaw moved in her front door stayed open, chain off. The kettle whistled on the stove more often than that black baby cried. Nedra ignored those rare cries but kept welcoming the local kiddies she minded for next-to-nowt and those she didn't who wanted fussing over as well and so invited themselves. Noisy buggers; always running. Dancing hair flashing past Carol at waist height to see Nedra in the kitchen. No quiet. No stillness. Not like now. Behind the sittingroom window with the baby upstairs so quiet he might be forgotten and the house so quiet it was another house again and still not hers. Its walls leaned in, waiting. Dead Dodds men hung, framed, waiting.

Next door's two had been round earlier: the littlest lad on their street, who was always in and out, who was never still and in motion looked like a prancing marionette; he even had Joe 90's white-blond hair and horn-rimmed specs. And an older brother big enough to blow and tie balloons. Nedra hadn't shown Carol the balloons before today and hadn't asked for any help. Carol had been shunned in the kitchen earlier. The brothers there before school; Nedra recruited them with the promise of hot butties. Carol kneeling on the speckled green lino, arse up, head in the bottom cupboard, after the last pot to heat some powdered milk. When a balloon popped, she cracked her head on the rotted shelf.

Nedra clapped once from fright, then laughed.

Joe 90 burst into tears.

Carol reeled out the cupboard but stayed knelt on the lino. She plucked splintered shelf wood out of her bunned hair while she breathed behind her teeth, swallowing the pain. She just glared, creating a bubble of silence till –

the small lad, fretting round the kitchen, resumed wailing. He ducked Nedra as she tried giving him another tied balloon.

Nedra had his brother do three more then gave him Carol's seat at the kitchen table and a drink of water and a hot ginger biscuit. She'd already given one to Joe 90, which stopped his tears. He chewed it slowly, still prancing round the table.

'Making me dizzy this morning, you. Can't be having no fall at my age. I'm already a cracked plate.' Nedra scraped a chair and sat beside the elder lad, finding her rosary in her apron pocket. Then squinted low: 'What you still doing on that floor? You want bloody sweeping up.' The small lad crossed their vision, lapping between them. Nedra's eyes broke from Carol's to give chase. 'Now, now. Pack it in. What've I said?'

The next time he passed behind his chair his brother grabbed him, catching his twiggy wrist. He shook him, not hard, but again the lad cried. It reminded Carol of her son at that age.

Nedra got rid of them early so they wouldn't touch any more party scran while she busied about under the endless stare of her saints and dead men.

Now the house held its breath, ready with a Welcome Home spread; the months of powdered-milk smell crusting all drapes, carpets, cushions, snuffed out – at least downstairs – the witch's promise of all things sweet offered up instead. Carol's front room was full of wait-ing even if Carol didn't feel full or empty and wasn't really waiting for her son or another Dodds man. She stood at the window and warmed her shins on the radiator through her cosmic-print leggings. The glass was clean. The netting was clean. For a while Carol watched the street. She heard Nedra's walking stick tock the pavement. Nedra didn't need a stick. Nedra only took it to town. Maybe to school or church some days in bad winters when the capillary streets she knew as hers became as foreign and sequestered as frozen blood. But the poor cow didn't realise she and Carol were the ones cut-off, hoar-frosted, long lost. Nedra was forever busied with the grand nothing of everything. Religion, roots and blood.

But Carol felt buried now that the world was turning faster and faster yet she saw none of it herself any more and only sensed life happening in other places and its happening reaping her no reward except adding to the soilweight on top of her, increasing the depth and comfort of her own burial, so she felt bitter and safe in that the world would hide her without her asking to be hidden, and would forget her before she knew she was forgotten and realised that things were always rigged for her to be forgotten. She could only blame the Dodds men for so much. What they'd done so had she. Poor Vern. Realising this, way before she became a widow in her house of two and a half widows, she had decided the fight had left her. She was glad to be lost. She wasn't waiting to be found, only for Vern to visit, to nightly manifest. Not even death could stop Vern from bedding her.

So Carol turned from her window but left her shadow there on the netting *without her*, out of time, since Carol could resist the second the minute the hour the day the week the month the year the clock the heartbeat. In time, Kelly, her only son, would be home. This was her life. Her house. Her dead men. Her shadow unstitched, left there like dirt on her clean netting as she brewed up and went back to bed, wondering when the last living Dodds man would die.

NEDRA DODDS GOT OFF the bus nearly dinnertime, with her grandson Kelly and his half-caste slut from Hulme.

They walked through Violet Court with its battered cars and battered concrete, across what she once knew as Top Fields. She tutted and smirked at the skivers: their school uniforms sketched, incomplete and outgrown before time. Young girls with their lads – sat on bonnets and bollards, sat on each other, scoffing chippy chips, calling after her *Missus Dodds, iya!* And with her stick she pointed out her grandson for them but the coloured girl, gabbing, walked him ahead.

The day was bright and dry. The streets quiet. The houses quiet. The trees very green and quiet. She followed a cheap sharp scent: the girl keeping him a few paces in front. Wrapped round his elbow she was, her cheek glued to his jacket shoulder, dragging him up Ruddpark Road. She bloody knew the way. Queer that both grandkids would chase after coloureds from town. Which was summat Kelly had still to discover: his little sister having conceived and concealed, carried and delivered, kept – only to deny – her bastard baby, all while he was put away. Only their Jan could be that devious, that daft. By the mercy of Mother Mary, Nedra and Carol had managed to keep the news from him, even with local men doing time in that place alongside Kelly. They had left the reckoning for today.

Kelly had brought this girl home before, but only the once, last year, and Nedra couldn't remember if she'd fed her or just seen her

9

through the window, leaving in the morning, or if she'd sat with her in court or if that had been another pretty half-caste girl – because pretty girls went mad for her grandson and her grandson was mad on pretty girls. But this one hadn't rung the house or shown her face after he got sent down for ten month. Had she visited him? Nedra wouldn't ask. She was tall and bone-thin and nice enough, even with the cheek scar, which showed now in the noon sun when she glanced back to grin at her, brazen, still gabbing to Kelly – the scar that Nedra had maybe not seen before today, and so had at first made her think the girl *was* new to her, even after the girl had recognised her, and spoken to her, thinking she'd been recognised too. Nedra had arrived early at Strangeways to find her already waiting. That smile: like it was *her*, not Kelly, she'd been waiting to set free.

At Ringway shops Kelly and this girl turned a corner, not waiting. Nedra followed, not gaining.

The girl glanced back again, smiling again –

the line and patterned seat of her underpants showing through a thin orange frock, her dark legs indiscreet. Not that it was warm enough. Cold sun paled the frock and the mucky pavements and the housebricks and greened the leaves and privets. When the girl offered Kelly a cig they stopped to face each other and Nedra raised her stick and caught up while the girl lit up with his lighter, which had been his dad's *dad's* lighter, her Jim's lighter. . . salvaged from the smashed glovebox of his upended Triumph.

From nowhere little Joey Harvey's white staffie, Snowy, swaggered over to greet them. This albino crocodile. Collarless and intact. It stood panting like an idling mower.

'Who's gone and let you out?' the girl said, looking up the street for the owner.

'You asking *him* or *me*?' Kelly said.

That smile again got offered her, then Kelly.

'Fuck me,' he said. 'That's not little Joey's pup?'

'Is,' Nedra said. 'Aye, that's little Joey's dog.'

'And he's kept hold of his knackers.'

'Good luck getting your post round here,' his girl said.

Snowy's coat shone like a burn.

'Thinks he's a cat, this one,' Nedra said. 'Walks his self. Lets his self out. Oh aye.'

'Looks like he'd *eat* my cat.' The girl returned the lighter to Kelly's pocket but left her hand there.

'Snowy likes having a wander through the week while Joey's at school and Linda's working. He's no mither. A'yeh? Always finds his way home.' The girl looked from the dog to her. 'Won't bite you.' The girl bent from the waist. Snowy grinned up, shaded by her; his damp nose followed her reaching hand. Kelly nudged her – last second – toppling her forward, exposing the red stitch of her underpants. Snowy danced to avoid being stepped on. The girl shrieked and Kelly caught her.

'Cheers, Kell. Tryna feed me to wild animals.' She swatted him, clinging to his jacket sleeve, before pressing her ear to the meat of his shoulder.

Snowy began to follow them but lost interest and crossed the road, slanted. A gold Granada from Fellside Road (Nedra had yet to work out whose, having seen plenty driving it) braked; the dog grinned it gone.

Kelly freed his arm to smoke, his eyes and ears elsewhere till she muttered to him and he answered quietly, and her smile came back full; they spoke only to each other.

'What did you say your name was, love?' Nedra gripped her grandson's other elbow to talk across him.

'Nana,' he said.

'That's *my* name,' she said. 'Am asking hers.'

'It's Zuley. Remember?'

'Not *Julie*?'

'Kin 'ell, Nana. Leave her bloody be.'

'Odd name that.'

'Yours is too. Dead nice, though,' the girl said.

'What, "Missus Dodds"? Is a nice name, that. Dodds is a name what means summat round here and always has and will.'

Kelly sighed. 'So, what about that lot? Time they coming?'

The girl pinched the cig from his gob, talking smoke. 'Dunno. They've all got work.'

'Who has?'

'All the naughty heads. Proper jobbing lads now.'

'Working? What work? There's fuck-all work.'

'I've had to take day off, me. *Unpaid*, mind. Kelly Dodds, you might think you're God's gift but you're an expensive habit.'

'Y'hear that, Nana?'

'Takes after his dad. Handsome and trouble.'

His eyes held her for the first time that morning, held her for the first time in ten month. Her grandson: an hour freed, under Wythenshawe sun, proud and charmed and a bugger, as his fathers were. But the differences frightened her when she saw them. There were things in Kelly's stare she didn't recognise; and it wasn't youth. Youth, Nedra dealt in. However old she got there would always be the young to feed to wash to clothe to pray for and to put right. She knew what sins they committed as they mixed and strayed. With duty, with love, she grandmothered half the estate. But her Kelly was technically the last living Dodds man and so it was she who shied from her grandson's eye, sensing in it for her a faint pitying warmth instead of his fathers' scalding blood.

'Where's it you work then, love?' Nedra asked the girl, breathless, almost shouting. 'Town?' And the girl said, then said whereabouts, but the words meant nowt to Nedra, who trotted now, not to fall behind.

'We've missed him like mad.' The girl, twisting: 'Haven't we?'

'What's she called again, this one, love?'

'Stop mithering, Nana.'

'Zuley.' The smile answered.

'Funny name.'

'*Un*forgettable,' Kelly went.

The girl giggled. Nedra had heard that before, and not behind walls coupled with bedsprings at daft-o'clock in the morning. *This* girl, this one, *had* sat at their table late one evening early last year when Carol still jobbed all hours at the Kipling cake factory, and Jan was off out, in a rush to ruin herself ten minutes after *Top of the Pops*. He keyed the front door but didn't shout and just brought her through by the hand and into the kitchen and she sat there. Black and pretty. Dressed for dancing. Smelling like left-out fruit salad. And Nedra fed her from the chip pan. But the girl barely touched her plate. And when Nedra asked if she were poorly it went ignored since Kelly was there to tease them both, these women his. And the girl had giggled loud in her kitchen, as she did now, showing off. Nedra still didn't remember the scar.

'Who give you that, love?'

'What, *this*?' Touching her cheek.

'Nana. Don't be nosy.'

'Well it wasn't your Kell, so don't worry,' the girl said.

Perfume tickled her nostrils. Nedra tucked two chins inside her scarf.

Kelly blew smoke at the girl to devil her, then flicked the cig at a drain and for a bit they leaned together, quiet.

Gulls drifted overhead, talking about them.

'Can see you two getting ideas already,' Nedra said. 'Do you no good. Especially you, laddie' – her short shadow, shortened at dinner-time, jostling theirs on the pavement.

They turned onto their street: weed-choked plots, ashy doorsteps behind cracked gates and lush wonky privets.

Snowy was waiting at the bottom of the road, funhouse-doubled in an open car door – number thirty-three's kerbed Cortina. He stood grinning them.

The girl passed their gate and kept on, towards little Joey's dog. 'How'd *he* get there first?'

With her stick, Nedra unstuck the gate and let her grandson go in. Another clot of pride sat in her veins, with her faith, her cooking, the kids.

They entered the house as Carol came barefoot down the stairs. Her daughterinlaw had slapped on a bit of tutty but hadn't changed. Filthy leggings, a bloke's shirt (Oxfam; not one of Sefton's) stained and gone at the collar and missing buttons so not even fit for house-work and her figure beneath it going too. Even with makeup she looked chalky and sour. Their Sefton, God rest his soul, not missing much. Carol greeted his and her son wordlessly, held him a moment and kissed him quick on the mouth. His eyes on hers; they were hers;

their eyes were tin. She left her lippy on him. He spoke but Carol saw the coloured girl step in behind her.

'Iya,' Carol said. 'So, you've put up with all this, have you?' To Kelly: 'Lucky lad.'

'Dead right,' said the girl, chaining the front door without need.

Nedra peered at the ceiling and listened. Then shed her scarf, hat, anorak, expanding without them, not shrinking. She hung them in the hall, then propped her stick in the corner by the doorjamb after poking the girl's bare calf. The girl hopped aside, said *Oh sorry*. But Nedra never looked up, just unchained the door and went for the kitchen, half-humming, half-singing, in a cheery waver, passing between Kelly and Carol, bringing Kelly's face down to hers with both palms for another kiss. Her gold necklaces – heavy and dull – clashed on her chest.

Her Kelly home. A Dodds man.

She tied her apron in the kitchen doorway while they stayed in the hall. The girl's laugh, Carol's barbed voice, answered and included:

'Don't tell us this one come and met you at the gate?'

'Aye, she did, Mam. Got there before me nana.'

'She must have no mirrors in her house. Or else she's bloody mad.'

'I know,' the girl said.

'To know is worse,' Carol said.

'Mam, how come you sent Nana to meet us?'

'I never sent anybody anywhere.'

'Why'd you stay home?'

'I had other arses to wipe. How long you stopping with us?'

Kelly gave his mam's head a kiss, gave the kiss a sound.

The kitchen was flooded with sun. Nedra stood at the window. The sky was fixed. She twisted the handle shut to kill the draught and saw a row of brown tiny birds lipped across the garage roof. She watched them do nothing, her eyes watering. Again she tightened the apron, frontways, tying the bow so the string lanced her diaphragm until she felt twisted and separated like a balloon animal and it made summat else inside her that was in the vicinity of this pain rise into her chest, into her throat until she felt she could choke it up. Whatever it was. As she hum-sang at the kitchen window, with the birds. Aproned

14

and relieved. Her Kelly home. She: a big-boned fatnecked Catholic pear of a woman, who drank a swallow of straight vinegar before bed and did so from being a child and only denied herself once she was widowed. Nedra the widow, Jim Dodds' widow, she who shared her widowed daughterinlaw's house and widows' bed, which she and Jim had given as a wedding gift: *a tidy bedroom suite for the newlyweds of '62, Sefton and Carol Dodds. Bless, Jim. And don't you go forgetting the kindness of his soul. I'll hear not a bad word said of our Jim.* And for nine springs now Nedra had shared that death-scented bed on which her son had wifed and lain for fourteen years only to rise from it one morning and never return to its pillow. For nine springs she had cooked aproned in Carol's kitchen, wearing a tangle of necklaces that were older than Wythenshawe estate and rattled through the house, saying more than her whereabouts. Even now she could be alone and busy in the kitchen or minding the street's kids, keeping next door's Joey Harvey and the rest occupied, and suddenly think: my husband and my son are dead.

How can this be?

How can I be here now, alive now, with our Jim and our Sefton dead?

Funny that.

The brown birds dominoed off the garage roof. Tiny. Wingless. They rose, skimmed over next door's fence.

Kelly entered the kitchen, the girl's hand in his, Carol last.

'You two didn't cook all this?' the girl said.

'One of us did,' Carol went.

'Oh, it's nowt.' Nedra pointed at more savouries and sweet dishes on the counter. She opened the fridge to show him what else she'd made him. Only the girl peered in.

'Ee-ah.' Nedra broke off a lump and gave it to Kelly. 'Watch your fillings. We'll all have no teeth, won't we?'

'There's so much of everything,' the girl said.

'Well. It were in case you wanted a do,' she said.

For a long second Carol eyed her, expressionless.

Nedra tried lifting yesterday's stew from the counter back onto the stove and the girl came forward again and helped with the heavy pot, then took it from her entirely, spinning with it first saying: 'You've got it made here, Kell. Should see him round mine. I might tell him where the grill pan is if he's good.'

They watched his girl against the sink and sunlight in her thin orange frock and red knickers, sucking stew from her fingers before the kettle whistled.

When the girl crossed the lino and backed into his arms, Carol asked quiet things that Nedra couldn't catch, the two of them whispering almost and Kelly sometimes listening. Nedra hummed at the ceiling and heated the stew. She spoke to the wall clock: 'Me kids, they'll soon be in to see me grandson.'

Kelly bobbed and weaved as the girl thumbed lippy stains from his face.

'Am getting it off,' the girl said.

'This isn't getting me off,' he said.

Nedra scoffed: 'Talking like that. You're not at the bloody Embassy Club.'

'You tell him,' the girl said.

'Mam,' he said.

'What?' Carol said.

'Where's our kid?'

Nedra stirred the teas. 'That one never comes home for her dinner. And if our Jan's not in school, and I say she's not, cos she hardly goes, then she should be here to see her brother back.' She felt her daughterinlaw walk behind her, the length of the kitchen, her crusty shirt not scratching, her naked feet not even patting the lino before she sat.

'Our Jan goes to school,' Carol said to the clock, not raising the temperature of her voice. She could talk like she was being steadily throttled by a hardworking pair of hands, the clock's hands, a Dodds man's hands, hands for which she'd begged, or dared, if only to test their grip.

Nedra checked on the stew. '. . .Ee-ah, you lot.'

Kelly sat diagonal from his mam, in his old place, his back to Nedra, the cooker, the window. The sun in his hair. Nedra put a brew in front of him and stood there and squeezed his shoulder. He didn't turn. She felt the thing inside her that was and wasn't pain and was awed. Quickly she took her hand away. She passed the girl another brew.

'Ta.' The girl sat in Nedra's seat.

Nedra slurped hers standing at the stove. There was only Carol without.

She saw Kelly and his girl conduct a whole conversation across the table with looks. She saw just the girl's half. As good as heard her and what she heard was depraved.

Then Carol scraped her chair and rinsed the cobwebs from a cup out the cupboard. There wasn't enough in the pot for one more; Carol relit the stove.

'Now what?' Kelly said. He drank his tea too hot like always.

The girl blew hers watching him.

Nedra dished up the stew and gave him the first bowl.

'Can I help?' the girl said.

'Aye. Keep still.'

Nedra brought Carol's and the girl's to the table.

He hadn't started. 'Where the ashtrays, Mam?'

Carol checked the ceiling with her, stood with her, by the stove, fiddling with the gas ring.

'You're *eating*, aren't you?' Carol said.

Nedra chimed: 'You know when our Kelly was a babba he would cry to be fed and then he would cry once he'd had the lot. We all thought he'd be a fat little thing. Look at him. There's no fat on him.'

The girl continued the laugh she'd begun in the kitchen late evening last year.

'Nana.'

'Tis it, love?'

'Guess.'

'Eat, you.'

He took up his spoon.

The front door went.

Joey Harvey came through, and not running. Behind him were Kevin and Roger Burton and Susie-Ann Stone. Susie-Ann was tall and serious for almost twelve. Joey not seven till November and of course little. Kevin eight now and Roger ten. Kevin and Roger chased black cats and brought her tadpoles and singing frogs, and now in the lengthening spring days after school, they dripped Painswick pond through the house. But Joey was a delicate bird, sickly-pale all year round; he normally hopped and hovered everywhere, even when eating or after punishment. Nedra wondered how he managed at school to sit still or sit at all. But now he crept over in his little uniform, the Milky Bar Kid, moving towards Kelly, and not everywhere at once. Like the others, he hadn't yet noticed her cooking or the coloured girl in her kitchen chair.

'Alright, mate,' Kelly said.

'Who's that?' Nedra said.

'It's your Kelly,' Joey Harvey said.

'You at Poundswick yet, mate?' Kelly said.

'No.'

'Why's that?'

'Am six.'

'Ay, we met your Snowy out there knocking about solo. He tried taking our Zuley's arm.'

'Take no notice of him.' The girl gave Joey the smile. 'Your dog behaved himself. It's Kell you've gotta watch.' Her chair was turned out and she held her kneecaps.

'He's never bit nobody. Not never.' Joey Harvey turned to her to say this but his eyes got no higher than her knees before he turned back to Kelly and he was standing dead stiff but Nedra could see the effort this took growing, the need to be moving growing, the more he remembered Kelly; as the strangeness of expectation wore off, the more himself he became.

'So, what you been feeding that dog?' Kelly said.

The boy hopping now: 'Allsorts.'

'Bet you have. He's been having your hot dinners and that's why he's grown so much.'

'Have *I* grown?'

Kelly tossed Joey straight up and checked the clock with the squealing lad midair, catching him before his plimsolls met the lino.

'You've shrunk. What you reckon, Susie-Ann?'

Susie-Ann blushed.

Joey squealed till he was released.

Before Nedra lost the chance she pinched the filthy crooked specs off his face and wiped them on her apron and replaced them neat. 'That better?'

Joey Harvey saw her treats everywhere.

'Butties first,' she said.

'*Butties*.' All Joey Harvey would eat were butties. Breakfast, dinner and tea. And only without spread. He could not eat sitting, at least in this house or his own, but never complained of bellyache so she'd quit trying to keep him in a chair, though long after Linda, his own mam, had given up. Each Friday morning Joey Harvey had a twisted-damp tenner for Nedra, which paid for his week's minding and his butties, though she'd told Linda she'd gladly do it for nowt. This also covered walking him from the schoolgates to the house whenever his older brother couldn't or wouldn't. Little Joey would join the gaggle of lads and girls whom Nedra was scheduled to meet and herd, feed and mind, and usually some left-behinds as well, needing haircuts, hot dinners and mothering, who belonged to troubled souls: the ones who skipped Mass for months and only slipped in the odd Sunday, wearing tall noisy shoes and trowels of tutty, because their husbands had blown another wage packet at Belle Vue. Nedra never turned her head when those sorts came in. She only looked when Father Culler comforted them, arranging house calls, while Nedra stayed after Mass to knuckle her rosaries, bent before the tabernacle, mouthing to Our Lady to watch out for these women who were wicked enough to stain Father Culler's vestment with mascara or even raid the cruet for Communion wine. Little Joey Harvey wasn't son to one of those women. Not that Linda didn't have husband troubles. Pray, how that woman had suffered. But her Joey had learned to stop crying before church and even to sit if not still in their second-row pew for Mass, rocking like his backside was burning for his sins when Father Culler rained holy water on the congregation.

Carol slurped her brew before asking him: 'Your name really Joe?'

He searched for her at the sink, squinting with the glare on his specs. 'Joseph Harvey,' he said. 'Two ninety-two, Fellside Road, Wythenshawe, Great Britain. Roman Catholic.'

Carol gave a frosty chuckle and went out.

Kelly put down his spoon. 'The lad's born next door and's been in every day. How's me mam not know his name?'

'She's no interest, love. None whatsoever.' Nedra unwrapped the butties she'd made this morning and gave them out. Kevin and Roger took theirs in the front room now they'd seen him. She said she'd fetch them summat to drink. But Joey stayed at Kelly's side and watched him thoughtfully while they ate.

Nedra gestured and Susie-Ann took Carol's place and untouched spoon and when Kelly's girl said *Iya* Susie-Ann blushed again.

'Blow on it,' Nedra told her. 'Or you'll burn your gob.'

The coloured girl smirked.

Nedra went: 'You know, Susie-Ann, this young lady lives in town. Remind me, love, whereabouts?'

'Near Princess Parkway.'

The girls twinkled, allies.

Susie-Ann said: 'Me cousin Charlotte lives round there with her new boyfriend but me mam says I can't never go visit.'

Nedra brought Susie-Ann her apple juice and stroked her long sand-white hair while she ate, having braided it like a palm branch for her yesterday before school. 'Your mam's right, love. I knew of a nice young girl who wouldn't take no notice of her mam and went in one of them scruffy cafes under Princess Parkway. See she liked the pretty lights and wanted to listen to the records and play on them games machines, and well: all it took was one prick of a needle in your arm, like that, and – *fffsssp* – that's it.'

'That's *what*?' Kelly's girl said.

'I'll tell you *what*. After that you wake up in one of them shebeens because you've fetched a good price and then you're sold and shipped abroad. And it's too late then for prayer because even the Blessed Virgin can't hear you in them places. Now think of that poor nice girl, love, and be sure to light a candle for her Sunday. But for now, you best eat up, otherwise you'll be late for your afternoon lessons, and you don't want that again, do you, love?'

Kelly's spoon, scraping his bowl: 'Oi, Joey. *You* seen our kid?'

'I seen her. With Alice Willows.'

'That girl never comes home for her dinner,' Nedra said. 'I don't know what she lives on.'

'Ay, has she been looking after you, mate?' Kelly said.

Joey swayed, chewing on his butty.

'No? I'll give it her when I see her.'

'Did they have telly in there?' Joey said.

'Where? No. No telly. No nothing.'

'Did you see me dad?'

'Oh, aye. He said to us I've to tell you to behave for your mam. He said the better behaved you are the sooner he'll be back. But you've gotta eat more first. Otherwise, you'll keep getting smaller and smaller. . .'

'Kell,' the girl said.

'Love, fetch the balloons,' Nedra said.

Joey lingered, cheeky.

'Go on.'

He ran into the front room.

Carol made her feet heard in the back bedroom, above. Kelly's old room.

'We babysitting?' Kelly said, when it finally wailed.

She saw Kelly's girl hug the wall while the kids raced out, batting balloons, their gobs stuffed with baked scran.

'Back to school,' Nedra shouted. 'Go on.'

The girl's eyeballs rolled around the emptying front room quick. Nedra straightened the painting she'd nudged letting the kids past. Her grandson was still in the kitchen, entertaining Joey and Susie-Ann. His girl had detoured on her way back from the toilet. From the mouth of the kitchen Nedra had seen her heading for the front room and followed.

'Me husband Jim got us this,' she told her.

The girl glanced.

'He took us to the Midland for a do one night – oh, years ago, when we was first married. He saw this there and asked us if I liked it and I said it was quite nice, you know? Quite nice. So he goes right up and takes it off the wall. This great big bloody picture. Went and carted it home. See, that was our Jim. Of course, he'd made them all think he had a gun in his pocket.' *Gun* got mouthed instead of said. 'Well, you see, with a Dodds man, you never know. . .'

'God.' Now the girl watched the painting like she expected it to pounce off the wall. 'And is that him, then? Your Jim, you've got framed out there?'

'That's right. Kelly has a look of him, so mind yourself, won't you? Our Jim was a rum sod, same as me son. But well what can you do? Have to laugh, don't you? When you can. And then you've to pray.'

'Your Kell's promised me he'll be good.'

'Oh well.'

The front door kept banging for Kelly. They swarmed in from town. A blanket noise of cassette music and voices grew thicker as the sun gilded the kitchen before fading. Lights came on. The coloured lads bunched in the hall, supping cans against the radiator and pictures. Brassiereless girls in tight patent shoes and shiny belted frocks waddled in and out of her kitchen. Lips like glazed cherries. Some went from lad to lad, evading hands, letting some wander awhile before brushing them off. Wanton girls. Gobby. Ruined. She thought of Jan. Catching her by the shops at weekend; that girl not mithered about getting caught, especially since the worst had happened already and happened because she was cursed like her mam, being her mam's girl – *Carol's throughnthrough* – and not Sefton's any more. That's if she ever was. And where *was* that girl? Her brother's do. Gone six and still not home.

At first the air was thick with stew and sweets and the lemon suds of rewashed dishes. But now the house stank of perfume-sweat and shampoo and summat else.

Alone Nedra sat at the kitchen table, the other chairs long since carried into the front room. From here she watched the congestion, behind a replenishing skyline of brought booze, between towers of her empty bowls – the sinktop too full – smiling only when her Kelly appeared for a refill, drunk as a lord, pecking her forehead and cheeks as she served him, telling his nana how he loved her, before the girl plucked him away, sometimes without the drink. But each time he returned he was more drunk, looking more like his dad, her son, Sefton Dodds, but the charm his own, the way with the kids his own, the sly softness his own, which he never extended to her sober and so was foreign to her and painful; she needed a Dodds man for waiting on, and could settle for a young lad's thoughtless entitlement. Dancing with this lot, jammed in her kitchen. The music not music but thunder, from a boombox in the front room that the first wave from town had arrived with: four or five lads, who'd come early enough to be introduced, although now she couldn't pick them out from the rest. *Thunder*. His girl turned her hips to it and tattooed herself on him in that orange frock cut low in the back, her dark shoulders sweaty. Nedra watched, appalled, until the girl broke off to pour another drink, then one for Kelly, then led him out again –

as Carol roamed with a plate of food, topping it up from the kitchen regularly, as queer and sour as ever with those sleepless eyes hooded and nasty and her smirk inscrutable, showing no surprise or fear at the mayhem, at the invasion swallowing their house whole – and outright ignoring some of them, the lads asking her summat, and not seeing or hearing them it seemed like to Nedra, even the mob in the hall, who were crushed to the kitchen now, right the way to the foot of the stairs. Carol wasn't mithered with any of it, except for smokers. She shooed them outside. Nedra saw this. Twice Carol heated a milk bottle and took it upstairs. Later she brought the thing down kipping and dribbling and clinging crooked to her as she stalked the kitchen somehow cutting out the din with her glary silence so nothing touched either of them – and all the while pacing and jigging to keep the thing in dreams. Carol paraded it through the house. Carol bloody wanted these strangers seeing it, asking after it; she'd no shame.

Joey Harvey was back having changed into his playing-out clothes. He couldn't hop or run inside. The house was that full. Other children wandered in to see what the fuss was and to be fed what she'd promised them but none except Joey stayed, as the intensity of the spectacle seemed to frighten them, and they went back out and watched from the street. She saw from her frontroom window those sitting on forty-nine's wall opposite, not speaking. Like her house were on fire and they had come to see it burn. Only Susie-Ann had to be dragged home by her dad. Nedra, too ashamed to apologise. Other neighbours stayed away. Even Linda next door. For the first time in her life Nedra thought about ringing the bobbies. Especially now, seeing Joey Harvey dance with a corner of the short orange dress as he mithered for the girl's attention. Attention which Kelly's girl was keen to give. He was as tall as her legs. He had found an orange balloon and wanted her to have it since it matched her frock. But Kelly tapped the balloon away as soon as it passed and lifted Joey and kept it airborne with Joey's head. Kelly flew the lad out the kitchen after it, both of them laughing. Some of the mob had spilled outside and with the backdoor pinned open she could feel the draught – her chair aimed at the hall: an arrow from kitchen to front door – even with all those people between. Some of the bigger lads wore sporty garb with women's jewellery, fat earrings and chains, and those lads might've been the darkest she'd ever seen and they were in the house filling it with talk and dance and drink. They stood over her at the table, bloody great big lads, lingering, polite, bold as brass, asking her to mind their cans or look after summat while they went for a smoke and not before asking if she was the cook and when she said yes complimenting her scran and asking from where in town she got her ingredients and nodding as she told them. Then they shared their own mams' and nanas' recipes for this and for that *and if her Jim could bloody see her. . .*

Carol came into the kitchen again with it and Kelly's girl quit dancing to the thunder. She asked and Carol gave it her – the baby – and even then it didn't wake.

'Isn't he gorgeous? God. Just gorgeous.'

'Sleeps through anything,' Carol said. 'First I thought he might be deaf.'

The girl glanced about, suddenly embarrassed.

'Look at you. It could be yours,' Nedra said. 'Is the right shade – look. Could be.'

The smile strained thin, the scar like a stuck zip on her cheek. The girl wasn't peering at the baby but at her, trying hard to read her. 'What's his name?' the girl asked.

'Still not got one yet,' Carol said.

'How old's he?'

'Depends. He was eight weeks early.'

'God. Looks like he's doing well, though. Both you look well.'

'He's not mine.'

'Oh. Was gunna say.'

Carol spotted smokers in the hall and left the girl holding it.

Kelly kissed his mam's cheek as they met in the doorway.

Then:

'Whose is that?' he asked his girl.

'Yours,' little Joey Harvey said, being carried like carpet roll under his arm. 'It's a secret. We wasn't to tell even Lord Jesus but I forgot and told him before bed but—'

'How'd you mean, *ours*?'

'It's your Jan's.'

'Mam!'

IN THE WOODS IN the dusk the Didsbury lad was just for her. But when he spoke Jan was surprised to be sad he said nowt worth hearing. Nowt was happening, except the usual – never mind the lad, who could be white or wog; her age or older; rougher, or posher like this one – and the usual was never enough. She would finish with him, there, in the woods in the dusk after their second tryst; Jan Dodds was no timewaster. Shame though there was nowt in his eyes but moving light from cars beyond the silvered trees and the whispering canal. Or in his daft voice, which he had scuffed up for her but could not unsweeten. Not in the gorgeous halfsight of him. Not inside her, either. Nowt burned in secret. What Jan had instead was dead easy to find and she would give it this one gladly: settle for his heat, his smell, his weight against her heart. Whichever the lad, Jan was after those things and caught them, first cast. Jan stood up some of them on the second go. Even the older lads. She might've done that today, if she hadn't had other places she'd been told to be: the classroom, the kitchen, the pew. Sod them. Sod Kelly. Sod the welcome home do. After Poundswick hot dinners she'd suck anyowt to swap the taste, eat anywhere except Fellside Road.

They'd tramped the dry mud of the canal bank, flattened grass over Millgate Fields, Alice Willows trailing them – with two satchels on one shoulder – docile, shrugging off three of his mates feeding her vodka. And now at dusk the mates had given up and gone and the woods and earth smell were in Jan's hair and clothes and it pleased her.

She wasn't cold or afraid. Backed against flaky bark shedding into her knickers, her school tights to the knee.

The Didsbury lad pawed her, dithered, his nose stabbing her eyelid.

Breathing him, Jan scanned the gloom one-eyed, sensing the paler lines of a girl against the next tree. Alice drifted closer. Their satchels dropping. Her uniform shone apparent while the wood was silhouetting in the last crumb of light, as if the new dark not the dying day were keeping her solid.

Jan clenched what the Didsbury lad offered; he swore like a dormouse and undid his pants blind.

More headlamps made them. This light didn't find Alice. Jan looked but the trees had changed and blocked the thread. Jan's white thighs glowed, then didn't. Glowed. Then didn't. He touched them, afraid.

'Ay, Alice, he's all yours you know after this. *If* you fancy him.'

'. . .Fuck off,' the Didsbury lad said and kissed her.

'It's not even in!'

'Yerrit is!'

Jan stopped him rushing. 'Oi, give it here, you.'

He was broad and skinny. A bit older though not as old as he'd said. As she put it in she wanted to laugh but it would push him back out and end it there and she didn't want that yet.

His fingers did guesswork. He dragged her skin but when she bristled he rubbed lighter, and with pressure and pace half learned she had him conduct her, had him collect their heat – letting it run onto his thumb. Both her eyes stayed open; his scared shut.

Ordinary feeling returned to her piecemeal, even before he'd finished.

He pulled out already shooting –

smear-shot the rest on her right thigh, which glowed in the next wash of headlamps crossing the canal –

leaving her chilly but too proud to cover up straight away. She wanted him to see the lovely mess they'd made but he wasn't bold enough to admire what he'd done.

Behind his back she gave Alice a thumbs-up in the ghostlight. She knew when it came to a shag Alice either would or wouldn't and no amount of plying or pressure decided for her, which couldn't be said for owt else; Alice let Jan rule her; the girl was meek and mild in every way but appearance and had none of Jan's gobbing fire, and was immune to it even, and never caught from her a contact flame, not even after all their budding years living in each other's pockets. Yet Alice could be unreachable in sickening ways. A natural with secrets, decisions unshared: like the school morning she clippered her hair off beginning a spate of Poundswick suspensions successfully appealed by her mam Bev. And the ten piercings needled in Affleck's Palace. Jan had been blind to the truths of this transfiguration until a January Saturday last year when she had seen Alice waiting cold at the bus stop full-formed. A grade three and slathered kohl and tangled earrings that winked like fishing lure. Alice's mouldy bedroom got re-postered with shite bands that she sung to the tropical fish in her front room as she nosed their tank, the breathed-on glass mucked with crisp salt, makeup. The way biddies spoke to babies Alice spoke to earthworms, garden spiders, not just cats and dogs. Even Bev's own dog, Bully: a staffie like Joey's, but which barked forever and chewed their unstarted homework and shoplifted clothes. (It hated the stink of blokes Bev said, which was maybe why it always went for Jan.) Alice had even had a terrapin for a few hours which Jan had traded off a ginger mong in the year below after he told them his cousins would tie it to a balloon. Ginger wanted to cop a feel at break but Alice changed her mind behind the science mobiles, and so Jan took her place. (This was just after Jan's house got dawnraided, when her brother got pinched. This was before she had a term off from Poundswick, when the lasses that she'd thumped and robbed and nicked fellers from for a day or two would spread word that she'd been up the duff all summer because of one night with a *Longsight nigger*.) Come hometime Ginger gave them the terrapin in a crushed shoebox. But as they dozed in Painswick Park by the pond, the terrapin ate its way out and went swimming. They'd been lain on their fronts, Alice talking her dreams and Jan tracing a scab on her elbow with a blade of grass. Jan had plucked a dandelion and rolled it, juicing it, till the scab perfumed and stained. When Alice saw her doing this she stopped talking. They sat up together. Jan spotted the terrapin as it plopped in the pond. Alice, checking the empty shoebox, seemed almost glad, but cried later, at her mam's. Bev just laughed when she heard what had happened and said thank God because their staffie would've no doubt *et* it if Alice had got the thing home; and from the backdoor their staffie barked on cue and Jan laughed, laughing more at Bev.

But Alice hadn't cried in front of Jan since.

Now in the woods her distance from them seemed to close without any movement from her until it'd happened and Alice was right beside her and the Didsbury lad and the rotted tree in that dip of land. Letting herself be led. Her kohl eyes stayed open and upward into his until he turned her and bent her and flipped her skirt – and then looked down at her own scuffed green Kickers, bridged apart beneath her.

'Is he in?' Jan said, not dressed.

'Dunno' – Alice's voice flat and her face for a moment lit and not blank-scared or blank-sad but Jan didn't know what this meant.

Still soft, he spun her hips to try again. Jan cupped his arse, humping away.

'. . . Fuck off,' the Didsbury lad said.

Jan cheered him on till it was useless and both girls giggled.

Before he could get his pants up Jan grabbed it. In her sticky palm he squished to nowt, like a dishrag under a hot tap. Alice moved and Jan took her place kissing him away until they almost fell over and had to break for air. 'She not getting a go then?'

'Fuck off,' he said.

But then the two of them were caught inside a yellow-moon net. The Didsbury lad bolting instantly, tripping through bramble. Twig-snaps. His pale arse chased by torchlight.

Jan called into the yellow halo and danced, spotlit, giving two wagging sets of Vs, which she worked into her routine. On a mound of exposed roots near and above them, between slanted, shattered trees, a silhouette watched. Shining them.

Alice jumped her tights up, then lifted their satchels which the torch found for her. Jan pulled Alice's free arm and ran her right into the halo shouting 'Have a nice wank!', both girls floating above tree stumps and blurring under a roof of branches and Jan catching bloke's fingers filthy on her shoulder before they were free of the woods and the torch and free with their shrieks and weeping laughter across the field and canal bank to the bridge then the road.

'Am gunna be sick, me,' Alice said.

'Least you don't need us to hold your hair back.'

'I mean it, Jan.'

'You've not had enough to spew.'

'It's all that running.'

Jan veered off into a tiny front garden through its missing gate. She squatted in the dim, pissing out the Didsbury lad. Shrubs with fat teacup flowers gave off a sweetness and hid the girls from each other as liquid staggered from them both – Alice's slapping the pavement; Jan's pattering dry soil.

'So has owt happened yet with you and whatsisname?'

'. . .No,' Alice said, her voice thicker: 'but his mam and dad've always been dead nice to me, and our Bully never barks at him.' The new voice carried like she'd walked on, forgetting Jan wasn't there.

'Oh well, that's it, then. Meant to be. You two might s'well get wed next week. . .' She finished watering the garden. 'You know I wouldn't waste a wank, me, over that lad.'

'Bet *he* would. Bet he likes *you* best.'

'Nobody likes me best – I'm just easy.'

'They do like you. Jan, they do.'

'You've had whatsisname living next door to you for donkey's, right? Goes Poundswick, same year as us. Same everything. And you never looked twice till now?'

'I have. Just never said.'

'He's a no-mark.'

'You don't know him.'

'And that's how I know.'

Green Kickers, scudding closer again.

When Jan finally rose her thighs for a second seized up like her nana's. 'You wanna wear you mam's stilettos round Civic.'

'She can't walk in um neither.'

'I'll teach you.'

'He don't fancy us.'

'I'll knock on for him in the morning before I knock on for you.'

Alice ignored her, said: '. . .Who's he shagged, d'you think?'

'Just his hand, I bet. Unless he's had that Sharon.'

'Sharon who?'

'Posh bras. Take her tits up to her chin.'

Alice retched again.

'Look, *you're* the one what should hear if he's dipping his wick. When his mam and dad aren't in, put your ear to the wall and find out.'

'He plays his music.'

Jan's water had gullied the soil and glistened with the upstairs windowlight. The house was pink-cladded, a telly going in the top bedroom. Applause or a gunfight. From somewhere behind the shrubs Alice said, lonely: 'You gunna keep shagging Mr Somerville then?'

'Yeah, course.'

'. . .'

Hopping to dry land, Jan took three empty milk bottles off the porchstep and loaded her satchel, which Alice had carried all day. She returned to a dead street of dark windows, without kiddies playing out, and got spooked by its stillness. Her bag swung as she dodged Alice's pools on the pavement; the milk bottles clinked on her hip. She undid her bag and bent her torn exercise books to stand the bottles separate, the gaps stuffed. Alice was patiently swaying by herself, head down, ankles together, stage solo under the cut of a lamppost which spotted her without so much as a Cortina parked for the corner stretch of road, so that before Jan reached her Alice seemed to be drifting in outerspace.

'Please don't, Jan.'

'What?' She caught up and kissed her temple. 'Sup with you?'

They walked touching. Conquered street after street.

'Jan, is he really seeing that Sharon?'

'Whatsisname? Fuck knows.' Answering, she took a milk bottle and threw it over her shoulder, giving it spin. It smashed on the windscreen of a parked van. Alice turned at the bang and shoved her away but Jan sucked her close again.

Alice stared at her, transmitting nothing.

Jan loved her: even though Alice had become dreary music and jangly tat. The Willows were lapsed Catholics too. Bev had her girl-hood rosaries buried in a jewellery box they routinely raided. Jan didn't care for Slaughter and the Dogs, the Fall, Blue Orchids, the Chameleons or any other noisy whingeing local bobbins that knifed her spirit. She liked *Top of the Pops*, Mary Jane Girls, Terri Wells, Five Star, and knew Alice did and all. She'd switch off Alice's two-stack turntable – tape deck missing, a car boot sale find – and tune the radio, after some Prince or D Train. Last week she had done this and Alice had said nowt; stayed lotus on the single bed by the window and watched the shared wall like she could see through it, into whatsis-name's bedroom next door: another gormless lad tugging his prick.

Jan had watched her watch the wall. 'He's not even that good-looking. He wants his hair cutting.'

Alice blinked. 'Sounding like your nana now.'

Jan went over and slapped the shared wall: 'Oi, knobhead. Do you even know what you've got next door? Lucky sod, you are. So get your arse round here and don't forget your tiny cock—'

Alice had leapt to spike the radio and upset the aerial when she kneed the bed table, scattering pic-n-mix and lashing vodka. Vanity 6 fizzed from the speakers, then blasted. Bully barked downstairs. The bassline made the shared wall come alive. Alice's new posters warped and shivered, their corners curling off their Blu Tack to flutter like shy insect wings. . .

Now Alice coughed on her shoulder and the midweek night was cold, the houses already asleep. They came to a posh main road with a little traffic but the pavements stayed empty. The set-back houses grew, were lined with high privets. A bus hushed past them; they didn't know its number. Their stolen clipper cards each had only one ride left, which had to be saved for going town.

'Freezing now, a'you?'

Without leaving her shoulder, Alice yawned into a nod.

'Stop. Give us your thumb.'

Alice gave it and Jan posed her into a teapot with her spout to the road. She stood back; a dozen cars went by; Alice yawned at them.

Jan tried instead.

The seventh car pulled in. A greasy frowning woman about her mam's age wound down the fogged window while the car rattled. The woman had a loose, chestnut perm and spread-out features like a cartoon rabbit – her forehead oily under the cockpit bulb. The other car seats were empty. Jan was only sure the woman was looking at her and not Alice when she cocked her head.

'Why you young girls cadging lifts round here this time of night?'

'We've to get home, miss.'

'You two've been drinking.' Her eyes were like frozen peas.

'Y'what?'

'Don't tell lies. Must think I'm daft. Can smell it from here.'

'With that nose you can.'

The woman sped off, checking her mirrors.

Already Alice had her thumb out again.

The dash clock said eleven eleven. Crinkles of smoke patterned the spaces between them till he cracked his window.

'Give us one.'

He handed Jan a pack of Lamberts and she sparked up with the car's lighter, then pinched two more and started jabbing buttons on the radio but each gave her static.

'What do you want on, love?' he said.

'Dunno yet, do I?'

He used her fingers to tune the radio, holding them tightly, carefully, not crushing them, said: 'How's that?' – Jocelyn Brown needing you to remember days shared in the sun. He let her go to drum the Granada steering wheel, but his belly didn't leave much room. Pork skin and grimy nails, long like a woman's.

He drove slowly on the quiet roads, baring his teeth at her each time he turned right, letting her fiddle with everything. Whenever light swept in she glimpsed the oil-stained roof fabric or the page-three

34

girls papering her footwell. Constellations of silver nuts and screws twinkled around her satchel. A tape measure in the cup holder. Jan tapped her fag ash between her knees, then tried the glovebox.

'What you doing, you?' he said.

Fluffy winegums, betting slips and blue johnny wrappers fell out and she found a cut envelope creased shut which he grabbed before she could unfold.

'Oi, don't go messing with that.' He stuffed the envelope down his door pocket. 'Lad from work left it in there.'

'Can we not have a bit?'

'Have a bit of what?'

She slipped her skirt right up and untwisted her tights, fixing the gusset. His glances came quicker.

'Oi, you're not a nutter, a'you?' Jan, wriggling.

'Am I 'eck.'

'Some fucking perv.'

'Listen to that gob.'

'Who a'you, me *dad*?'

'No. But I might know him. What's his name?'

After a beat she said: 'Sefton Dodds.'

'. . .*Sefton Dodds*? Bloody hell. There's a name what takes me back. Aye, I know Sefton, yeah. . . His old man, Jim, you had to watch, mind. Had a right temper. Always good with his mitts. Well, they both was. But not seen Sefton for *donkey's*. We moved away you see when I got work down south. Worked all over, actually. Before me and the missus moved back. How's he getting on?'

Jan unshut her legs.

He glanced at them, taking another drag. 'By God, ay? Sefton bloody Dodds' – to the road, then to the rearview, tapping the wheel harder, losing ash.

Wake up, Jan mouthed between the front seats.

In the back Alice swayed, kipped. Once last summer Jan had got her so drunk that she slept standing against the outer wall of the Golden Garter on a Friday night that was still day, holding chicken in a basket while they waited for Bev to be chucked out or for their lives to begin, or at least for their legs to be noticed; to be taken for a joyride in a twoc'd Nova by a Magnum-tashed pisshead who was last in line for a Sharston factory job; otherwise Jan and Alice would have to walk Bev home – clasping her from each side to keep her up as she sang the gossip and the grief she'd wrought. Sometimes it was Bev climbing into a Nova, waving them ta-ra.

Headlamps scrolled over them now and for a moment Jan saw Bev's face atop Alice's, busying her dreams, and Jan saw through the faces and saw the woods again. Then Alice was wide awake.

The fat bloke coughed and went: 'Am Bryan, by the way. Shoulda said.'

'Sharon. That's our Gina. She's missing her bed.'

'Oh. The wife's name, Gina. Iya, love.'

Jan said: 'Where was you going?'

'On me way home,' he said.

'To your Gina?'

'That's right.'

'Where we going now?'

'Wherever. Wherever you want.'

'Gina? Where d'you wanna go?'

'Home,' Alice said.

'Drop us off Civic.'

He flicked out his cig. 'What's matter?'

'Don't want your Gina worrying, do we?'

'Fair dos. Ay, Sharon – remember me to your dad, will you? Say hello for Bryan Banister.' He touched her thigh for this. When she touched his it was damp. Polyester pants like skin. She smudged his fallen ash. His polo shirt packed him in like a girdle and before she'd got under the dome of his gut her wrist vanished. She almost gagged at the vinegary stench when she tried curling to his lap. There wasn't room for anything and he soon yanked her up by her hair and kept hold of it. Alice screamed then. He waggled the wheel one-handed – the car rounded a bend on the wrong side of the road – and the girls slid from their seats before he snapped the car straight.

Jan freed her hair. He was shouting at her now but all she heard was Alice.

'Take a breath, you fat cunt!' she said and held his stare till he turned his head to keep them on the road.

Jan cranked the radio – 'Nasty Girl'.

He drove on, snorting like a bull in between little laughs of fear. She knew.

Her own fag had gone in the footwell; it was smoking the newspaper tits. 'Am gunna tell me dad.'

'Ay now. Don't go telling your dad. No need for that.'

'Well,' said Jan. 'You best give us some of that then in there before we go.'

They hadn't far to go but he turned off quickly after the Sharston factories and pulled up at a blacked-out strip of shops with glowing flats above and name signs so worn they were secrets only Nana Dodds would know. Knuckled trees stood in tufts of bluebelled grass. Tall weeds gridded the flagstones. A lamppost was on the blink.

He turned the key and the radio went off but loitered in their ears while they waited for him to make up his mind. He took the creased envelope, gaped one end and flicked the other, then spaded some powder, squinting so he didn't drop the key. 'Not like me, this, not during the week.' He bared his teeth at her afterwards, offered the key, then hesitated before giving her the envelope.

'What is it?'

'Just a bit of whizz.'

Alice, slapping the passenger door.

'Gina?' he said. 'This'll keep you going.'

'Let her out,' said Jan. 'She's gunna spew.'

'It's not locked.'

As Alice leaned her door open, Jan swung out her own – tossing the envelope up – frosting him and the page threes as she legged it, Alice dashing with her. He revved off, but Jan returned for her satchel when he threw it out.

After walking Alice home she needed summat to do. The two milk bottles she had left were broken. She tipped out her bag, nabbed two more off next door's step – off Alice's boyfriend-to-be – and took them to the carpark behind Portway shops and lobbed them to hear them smash. She'd aimed them at holes in the wall when she saw a ginger tom poke through a missing brick. The noise was good. But the silence returned vast under a low sky of hoover dust. Streetlamps hummed and the trees between them kept their leaves still. Jan grew hungry, invisible. She mooched along the streets' grass banks, no longer feeling the cold, noticing things in the branches above. When she was alone after dark everything was different but it wasn't enough. She wondered how late it was, if she'd skive off tomorrow, sleep in. For ages she listened to a car before seeing it, so when it shot up the road she forgot it was coming and she jumped. It was gold and beside her for half a second – full of blokes and one in the back had his window down to yell at her: *Fucking gorgeous.* They made eye contact on *geous.* Jan stopped where she was, visible again under the sudden wag of the leaves, her grin wet as the gold car went from sight again to sound. After that, she was called to Civic by the screams of the joyriders' tyres in the courts below the eyeless blocks of flats. A few ex-Poundswick lads were bunched around the callboxes, toking dope. She was by herself on the sidewall at the entrance to Violet Court, thinking herself invisible again, when a ghost said her name. No one else seemed to hear it. Hear him.

'Jan.'

She looked.

'Jan, love.'

On this went. Livid, she almost said: *Where a'yer?* But she was cold again, her feet hurting, taking her home.

She kept the house dark and helped herself to whatever had been left out – scranning it without cutlery since there was none in the drawer, not even a clean plate.

Undressing as she went up the stairs –

missing the squeaky steps. She walked her tights insideout. Debris stuck to her feet. And then with full weight she heel-crushed

38

a drink can and tipped backwards but caught the wall rail. The can bounced down the stairs. She breathed through her nose, her heart ticking in her neck while the house slept. When the kitchen clock ticked louder than her neck she picked up another open can of super lager on the second-to-top stair, swigging the lot on the landing in her underpants, leaving the empty there before she went into the room.

Black it lay in pilled, frayed, corn-coloured blankets. Its eyes moved beneath their lids. Fists to cheeks, uncurling in peace. Sour milk and eczema cream it smelled of and when she peered closer it smiled at her in its sleep. She spat on it but it didn't wake. Jan opened the window and let the night's draught in.

Naked she prayed over the flimsy cot for it to die. Rags on the cold radiator. Dirty towels everywhere and sealed nappies and handme-down garb piled into shadow. Her pit-sweat dried. Her nipples went sore. Goosepimpled. Her heart ticking now through her fingers gripping the cot bar.

It stirred and began to whimper, like it was –
falling
falling out of a dream.
Jan shut the window, leaned over the cot –
gozzed again and went out.

At the mirrorstand in her room she kept ticking. The cracks of streetlight from the curtain split lemoned her skin to butter. She was already tender but she put her fingers there and did it and did it so fast she got tennis elbow and kept having to swap hands. Her stretchmarks dimpled. The knots of cramp hardened. But standing there, her toenails raw from clawing carpet, she came as she bit her lip panting and freed her ticking blood.

Too spent to stand she lay on the carpet to change her knickers and climbed into bed.

Kell belched next to her on the pillow.

She yipped and covered her gob. He turned over, with the duvet. She rolled his wiry body further to the wall and let him keep the covers. His heat was enough. Their shared blood enough. An odd calm held her. She combed his hair with tired fingers and kissed the back of his head a dozen times, each kiss softer, then put an arm around him to sleep, accepting her fate –

her ticking to his ticking

You you you you.
You you you you. You you you you.
You you you you. You you you you. You you you you.
You you you you. You you you you.
You you you *you*.

When she woke it was dim-night and he was sat on her waist in his vest and underpants, strangling her. A blocked-out head and shoulders shivering against the ceiling grey. He had the bedsprings flat, his thumbs on her windpipe so she couldn't scream. She kneed and kicked, flapping and scratching. Blue crystals began to pop the edges of her sight and jumble his shape. She swung out, cracked his arse bone, then shinned him in the bollocks.

He leapt up, howling –

as she sprang to the floor – dry-heaving – and thought she'd gone deaf but it was only her voice that was gone and she tried to shout it back but choked.

'What did I say? What did I fucking tell yous before I went down? Can't keep your legs shut for five minutes.'

Jan coughed a sound.

'You're *fifteen*,' he said, 'Stuck with that wailing shitting thing. Unless they take it off you. But Mam's having none of that, is she? Can always do with more misery, our mam, can't she? Least I know why she stopped visiting. Fuck me. Nowt changes round here, does it? Except when it does.'

'Get out. . . me room,' Jan croaked and stood.

He knocked her back to the floor. 'I tried mine. No bed, no nowt, except a black baby in there; have you not seen? See, Mam's got rid of all me gear, hasn't she? And you let her. Sold the lot to make way for that thing, which I've heard you won't go near. Guess Mam reckons I won't be needing owt cos I'll be back inside soon enough.'

'I said not to get rid of your records,' Jan croaked. 'I told her!'

Kell thumped and bashed the wall. Once he'd tired himself, he sank to the bed, rocking, breathless, then he said to her slowly: 'How'd they keep quiet about *you*? How'd *you* manage to keep secret from *them*? That's all *I* wanna know.' He winced and lay coffin-flat. After a while he raised himself on one elbow. 'Spose that's why Nana never come see us. She would've let it slip.'

Jan stayed coiled on all fours, glazed with fright, her nose bleeding or running. Her throat on fire. And when her sweat cooled she trembled and Kelly threw her his vest, saying: 'Might as well have the shirt off me back, our kid, you've had everything else.'

Jan wiped her nose with it and threw it back.

AT 2 A.M. CAROL Dodds let Vern Jenkins – gleeful, bow-legged, old-book-smelling at just thirty and sixteen-years-dead come October – enter her marriage bed and make love to her. Let his soft woman hands between her legs. Let his whispered jokes ease the pain as he pushed inside her. Squared up against a Strangeways shark like her late husband, Vern was lean and slight. Hopeless with his mitts. But Vern Jenkins alive or dead was twice the man her Sefton was and not just where it counted. At least her husband stayed dead and didn't visit. But her Vern was a randy sod. Prick like the Eiffel Tower. Balls big as tangerines. Some nights he hurt her which made her glad; she never let him know because the pain was brief and rare and felt like penance. And only in the pain which Vern caused her, Carol came close to forgiving herself. But Vern was always gentle and in the pool of her collarbone he told his daft jokes. New ones tonight. So bad they tickled her. The jokes' vibrations tickling as much as the jokes themselves. He had to trap her mouth shut – his palm sweat tasted like Ovaltine – whispering: 'You'll wake the whole house, love.'

'Sod them,' Carol said, or tried to.

They laughed into each other's bodies afterwards, standing in the bed as he got her out of her nightdress. Then he helped swap the bedlinen.

'Carol, love?' he said.

'Yes, love?'

'It's a shame I'm dead.'

'Forgive me, love.'

She laid flat. Vern rubbed her belly. His touch painful because it was painless and not entitled like a Dodds man or a baby, not trying to grab all of her at once and keep her for only as long as she was needed. Some nights she would cross her landing, and she would nurse their delinquent daughter's baby on her empty breast. Some nights, already fed and sleepy it would indulge her. And she would pace and remember:

Vern was gap-teethed, clever and working. Lovely, talky and daft. The librarian's assistant learning Pitman shorthand at night school, having passed his eleven-plus and gone to St Augustine's and wound up with two rooms of his own above a closing-down greasy spoon near Sharston Baths. In one a giant aspidistra that he crossed-his-heart-hoped-to-die had belonged to Sydney Howard. Books bricked into furniture filled the other. The first time they did it fully was on his floor, fighting to get undressed, toppling columns of Woolworths' paperbacks, their kissing lips papercut, laughing.

Carol hadn't seen Vern wearing clothes since 1969, even in dreams. Vern turned her body over now and fingertipped an S from right shoulder to left hip to right calf to left toe – bunching the covers away.

'I'll catch me death,' she said.

'Very funny.'

Noise came from behind the wall. 'What's that racket?' he said.

'Be our Jan getting in from another night of sin.'

'Want me to have a word?'

'Imagine.'

'. . .'

'She's safer outside.'

'Is she?'

'No.'

'Wish we'd made a baby, me and you.'

'But we did, Vern. We did.'

'Such a shame I'm dead.' The words were shrugged, lighter than love. He got up and the bed rose. She had a drink of tap water on the nightstand and he downed it and glanced at her and grinned while his prick went up slowly by itself like a drawbridge in silhouette.

'Thank me,' Vern said.

'Thank *me*,' she said.

Vern visited her of a night not because he forgave her but because he couldn't forgive her because he thought he had nowt to forgive. Carol was sixteen years' sure that was it. That Vern's forgivelessness kept her his and kept her in pain and of both she was glad.

Vern only lived between her stagnant days. Dead days in the cake factory when she had worked, and in the house; only her sleep possessed momentum. Days before their daughter's baby stole her son's room while her son spent a year at Her Majesty's pleasure, before even her husband and fatherinlaw were killed. Before her maminlaw moved in. Days so brutish and eventless she could barely sift them for a single feeling or memory. But her nights with Vern were printed catalogues. Black honeymoons. Bound and spined.

'Forgot to ask you. How was the do?'

'Messy,' she said.

Vern stretched, unwilted. 'I'd love to help tidy up tomorrow, like, but. . .'

'Men.'

'Where was me invite?'

'Our Nedra must've run out of stamps.'

'Your Kelly's a nice-looking lad now, isn't he? Takes after his mam, of course.'

'Does he?'

'He's not his dad.'

'He's turned out same.'

'He's young and daft but he's out now and now he's out he might decide he'd rather *stay* out, for his nana's cooking.'

Of course, Nedra hadn't visited him. Carol went every week until Jan had the baby. Nedra lied for her grandson and for herself and to herself and to anybody polite enough to do it back. Even Dodds women:

Eunice Barry née Dodds.

Carol's sisterinlaw; her latest letter: a tepid postcard which had arrived a fortnight ago and lived amid the saints on her clean, crowded mantelpiece of votives, idols, trinkets, bibelots, blurry snaps of Pope John Paul II in Heaton Park, and other notes from Eunice, who had emigrated to Canada, intact. Some of Eunice's bleached correspondences Nedra hid in her bedside drawer after months on the mantel. But Carol didn't know why.

21st April 1985
Dear Mam, Carol, Kelly & Jan,
Glad our Kelly is still doing everso well. Hope he keeps the job. Has he got himself a nice girl yet? Went to an American wedding with our Freddy last week! A feller from his works. Bride was a _real_ Yank. We stayed on Delaware River, Trenton, New Jersey. Lovely ceremony. Freddy said she was up the junction but you couldnt tell. Lovely slim figure. Never touched her own cake! Our Freddy had plenty. Just as well. No currants in American cakes. I miss currants. Sorry we cant visit this year. I know its been forever. How is our Jan doing at school? Any boyfriend trouble? All that still to come I suspect. Hows weather? For us Saturday Fine and Dry. Sunday Wet and Windy.
Love Eunice & Freddy

Carol had read the tight chicken scrawl to Nedra first. Then reread it to herself. The postcard showed an aerial photo of a grey city river. More crime scene than wedding resort.

'Lovely,' Nedra said, stirring a pot. 'Just lovely.'

'It's not even Stockport Viaduct,' Carol said.

'Catholic wedding?'

'Doesn't say.' She gave it her to check.

Nedra went out, aproned, humming, to put it on the mantel altar with the rest.

Carol remembered Eunice as a fat, freckled girl of the sixties; smiley and inscrutable. A nail-chewed typist for a Jewish sewing firm in town with a week's wardrobe of wallpaper-print blouses and suede skirts. A girl who told her own mam and dad and brother that she didn't smoke, then showed Carol that she did without conspiracy. Eunice fled to Canada in '66, between Kelly's birth and Jan's, having eloped with this Freddy, a Protestant clerk from Heaton Chapel. They'd found that out in the post too. After that, Carol met her sisterinlaw again, nine years later, when she flew back for the double funeral. Dodds women were only as good as their secrets. Freddy was fatter than Eunice. Silver tash, red sideburns. Carol suspected he was rich. Eunice had worn pink specs thicker than her mam's reading pair. All through the Rite of Committal she whipped them off and on and off, weeping like the Italians in old films: with her whole body. Carol had wondered if it was relief. . .

Vern picked up Carol's nightdress now and sniffed it. 'Thought you hated blue?'

'Sefton liked me in blue.'

'He was right to.' Vern hooped the shoulder straps over his stiff prick and hung the nightdress, then unlatched the window.

'I wanted a different colour but it was all they had.'

'You could change the colour yourself.'

'Check the label.'

Vern rotated the nightdress like clock hands – from six thirty till midnight – to read the hem label by the window's grey light. 'We've been to the moon and we still can't dye nylon or polyester.'

'I haven't been to the moon; have you?' she said.

'This *is* polyester?' he said.

'You should've been a woman,' she said.

At the do earlier that evening to welcome her son home from Strangeways, a coloured lad from town, stocky, half her age, had said sweetly and confidently to her in the crowded kitchen: 'How nice it would be fucking you.' She'd taken his lit cigarette and walked him outside and given it back. The evening sunshine smelled of dope and wisteria and her flagstones and weeds and scrap of lawn were hidden by feet. There, off the step, they shared a bizarre moment of silent communication where he didn't even undress her with his eyes but kept them on hers and when he broke it to finally smoke she saw the gorgeous young black girls nearest them posed with jealousy.

Carol had tripped on her own doorstep going in –

and remembered:

the accoutrements of jealousy. True jealousy. Colourless. Not male or female. But both reasonable and incommensurate –

as in October '69, when her husband Sefton was freed from Strangeways on a Friday, swallowed the gossip with his mam's cooking by evening, hunted the pubs and rallied his cause Saturday, and had a name and address by Sunday. He'd driven round on the morning with his dad, while Nedra sang hymns in St Michael's and confessed to not putting enough flour in the charity stall cakes. They rang Vern's doorbell uninterrupted. They got poor Vern out of his bed. Sefton battered him to death on his own doorstep. Behind the shut greasy spoon. While Jim, her dadinlaw, dragged Carol back inside and perched her bare arsed on the cold radiator and shushed her with his savage yellow stare. A dog stare. Eating her. Vern's bones breaking in their ears. Jim not hearing a thing but *her*. A sheer and animal auscultation. But the instant Sefton was done, or maybe not even done, just breathless or bored, Jim still knew because he patted her knee. Then Carol could lift herself off the radiator and put on her new dressing gown. Jim took her upstairs and packed her bags while she got her young son up and fed and her Sefton brought in the body. She rinsed the teeth and gore off the step with Vern's sink bucket, then put on Sefton's favourite frock. Her oldest frock. Faded navy, white polka dots. *Already then too tight in the waist.*

By midmorning their son, Kelly, who was crying and seven and buckled into the back of Jim's Triumph, goes: 'Where's Uncle Vern?'

Carol ducked in with him and blew his nose on her dress sleeve. 'We're going back to Daddy and Granddad.'

Now Vern was in her house, gently swaying his tackle in front of the nightstand, seeing his death play through her mind. His grin kept. He looked on her with absolute calm. '"Wolves are Things. Keen and ruthless. Strong, even if they are cowards."'

'Who wrote *that*?' Carol said. 'Shakespeare?'

'Somebody.'

'Will have been a bloody bloke,' she said.

Dead Vern got in her bed for another fuck. They were gentle and giggly and he couldn't hurt her which hurt her and the love she felt

48

for Vern was so strong still she had to squeeze him each night until her arms were tired, just to sleep.

In black she woke blinking with her eye mask on. The blinks sounded: footsteps in snow. She rubbed off the mask, blanched and fraught and listening. Her bedroom was alive, the darkness alive, her ceiling dotted like an untuned telly.

Carol felt the wordless bass of her son's voice through the wall and remembered he was home.

Vern was gone –

and the fresh linen was stale linen again. Nedra lay on it with her back to her, sinking her half of the bed.

The old marital bed a tomb, halved then wholed again by widowhood, with her maminlaw's half by the door, Carol's to the draughty window, their bedtables cluttered with more saints, more pictures of their Sefton and Jim, their weddings, Carol-dusted and Nedra-framed. Watching. The Dodds men were forever watching. Vern would wink at them, her Sefton, mid-stroke.

Now her son was twenty-two and free, banging and yelling.

Now their daughter was crying to her for help.

Kelly, clouting her.

Carol lay there and listened.

'If her babba can kip through this, then so can bloody we,' said Nedra, in the dark. 'I say leave them both be.'

And for once Carol agreed with her maminlaw, and so she did.

THOSE CHESHIRE BOYS IN tonic suits in cricket club neckties in a big borrowed car hit her Jim's Triumph on Wilmslow Road before midnight Christmas Eve '76. Her Jim was driving, good as sober; her Sefton beside him and already gone after an evening in the Woodpecker; both strapped in, heading for town. Those boys, Protestant sons, good jobs, plenty money, those boys were drunk and lived. While she –

got rung at witching hour, called from church to station to morgue to identify their bodies on Christmas Day.

Her husband, Jim Dodds.

Her son, Sefton Dodds.

But it was those boys not hers who healed and were redeemed.

Every night for eight and a half years Nedra had visioned the crash – every bloody night, awake or in dreams, even though she wasn't there. Newspaper clippings whose lies lived in the bedside drawer in a used envelope with a maple leaf stamp – *GANGLORD AND SON SLAIN IN XMAS CRASH; FATHER-SON VILLAINS IN FATAL COLLISION* – all of which she reread by dome magnifier, which she'd bought herself one year out the catalogue when everyone, even the kids and mams on the street, forgot her birthday. Eunice used to send monthly miniature parcels of soap samples, funny brands from Freddy's works. Nedra would test them all with tender suspicion. But now Eunice rarely sent her owt, even on her birthday, only ringing and writing sometimes, busy keeping a decent husband. At the funeral Eunice had wept constant, so barely talked the entire time they were back. Nedra cooked her allsorts but it never got touched. Not even a weak milky brew. (On burial day Nedra had swallowed her capful of vinegar at dawn, not having slept. Nedra learned ways to console herself, short and long, but didn't know how to console others without tea – especially her daughter, nine years foreign by then. Freddy had a drop of brandy at the old house, though; or was it *Lamb's* Freddy liked? They lasted two nights at the airport hotel, having insisted). And after years of trying, which Eunice stressed to her over the phone whenever Nedra asked, and Nedra asked whenever she rang: they'd no family. Her daughter, forty this year, and childless. Even with no history of barren women in the family and Nedra herself having conceived no bother, carrying Sefton, then Eunice uneventfully. Nedra had only lost the one – about five month in; a miracle bestowed upon her at fifty. She had worked up Jim over some petty business on the wrong night and, well, that was her own doing, as were the weeks of unstoppable mess and pain and private tears sometimes too spontaneous to be hidden, leading to more trouble. Besides, he'd been sweet afterwards and bought her a new Philips cooker – not even a rental. Anyroad, she had enough of them to mither with as a childminder and dinnerlady at St Christopher's Infant School. Jim had reminded her they were both getting on and she should stop being so daft. She prayed of course.

Her husband. Her son –

while those Cheshire boys' names got printed in the order of their fathers' wage sum.

Those boys whose faces were at first kept from her, while her Jim's Triumph Vitesse was shown: mangled, overturned.

Nine years this Christmas.

How can I be living and they be dead?

Awake the crash was loudest. But in dreams she was inside the car with them, cramped in the back, moving, the road empty and the night not night not day and her window already shattered and the breeze winging her hair. Beige leather creaked. Hard seats that'd had her rump aching on daytrips to Rhyl. Sometimes, in these dreams, it was her own blood soaking her seat through her layers, like that time she had lost one. Did Jim forgive her? Tonight Nedra slept in fits, riding repeatedly in the back of the Triumph to be washed with hot blood, feeling her son's life leave him while her husband's warmed her fat ankles as it climbed her footwell. Tonight the crash *mended* the windows, their glass returning to seal her in, as Jim's blood rose till it filled the Triumph and her Dodds men sat empty-fleshed. Tonight they drowned her.

Nedra woke without a flinch –

knowing why she never forgave Carol for leaving Sefton during one of his short spells in Strangeways so that she could shack up with a fancy man who dared to raise Kelly as his own. What with her Sefton and her Jim later dying blameless and together and having since found no justice, local or otherwise. Perhaps she had never forgiven Carol for doing what she, Nedra, never could, despite also having reason to, since her Jim had a temper too and could be tempted by an indecent waddle, although for this could he be blamed? That shameless slut Minnie, having thrown herself at him. And what sort of man would he have been to turn such a thing down, after fighting a world war, after him telling her and still having it shaken under his nose? But it was only now, with a Dodds man in the house, after all those strangers invaded her home and ate her scran, after he had learned the truth, it was only now, as Nedra grew old and awake in the dark, sharing her daughterinlaw's bed, that she knew *why*. Why she had never forgiven Carol for going back to her own husband, Nedra's son; for showing her it could be done only to undo it.

Now the thing inside her that was and wasn't pain woke too and climbed into her throat and she gulped it back down.

True –

Jim was a bugger. Sefton was a bugger.

These were witching-hour doubts; they gnawed through her, sowing sin, turning faithful hearts contrary. She waited; her heart was silent; the tightness left. But the thing inside her began to burn. It came up again and she swallowed it again. She turned over to keep it down and the old mattress complained.

She replayed the day – saw dark figures in her kitchen whenever she dared shut her eyes. If she kept them open, on the canvas of the ceiling, was the Triumph's crash.

Carol was awake too; she knew by her breathing. She looked across the pillow and found her daughterinlaw faced away, separate, cursed. Kelly's do hadn't been mither for Carol who nowadays seemed immune to surprises. Was that Jan's doing? But Carol had been that way since before her daughter had given birth. Jan had hidden her pregnancy from herself, not just them, hidden it until it wanted out of her, two month early, at which time she could foist her secret onto them. Carol had no shame or interest in her wanton, truant daughter; one might as well help the Devil shovel coals. Nedra thought of the neighbours tomorrow. But a Dodds man was home. She loved Kelly too much to have visited him inside. Tonight, Carol had said nowt to her or to him, not even with her face, not even when the do was over and Kelly knew everything. In the kitchen Carol had stonewalled him, taken his fury and made it clumsy and small, like a dropped spoon. But now with somebody sharing the dark with her, Nedra was less afraid, even if it was Carol. God had punished Carol for her adultery. God had taken her husband, Nedra's son. Why had he taken *her* husband too? Father Culler once said it wasn't for her to know. But she could tell Father Culler thought he knew the Lord's reasons and Nedra knew he didn't. And she finally confessed this vanity only to be given Hail Marys to spend on her soul for its penance in lieu of answers. For after eight and a half years Our Lady's prayers had gone unanswered. Now the thing inside her rose again. A tightness in Nedra that tightened every year but could not break her. But then, after they heard Kelly through the wall, beating sense into his sister, Nedra knew she would rise early to clear away the pots. Carol could see to the rest of the house. Tomorrow as well she would write to Eunice. She had spared her from Kelly's conviction, spared her from Jan's fall too. Nedra suffered too well to unburden herself outside the confession box.

Nedra thought of how many her cooking had fed. And not just at the do. Nedra wished to remain useful. All her life: feeding the bottomless stomachs of the young.

Nedra let the ceiling bleed.

Her special ingredient for any dish main or sweet was vinegar.

JAN GOT OFF THE bus with him at Longsight – with her white shorts wet, the skies red, her fingers and feet swollen with lust and good weather. Mad weather for a March Sunday of '84. This was after an afternoon she and Alice had spent traipsing round town, mithering sun-drunk lads in Piccadilly Gardens to buy them freezepops for a kiss.

He was off the bus second and had her wait while he patted his purple shell jacket – after his cigs, she guessed. Black and beautiful and making the world fork round him until he was ready for her. In red daylight fade she saw him: plenty taller than her but not that tall for a lad. Standing on the crowded pavement she could only watch him through the corner of her eye, blinded by his beauty, while the people went by and the bus went home, with Alice. Up the street a breeze as hot as breath skimmed a topless bin, overflowing. Jan felt lighter than the litter. She was already dizzy. If she flew off would he notice? He counted his cigs, ignoring her, and put them back without taking one. Jan was numb with concentration: trying hard not to care or do or speak, even though she had nowt to say as there was nowt to say and the only thing to do was to somehow outmatch his cruelty because she couldn't outmatch his beauty. But she was fourteen and off the bus in Longsight on a Sunday evening, and he was hers and she would have him.

The air hadn't cooled since town; Jan plucked at the damp frayed hems of her white shorts, then stopped when his arm touched her as electricity on her shoulder. Her legs walked fine without her. But she had to stop concentrating on not concentrating to hear what he said.

'Cav a drag?' When she realised he *had* taken a cig and was smoking.

'Ee-ah.' As they passed a bookies he lit hers with the one in his gob.

She tried to spit into the next bin but the breeze sent it to the pavement. 'Why'd you smoke menthols? Taste rank.'

He just laughed.

The shops were shut, the awnings rolled up, but some places glowed for evening trade and since the road ran straight the furthest places shone like desert cities in a film. They passed a huge pebble-dash pub with pinned-open doors, its entrance bright and shouting. Old restaurants and businesses. All stepped entrances and pigeon-shat granite.

He hooked his arm around her and swung her across the road into crawling traffic – more buses coming from town. Outside a jewelled takeaway with offers written in the window, he smoked at the menu while Jan pretended to read it.

'What you having?' she said, mad to be blushing as his arm left her neck to wax and wane her spine. Then he dropped his cig on the step and went in without her – ordering for them from a Pakistani girl who was older than her and prettier; her ponytail netted and plaited; someone who could work a fryer today and still be less oily than Jan. He leaned on the opposite end of the counter but the bitch came to him, familiar.

Inside Jan benched herself against the window, adjacent to the drinks fridge: kicking it until she broke the seal and the door stayed open, letting out ice fog.

'Fuck's she doing?' the bitch said.

He looked at her too as she ground the stones of her ankles together – the fridge chilling her sweat.

Benched Jan could only see the bitch from the chest up: the bare brown shoulders, the twisted green apron, white bra straps, pony-tail; the frown she wore *for her* that went away *for him*. Jan saw him make her promises across the counter. Then a white lad appeared in the back and made the fryers hiss. The three spoke about things Jan couldn't catch. The bitch though. Jan separated her, never blinking. She was chatting as he took 7UPs out of the fridge and shut it. Put one beside Jan on the bench and drank the other stood again at the counter, relaxed, with his back to her. The bench was upholstered in red vinyl like a barber chair and the cold can rolled into the impression of Jan's weight where it burned against her leg. She opened the fridge and put the 7UP back and picked a Dandelion & Burdock.

'Shut it this time,' the bitch said. Then to him: 'Tell her.'

With her drink Jan approached the counter to salt her chicken and refuse hot pepper sauce –

but then behind her the door jangled and lads' voices came in from the street. He turned instead of touching her. Jan left her food and ran through them – more shell-suited black boys, pleased to tangle her in the doorway, until she shrieked GET FUCKED and then they let her pass and she was running until one of them caught her elbow when she was halfway to the bus stop. People shuttled along the pavement nosy and useless, the red sky going. She fought him. She spat on his purple shell jacket.

He put her against the nearest shop window and kissed her, completely, her toes just touching the street. He was a bad kisser and breathless from running and his menthol and chicken mouth seemed untrainable but quickly there was pressure –

a body to hers.

She picked the net of his string vest under his jacket, aware:

No matter what was done or discovered or accomplished of a Sunday, it was never enough; the day would feel like a waste. By teatime, Monday looming, Jan was restless and aggrieved. But *this*, this was new country. And even if he pulled away now and laughed in her face, she would think:

Right. Good Enough.

By the main drag midway down a skinny crooked passage overgrown. This thoroughfare abandoned to lovers and muggers and ghostlit each end but not from above. Ripe with wild flowers and burst bin bags.

It was here she gasped when she saw a fox watching them and she hushed him with the pad of her thumb on his lip, but he kept rustling her against the bricks. Weeds sprouting from the cement tickled her calves. She dodged his bad kisses to give a lovebite.

Footsteps came, then a shadow: an old timer on his way home. Jan spied a button-shirted belly round enough to be carting twins. He was ancient and bald; she yelled as he passed them: 'Can you tell we've not had our tea?'

The old timer hurried.

Then the lad let her be and stepped away to see all of her; and he was shaking his head, half-laughing.

Jan stayed to the wall, nervous without him, not knowing what to expect after making him laugh this far in. She was suddenly, cruelly empty, and wished she'd said nowt. Lads only liked their own jokes. Not birds with smart gobs. So, Jan's hung open, stupid, wanting –

him against her again. To get all of himself inside her, *two'd* up together, wearing her like a coat.

'. . .'

'*What?*' This came out louder than intended.

He turned to the other wall. 'Nowt. Just need a piss.'

She looked over his shoulder. He was down to half-mast. Jan reached round and aimed him down the path:

He went like the moon-ray water gun that Nana Dodds had got Kell the Christmas before she moved in. When Kell was too old for toys. Jan being almost seven when she began going cornershop on her own with a list she couldn't read, but could give the shopkeepers; and always Jan skimmed the change and split it with Kell. He was fourteen then and had started pissing the bed. Before the crash. But Jan didn't mind taking the rap. She loved Kell that much she got giddy waiting for him to come home from school and if she'd drunk too much milk by the time she heard his key she'd wet herself, her bladder in concord with his. Their mam would slap her face when she got in from work, but Jan would run sobbing to Kell who'd make a fuss. If Nana Dodds was at Mass or hosting Father Culler it was Kell who fed her, bathed her, brushed her hair, taught her rude songs and only smacked her if she crayoned his record sleeves. But she knew neither of them would ever grass. Back then Kell read her stories before bed; he'd read one about ghosts that Christmas Eve before they heard about Dad and Granddad. Kell pissed his bed warm for her that night, when their mam got the call from the police station.

Kell had kept away the dead. . .

Now the piss lashed off the bricks.

The lad nudged her away. Jan nudged him back harder but he swivelled and watered her hands.

Screeching and giggling, she dragged her palms down his shell jacket till they dried: 'Dirty bastard. Dirty black bastard.'

Then she had him against the wall, thinking –

finally

the real thing

thinking afterwards

her calves itching from the wild flowers, the waistband of Alice's shorts cutting behind her knees, an elbow grazed on the bricks – her nerves good as gone. And she told him: 'Shagging is the most fun you can have with your clothes on. Alice's mam says that. She's filthy.'

He watched now, searching her for shame. 'Who's Alice?'

'That was her on the bus. Me mate.'

'Got tissue?' he said.

Jan pulled up her shorts then cleaned him, stuffing him away half-mast. 'There y'are,' she said.

'Fucking hell.' He turned from her to rearrange.

'Where'd you live then? Best not be far; me bloody feet are dead.'

He turned tall, put his forehead to hers and backed her against the bricks.

But Jan was laughing and he laughed along.

The big light went on with its antique shade like summat from her nana's old house. Cream tassels gone grey and thick as pipe cleaners from cobwebs and dust. This was his bedsit above a launderette. He drew a curtain – a spare bedsheet draped over the rail – but left it part way. Then he switched off the overhead to put on the lamp.

An unpainted unpapered room. Smooth clay-red plaster: rusting the light. A kitchenette, water closet, a boombox long as a train carriage, a slot telly with Betamax, a folding bed.

Jan went: 'Who makes your bed?'

He fed the boombox a tape from a stack by the skirting board, then stood her in the middle of the room. Down on one knee, peeling her to Terri Wells' 'I'll Be Around'.

Jan talked along, pointing her foot like a prima ballerina so he could skin her damp sock. 'Told you. They're throbbing, me feets. Look.'

He kissed her toes. He felt his way up and then she sprang onto his hips and he carried her about, spinning while she raked up his string vest and sang: '. . .*Baayy-beee*. . . Oi, get your kit off now. . . Off! Off!' She wrapped her legs higher, hooped her arms around his neck, while he undid his pants standing, and shot inside her right away. Jan felt it and told him. The Kingdom of Heaven above a Longsight launderette. He floated them clean off the floorboards. Higher and higher until Jan had to brace the ceiling to stop them going through it. Jan pushed off and they changed course, gliding and turning like astronauts. For a space helmet Jan wore the dust-choked lampshade. She tried sneezing but couldn't sneeze with him inside her, not without him bursting her heart –

it having gone untouched by those poor Wythenshawe lads, like Tony Kinsella from Crossacres, who'd once tried it on with her and failed, by no fault of her own, a fortnight ago in cold February, behind the Golden Garter, with Tony's cousin Cid and his Perry Boys watching the initiation. But now. . .

Above the launderette, levitating. They did it until they were both sore and stupid – hovering drenched on their backs holding hands until they landed like an autumn leaf on his broken sofa bed a pond of sweat round her navel. She was so proud of this bird bath she wouldn't shift, even to lie on him when he asked. So he cooked rice for her nude while she sang along to Hi-Tension's 'You Make Me Happy', which she knew, thanks to Kell. They did it again and they took their time. Had the rice cold. They shared a joint, the strongest Jan had ever tried. It was raining by then. She smelled it through the walls even with the joint lit. It fell so hard against the window he got up to boost the volume for 'Juicy Fruit'.

He said: 'They play this twice a night at Caribbean Club.'

'Never been.'

'Lying cow. On the bus you was giving it all that.'

'Me brother Kell's mad on this stuff. Plays it before he goes town at weekend.'

'Where's he go?'

'Umm. . . The Man Alive, is it? The Reno. All over.'

'Bet I know him.'

'He loves it. Well, he says he does. But it's only cos of the birds. Always goes for coloured birds, our Kell.' Jan toked for too long; he was happy hearing her cough. '. . .Plays this one over and over. You know like when you try convincing yourself summat's dead good but it's not, it's shit. Not that this is shit. It's alright, this. It's dead good.'

He studied her.

She stared back, insistent.

'Yeah,' he said. 'Yeah.'

'Oi, what's your favourite animal?'

'Fuck knows. What's yours?'

'Walrus.'

'What's a walrus?'

'Give over,' Jan said. 'A walrus, right, is one of them great big bloody dock-off seals with whiskers right and teeth.'

'You're lying to us.'

'You're bloody thick, you are. No wonder you're not working.'

'What d'*you* wanna be? A zookeeper?' He pinched her, flipped her over. They wrestled. His dark throat she'd marked. 'It's not real,' he said.

'Yerrit is.'

'Chatting shit. First the Caribbean Club. Now this.'

'God. Listen to that.'

'It's Cheryl Lynn.'

'No. Out there.'

They listened to it like it was a song. Together: naked at the draughty window. Rain flooding the tiny carpark behind the launderette. A warm syrup darkness. Speckled and growing.

61

'Little dancing men. What me nana calls rain bad as this. Little dancing men.'

He rifled through kitchen drawers, then returned. 'Walrus,' he said, handing her a green felt-tip. She sniffed it first, till the walls began to ripple. He pointed at the moving red plaster, miming a big circle by the window. 'Draw us a fucking walrus.'

When the rain stopped she caught the first bus home. She beat the late dawn with his seed planted and the rest of him seeping away slow enough to always be leaving her, always there. And whenever Jan used a comb (usually one of Kelly's) she would find its teeth afterwards clogged with lampshade dust. All her life folk would tell her she had dandruff when she never.

The dawn raid began minutes after Jan got home. She had seen no unusual cars, no uniforms there in the warm lush silence of the street after rain with its green trees dripping fresh and full of birds scared to sing and its cloud-scrubbed gates and garden walls and house fronts. Curtains too tightly drawn. Jan knew it was all wrong, that it was about to kick off. She went inside and bolted the backdoor and crawled upstairs and into bed without waking anyone and fell into a strange sleep. So tired at having made it home, having been so loved, that the sleep was like a spell. A sleep shallow but unbreakable. It was the only place safe in which to sew back up her heart. The needle told her what it knew:

That Jan would never see him again.

From the winged vantage of dream she watched the pigs break in. Banging, barging, huffing. She saw one open her bedroom door before her mam leapt to shut it again: 'You can't be coming in here where *my* children sleep. Give us that. Give it here.' Jan just listened to the pigs slap her mam quiet. Re-enter her room, searching for what wasn't there. They ordered Jan up and dressed; but tough; she was hard asleep. Nana Dodds fainted reciting verse; Kelly resisting. They crushed him into a scrum on the landing and began reading him his rights. His smushed face, halved in the carpet, right outside her room. His smushed face, telling her to stay asleep. They couldn't spit more than a few words at him without him thrashing free. Their mam floor-sat dribbling blood that she cupped in one hand; Kell called to her through the forest of legs: 'Mam? Mam? Mam?' and she said *I'm alright* – her voice black, steady, unamazed, as the pigs piled on top of Kell and he couldn't talk again. Jan saw all from above. They looked heavy enough to sink the house. Taking turns to catch their breath they battered poor Kell until he was dreaming too and then carried him downstairs. The pig who had slapped their mam now had a fallen quiff and bright rashed cheeks. His nostril whistled. He sucked on his skinned knuckles. More blood spotted the rug between her bed and door. Jan woke at dinnertime and saw it there, carried from a dream.

Everybody had been on the landing, booted and uniformed or dressing-gowned, grunting or wailing.

Next thing, they weren't –

and the whole house was crystal silent. But peaceless, unordinary. It stayed strung. Only the faraway hush of Monday planes and cars had kept Jan dreaming after her mam and nana had followed Kell to the station –

leaving Jan to skive off school forgotten, to be woken when Alice came round on her dinnerhour to hear about the coloured lad from Longsight, who was gorgeous enough to get off the bus for.

She heard a frail shout: 'Jan. . .? S'me.'

Alice came into her room, spotting rain.

'Jan.'

She rubbed her eyesockets, yawned into a cough, then felt him leaking.

'Your front door's broke.'

She flipped the pillow.

Alice dropped her satchel on the rug and climbed the bed. Her denim jacket rain-kinked. Droplets bobbled the stubs of her clipped hair. 'I can't kip with a bra on, me.'

Jan saw out the window: slate cloud, carrot roofs, sagging trees. 'Get yourself a towel out of there.'

'You're like an oven in this bed. Am getting toasty from here.' Wet rinds of her Kicker soles were caked in grit, soaking the duvet.

Jan stared at the dirt expressionless. Alice absorbed the silence until finally she clocked the dirt, and that she'd tramped muddy rain through the house. 'Your mam'll go mad, won't she?'

'Can just blame it on the pigs.'

'Y'what?' Alice unlaced her feet in the air – flicking her shoes over her head. '*Pigs?*' They bounced on the rug.

Jan slunk to the wall and faced away.

'How was it?' Alice said.

'Best I've had in me young life.' Jan sat up again. 'Bet you was diddling yourself last night thinking of me and him, wasn't you? Don't lie. Seen your face?'

'Your mam never rang us.'

'Told you. She can't be doing with me.'

'. . .Was he nice?' Alice whispered.

'Nice? He liked me not you. Never even looked at you.'

Alice listened to her cry, then hugged her. 'Where's everybody?'

'Doesn't matter.'

***

Now Thursday morning, May '85, next door's little Joey Harvey opened her bedroom door dancing, hopping, squeaking: 'Nana Nedra said tell her *Get up, you lazybones, if you want breakfast or not!*'

Jan sat up quick and dropped the sheet. She shook her tits at Joey who staggered, clutching his eyes with fright, then raced downstairs. Jan stretched, beaming. She remembered she had Mr Somerville for English first lesson. She'd go in after all.

Joey had left her door open. There began a wailing; her mam, with it, shushing it, going *There there. . .*

Jan picked somewhere soft and unbruised on her body and pinched. Hard. Until everything was water. Though she could still see Kell, face down in her bed. He reeked of lager and farts. Her big brother, not a day out of Strangeways and already he'd tried to strangle her in her sleep.

Jan took the sheet and exposed his peaceful shape and without blinking stared at him long enough to air-dry her sight. Touching his scalp without knowing why, she wanted to cut off a lock of his hair and not keep it but bury it, somewhere only she knew about, but she couldn't decide on the place.

She got up and cat-washed at the sink. Dressed for school, whisper-singing as she dabbed her bruises with tutty. Kell was still dead to the world when she blew him a ta-ra kiss. Then she went straight out, even with the kitchen lively and breakfast-smelling – without even snatching a fistful of Sugar Puffs or her coat from her chair – having already nabbed some spends from her nana's handbag which was hooked on the end of the stair rail.

Jan could've emptied her purse and still eaten her toast in the kitchen and looked her dead in the eye. But Jan wanted her first taste of the day to be Mr Somerville.

IRA 'MAC' MCGOWAN, CHIEF of the honorary Dodds men, turned up that Thursday midmorning to raise the dead and rescue Carol Dodds from martyrdom and widowhood first by recruiting her son over a cooked breakfast followed by a warm slice of angel cake both courtesy of her maminlaw who after all knelt at the altar of hospitality, hypocrisy and false modesty, and might've welcomed Mac after all these years for Jim's sake, or, equally, spiked Mac's tea with oven cleaner for Jim's sake, then fed his bones to the white dog that patrolled their street and one night last November got loose and tore up a family of foxes on Carol's lawn who'd been at her bins for months, leaving Carol to find the magpies first thing, picking through dead leaf, plucking intestines like worms, while she smelled no blood only mulch and dew. But Mac reached her doorstep without running into Joe 90's white dog. Mac might yet charm her son into becoming the Dodds man his dad was or even his grandfather was: Jim Dodds being the Dodds man Mac once worked for as Fixer and Muscle. Mac had been a touch too young to be Jim's peer but too old to play second son, so had bagged the job of Right Hand – long before Carol ever met a Dodds man.

It was inside that Jim met Mac. Having grown pally with a young Brendan Behan in Strangeways who had failed to break a comrade out and wound up locking himself in. Mac brought him to Jim. But the Dodds man's sympathies, a generation from Limerick, were already thinned by the belief that politics and religion were just ways of making a few bob when they weren't getting in the way of doing so. Still, he admired the cause and the romance of it, which made Mac and others think Jim more emerald than he was. They also took Jim for a radical because Jim was unaccountably bright and had taken to reading aloud the *Manchester Guardian* to those who dared listen. Jim's audience of wingmates – many of whom thought to be illiterates or soft in the head – and even screws from the next wing, would come to hear Jim's riffs and editorials, delivered as homilies. The interstices of local government came with the latest ration list and price of beer (1s. 4d. a pint); trade union affairs and London banking disputes; Prime Minister Attlee's speeches; the Princess's engagement calendar; the King's health; the young Queen's coronation. Some men listened in blank terror and those men always sat closest to Jim, letting their cigs burn long. Others relaxed and shut their eyes and warmed themselves in front of the fire of Jim's voice which was steady licking those difficult words and never wavering to milk or acknowledge this communal awe. Jim repeated society obituaries alongside local barber notices for masculine perms at three guineas a piece. It scared them. Jim knew things he shouldn't, things they didn't. And what *they* knew didn't matter because at any moment he could bash them and open their skulls to learn whatever he wanted or rather make certain they knew nowt.

Jim was naturally the first Dodds man to leave Angel Meadows when the City of Manchester claimed Wythenshawe; and later, with Mac, Jim claimed Wythenshawe from the City, and became its guvnor. . .

So said Sefton –

who had first fed Carol *all* this, as the adoring son recounting his father's legend, reluctant but unprompted, that night in '61, not yet having done any time with or for his father, but having seen the inside of a borstal when Carol was still doing Whit Walks with Royal Oak Junior Morris troupe.

Nineteen sixty-one: they were just courting then. He was seething at her cool interest. Wanting to impress on her the savage history of the Dodds clan. Carol was soon up the junction with Kelly and had yet to meet Sefton's mam and wouldn't until she was showing and by then there was nowt to do but fix a wedding date. And so Carol found her approval the easiest to earn, and her respect impossible to gain.

But first Sefton brought her to town, to a basement spieler behind Peter Street, crammed with villains. Ageing Teds like Crombied peacocks. Bent bobbies goosed her and drank to her health. Pimped chorus girls doing blue ditties on the stage apron; their tired winks met her across the club through a fog of Woodbines. Carol was there that night as Sefton's bit, to meet Jim, and all the honorary Dodds men and their women. (Of course, not Jim's missus, Nedra, chained between stove and pew.) This was to be an audition then. And poor Carol, dead keen but no actress. No hope of bagging the role long-term.

Mac was the biggest and the brightest or at least the quietest. Minnie, his missus, the beauty. Carol took him for a Dodds man by blood and hid her surprise when Sefton said he and Mac didn't share a last name. Sefton drank to this like it was a blessing so small he needed reminding of it. Then ordered another round to forget. It was later Carol realised that the more Sefton drank that night the soberer he got. No bar tab. No shillings. No nothing. It was the same everywhere he took her in those first weeks, in town or on the estate, and the ridiculousness of it hadn't worn off, or the queasy glamour it gave her – completely changing how she held a Babycham, wore mother-of-pearl, filled her stockings. Any room full of boozing strangers could credit itself because she were in it, would tear to make way for her delicate feet; where before she would've been swallowed, now she would be looked at like food. *The Jean Shrimpton of Delwood Gardens, this one. Little more breast. Little less leg.* But that night Jim had approved. Of his son courting a mousy bit of fluff in tiny heels and brand-new ribboned polka-dot frock:

Dodds men, laughing.

Go on, then, Jean. Be a good girl and give us a twirl.

Cry later, Carol.

But really Mac's young wife Minnie had done the approving, had won her the job.

Though only Carol had clocked this.

Who took orders from whom.

How Sefton resented Mac.

How satanically sweet Minnie was that first night –

'I'd be well away in that frock, me' – perched cross-ankled at the sinktop when Carol came out of the ladies' stall. An arm ready to whip round her middle.

'Can borrow it, if you like,' Carol said.

Minnie stepped in front of her. 'Go on, then. Let's do us a swap. Imagine their faces, that lot. Those buggers won't know who to take home.' Minnie began to shimmy and moult her own chevron stripes like an insect queen. Joints bending round to unclasp what would on Carol be well out of reach. 'I'm not having you on!'

Carol nodded in polite terror, reversing to return to the stall, only to glance off the shoulder of another girl passing behind. Minnie stopped and giggled and with her thumb knocked once on Carol's lips and Carol opened her gob to protest and Minnie left a little summat dissolving on her tongue.

'On me life if you aren't the absolute cherry. Fucking best thing that handsome bloody brute's ever showed up with of a Friday night. And Jim thought we'd never get to have a look.'

Carol gulped. Burning all the way down.

'Do me up, love.' Minnie, half-spinning. 'Right. Come on. Let's make a few records jump.'

The kindest face housing Pendle-witch eyes. She being a touch older than Carol but a fraction of Mac's age and ruled him as she did Jim. Carol saw all this that night. That Mac's queen ruled the Dodds men, and ruled Jim, even years later, after her youth was spent and her beauty had grown into something seasoned and superior which men still acknowledged with passion and women envied too much to admire.

Carol soon learned Minnie.

Or maybe Minnie soon learned Carol.

Since all Carol really learned that night was that it wasn't just Minnie's body that was half-wasp.

In the cab home Carol shivered and Sefton sulked after she'd done him proud he said and said it like he meant it even if he said it to Oxford Road and not her. He leaned away, breathing, not mad at all but dazed almost, not wanting to be touched, though she needed his shoulder for a headrest and thought he might take her shivers.

'Want me jacket, love?'

'Am fine. It's them uppers Minnie give us to keep awake.'

Sefton, so chuffed with how it went and still deflated. Except for his prick, which scored a third pleat in his best pants. Showed in tides of carnival light along Oxford Road.

Carol, weathering Minnie's pills, sedentary in motion, a razorblade in wet tissue: 'She wants your dad, that girl. Seft, I'm telling you. She wants Jim. *And* did you know she don't wear any drawers?'

'And how the bleeding hell d'you know that?'

'We was in the ladies'. She pops more pills than cross-country lurry drivers. Black bombers, purple hearts. . . Tried giving us allsorts. Never seen anyone dance so much in me life. God, and she knows what she's doing.'

'Then what *you* doing?' He watched her fingertips walk.

'Don't be nasty.' Carol stroked his jaw instead. Five hours since his last shave and already enough grain to catch, to calm her shakes.

His mouth, turning, sodium-lit: 'Me dad. . . you know, he took me last one into the bogs first time I brought her out. Oh yeah. Give her a good time. Same story with the one before that, only he waited a fortnight with her. Though the lass wasn't so keen. Screamed the bloody place down, *she* did. Still never put up much of a fight, he said. . . And so that was that.' He kissed Carol's hand. 'Good job he took a shine to you back there.'

Carol did things inside that cab, things she could later blame on Minnie's pills.

When her front door went, Carol was bent double, in citrus fumes and squeaky marigolds, her arse showing above stirrup leggings and aimed at her front door. The visitor knocked in threes, politely spaced, on the warped glass. Her shirt scabbed with powdered milk and babysick. A red bucket of foamy slop with floating dog-ends was for sponging scuff marks off the skirting and for dribbling water into her maminlaw's handbag, which dangled open on the end of the stair rail, the chocolate purse inside it open too, like a thirsty mouth. The red bucket spread her bare feet. Carol glanced when water splashed them. The nails were sharp and yellowed, her feet otherwise like fresh bars of soap. They belonged to Carol but Carol no longer belonged to *them*; over the years she'd swelled like cake mix, though Nedra's baking wasn't to blame. She toed the crusty carpet daintily while she worked, dried her lovely feet. She heard six-shooters and horse-trot from the telly playing *Bonanza* to itself in a tidy front room. Then she heard the letterbox clapping and Nedra's tangled jewellery at the stove where a pot of summat bubbled. Heard the baby's contented silence in Kelly's room and Kelly's snoring in Jan's.

The letterbox clapped again. At her bucket Carol didn't stop, didn't turn. 'You can see it's open,' she said finally. 'It's always bloody open. Strays get welcomed in this house.'

Mac pushed the door, cleared his throat and stayed outside and she turned – not enough to see him at first. Carol knew Mac just by the mute of his manners. The solid signature of his presence. The huge quiet configuration of his space. With marigolds she tried raising her waistband and soaked her leggings.

'Lo, Carol.' Stooping, clean shaven, no clue where to look.

Her back twinged. She held her hips, wet through, and twisted herself right, grimacing at the hard brightness thinning his silver hair which was parted the same, exactly how it was, almost nine years earlier, at the double funeral. In this hard morning light Mac glowed strong and sheepish and handsome at sixty-five but no younger. His granite features florid. His height unlost and his boxer's hands liver-marked and drawn out from his body, like a gun fighter or a heavyweight champion in a gala suit, comically contained. Shy with it and boyish with it, but in Mac no younger.

'Carol, love?'

'Why now?' she said, going fat at forty-three, skinning those mari-golds. They slapped the red bucket and wet her dried feet.

Carol Dodds left Mac there midmorning and traipsed through the hall she'd lined with bin bags, passed the straightened pictures of her dead men on the walls, towards the kitchen and her maminlaw, whose wide hips blocked her, held the doorjambs. Necklaces chiming. Nedra crossed herself. Carol glanced round but saw only wet footprints in her still-to-be-hoovered carpet. She advanced and Nedra glared through her, to welcome or strike Mac.

Her maminlaw put the kettle on and refused his refusal to be fed. Had him tea-warmed and creaking his kitchen chair, the others empty, his brogues crossed under her kitchen table, on her mopped lino. Nedra hovered, twittering questions. Carol leaned waxen and stiff against a cupboard so his ox shoulderlines were to her with their polite, solemn geometry of violence and she saw everything he was and remembered –

the night she had clawed his back, Christmas Week '76 – four days after losing her husband – when Mac had finally asked her to bed. After the burials, after his wife Minnie became impossible to console in the Oaks where the mourners' finger buffet was held, and began laughing hysterically, in denial or ragged amazement, throwing gin and tonics at the flock walls and dismantling festive decor. Minnie's beauty no longer bewitching; she was just a strung-out mistress wilting without her stolen fucks. When all the drinks were smashed or held from her she began to sway-dance to Johnny Mathis – 'When a Child is Born'. Mac came to her but she snatched off a plum stiletto to javelin him with it, then ran out the pub carrying the other. Nobody but Mac would ever see her again. Humming 'Soleado' in the broken glass of Minnie's laughter, Nedra had dabbed his cut brow with a spill-soaked bar cloth and Carol had smelled rum and tasted rum when he sweated on top of her that night in Minnie's bed, hoping Minnie might come home and catch them. Carol had clawed his back good. Cradled Mac's sweaty head through the night, used his burly weight to trap her despairing giggles. He'd lasted hours, was more patient with her than real love could ever be. Like Nedra, Mac only knew what it was to worship. As he wore out her name Carol wondered where Minnie was. Expecting her to appear at the foot of the bed in ruined makeup with a kitchen knife or revolver. In the morning she left her whitest underpants in Minnie's empty knicker drawer.

Mac's marriage to Minnie was an unconsummated marriage to Jim –

Minnie's marriage to Mac was a consummated marriage to Jim.

Jim Dodds was much the same as Minnie from what Carol witnessed, only a man, so also a hypocrite.

And Carol knew Mac had suffered two decades' cuckoldry, with an ascetic pride and sickness. He had said as much to Carol that night, more concussed than unburdened. His talk was rare but it came freely then, and it was heavy as another body in the bed, fucking her.

For a living Mac had meted out Jim's cruelties, having been weak enough to hurt and be hurt, having needed only to hurt and be hurt. And so in the end, Carol reckoned, his soul was a spot cleaner than Minnie's and no blacker than her own.

She knew for years Mac had pined for her: Jim's son's missus. And she knew her husband had once tried it on with Minnie. But Sefton had no chance with his dad's mistress. Maybe the reason Sefton had toasted Mac's not being a true Dodds man in blood and surname was because unlike a Dodds man he had never been bewitched by Minnie; he'd married her instead.

That night Mac had shrugged his own abeyance onto Carol, to simmer and reduce, till it was burned on her for good. When, after her body's possibilities had been exhausted and these open secrets shared, Mac told Carol he was sorry. Dead sorry at having helped bury that bookish Sharston feller she'd been keen on for a time. Mac had known Sefton knocked her about and, with him being inside then, it was only natural she'd seek *comfort* elsewhere.

Comfort. Yes.

Carol nodded close. On Minnie's duck-feather pillow.

Mac nodded closer.

And still nodding Carol replayed Vern's daft jokes and drippy quotes inside her head so as not to scream.

Mac took her thin smile for forgiveness and slept peacefully beside her, spent.

The next morning, knickerless, she collected Jan and Kelly from her inlaw; Nedra, widowed too, would soon move in. When Vern climbed into her own bed the next night, Carol had whispered: *I finally had me a fuck with Mac. Decent stuff too. No complaints.* Poor Vern, resting his soft hands on her waist while she told the jokes for once. Vern was then only seven years dead. Laughing with his ear to her belly as she described Mac's prick pumping the content of his confession, Vern's laughter light and sincere. Carol's thicker. Crazed. Vern hadn't mentioned it since and Carol never brought it up. By now he'd forgotten because of course –

the dead soon forget; it's the living who don't.

'Sounds like quite the performance,' Vern had said. 'Especially for an older chap – even a big ox like *him*. For you he must've been on fire.'

'He sets people on fire, Mac does. For Jim. With petrol.' Carol held Vern's face. 'Laugh,' she said. 'Go on.'

And they did.

Then she'd rolled Vern to the other side of the bed: the space as warm as Vern's cheek since her husband's shattered body was but a day in the ground; Nedra's still to replace it.

So Ira 'Mac' McGowan was Carol's last living shag. Back in Manchester, shy in her kitchen expecting scran, and without Minnie. He even uncrossed his brogues and craned with his brew to show her the reverse tan of his ring finger around the curve of the mug.

'You've no need to be going to any trouble.'

'You're alright, cock,' Nedra said. 'Might as well have summat if I'm making our Kelly his breakfast.'

Mac looked at the wall clock. To Carol he said: 'How's the lad doing?'

' . . . '

'What age is your Jan now?'

' . . . '

At the cooker Nedra's twittering became humming became bacon hissing. The pot on the back burner; lard smoking the pans.

An angel cake cooled in a tin on the window ledge, its heat raising Carol's wrist hairs as she cracked the stiff window some more, then refilled the kettle and sat in her own seat, a space between them. Fry-up smells smothering the cake's, replacing yesterday's stew.

Mac was the same polite animal, afraid of women. His small eyes wet and lips half open, wanting and not wanting to settle on her. Everything here embarrassed him. She hoped he'd use the toilet and have to replant the orchard of varisized bras drip-drying on the racks just to piss standing up. But Nedra's shame would be greater than his. At the table Carol outglared him and he turned for help but her maminlaw kept her back to them, cracking eggs, nude tights wrinkled about her ankles and her enormous arse flossy with white dog hair. Carol never let that beast in her house but knew Nedra brought it in through the kitchen to spite her. Carol caught her the other day feeding it corned beef off the lino with Joe 90 prancing on the back step in his school uniform, looking like he could have done with the extra slices on his butties.

'Our Jan's fifteen now, isn't she, Nedra? With a baby upstairs she won't so much as look at. Me eldest Kelly's twenny-three in June and got let out of Strangeways yesterday. But you knew that. Be why you're here.'

He blew on his tea, tried again: 'So your Kelly's a chip off the old block, is he?'

Nedra dropped a warmed plate. It clattered intact on the counter like a coin losing its spin. 'Wait till you see him, Mac. Just wait. Grown up now, has Kelly. Would make his dad proud' – her voice so flighty her words took off and vanished into sausage smoke.

When he let go of the mug Carol reached across the damp clean table to touch his mottled left hand. She shaped her fingers over the mass grave of his knuckles as if hoping to find a name on a headstone. She kept smirking and made his frightened eyes follow hers to the ceiling. 'See for yourself.'

Nedra waddled into the hallway, hammering an empty saucepan with a wooden spoon, then returned as if she were still sounding her dinnerbell, shouting: 'Kelly's good as gold, Mac. Always they've crossed the men of this family, haven't they? Always. But by Mary's mercy he is home again – our lad – where he bloody belongs.'

Watching her maminlaw put spoon and pan in the sink, having failed somehow to raise Kelly or even the baby, Carol said: 'By here she means in bed on a Thursday morning at ten past eleven like the jobless ex-con he is.'

Mac picked up a knife and fork.

Carol folded her arms and leaned in. 'Where's Minnie? That bitch ever bear you any of your own?'

Neat cuts and stabs; he loaded his tools: 'You know what our Minnie were like. Nah, no kiddies. Not on your life.'

'Well?'

'Cancer of the breast. They told us just after Christmas. Give her some options, but she said *Sod all that*. Said they could fu— Pardon me, Nedra. She told em where to go. Fifty, she was. Picture our Minnie at fifty. Wedded at twenny-one.'

Carol watched her maminlaw: careful, worrying her rosary and necklaces. Nedra came over but changed her mind, retreating to the cooker. Put her back to them and said:

'Well, Carol wedded our Sefton younger. Of course, he never had much choice, but that's by the by. And I were eighteen with our Jim. It were the done thing then, you see? God rest them both.'

'And God rest my Minnie. You were at ours, remember?'

Still Nedra wouldn't sit. 'Aye, I do. Our Jim as your best man. He lent you a few bob for your wool suit and you was both such handsome fellers, the pair of you, with your thin tashes like in the films. And you wanted the reception at the Midland but had to settle for the Brown Cow and so I baked them little pudd—'

'When did she die?' Carol said. 'Minnie.'

Mac chewed and swallowed. 'Valentine's Day. You believe that?'

Nedra: 'Good God.'

'Good riddance.' Carol took a triangle of his toast.

Nedra dry coughed, almost a fit.

Mac poured her a glass of water using a dirty glass by the sink and sat again, pulling out a seat but she wouldn't sit. Then for the first time since the baby, Nedra made Carol a brew and Carol sipped it right away, let it loosen her teeth. Burning herself as the doorbell went.

Then –

the sound of Kelly's feet quick on the stairs.

Carol saw through the hall; her son slowed before he got to the door to belt his plaid dressing gown, (one which Carol could've sworn she'd got rid of) avoiding the bucket and bin bags of party rubbish to let Zuley in, golden brown in a red sunfrock which must have weighed as much as a first-class stamp. Shutting the front door with her back, to kiss her.

Zuley fought him off. 'Not even brushed your teeth.'

'Not had me breakfast yet.'

'Lazy get.' Zuley saw her sat in the kitchen and crossed the hall smiling like summer and he followed.

Who is it? Nedra mouthed, back at the stove.

You fled Manchester with Minnie, and in doing so finished Jim's firm. Dissolved its elastic web of honoraries and leeches: minders, doormen, drivers, scrap dealers, landlords, bookmakers, pill traders, pimps and armed robbers. You had finally renounced Jim and son by not leading an inquisition into their senseless deaths on that Christmas Eve, which our Nedra had expected then demanded then begged for – wanting summat done about the well-to-do young lads left alive on Christmas morning. Instead you skipped Wythie, and finally got one by Jim, after choking on your eulogy at the pulpit, for which Nedra repaid you hours later in tender nursing, stopping your blood at the Oaks.

Your morbid devotion to Jim: severed only when you let the dead lie. This –

Carol knew, had condemned Nedra to a phantasmal life of righteous nostalgia, blind sight and deaf ears, false memories and wilful distortions and indomitable resilience. With her wrath unfulfilled, her eternal soul came out Daz-white in the wash. In this way it was Mac's desertion of Jim in death which gifted Nedra the will to live, in stove pots and church gossip. Ira 'Mac' McGowan. Not Our Lord or the Blessed Virgin or St Christopher or St Agatha or that week's patron saint of Miserable Cows. And that was worth a warm slice of angel cake, an extra teabag and a fry-up.

Now her maminlaw glowered at Zuley's skin and scanty frock, a stirring spoon raised like a club. 'Oh, it's you, love. Thought you said you worked in town?'

Zuley said: 'Thursday I have off' – and Nedra turned, satisfied, and Carol caught the girl mouth to Kelly: *She forgets me name but remembers that?*

From behind, Kelly pecked his nana's cheek, holding her shoulders where she was littlest and not turning as Mac introduced himself but only nodding when he sat with him to eat.

Zuley said *Iya*; Mac asked her name and she chose the chair between them.

Nedra moved a pan to the front burner. 'Fraid the kitchen's closed, love, since we wasn't expecting company.'

'Was you expecting *him*?' Kelly pointed his baked-bean-juiced knife at Mac.

'*Kell*,' Zuley said.

Mac said: 'Ee-ah, love. Have some of me toast.'

'You're alright, honest. It's *this* one what's in a mood after yesterday.' Kelly scraped his plate.

Mac breathed in long enough to make his chair back creak. 'Heard you got out yesterday, lad. I've been in there meself twice. So, what reason in the world could there be this morning for you to be acting your shoe size?'

Chewing: 'Who *are* you?'

'Don't you know, lad?' Nedra said.

'He knows,' Carol said.

'. . .You one of them what worked with me dad.'

'Aye. And your granddad,' Mac said.

Nedra took Mac's plate, topped up his brew and cut him the first cake slice.

Mac smiled back silently, smiled at everybody, then tucked in. 'Champion that, Nedra.'

Nedra was finally in a chair, skimmed to the middle of the floor which had already lost its mop shine. 'Where did you say you was stopping, love?'

'Rod's putting us up in town for a few weeks while we sort out a job. Has himself a gaff now off Monton Street.'

'Not far from me, that,' Zuley said.

'Hope it's far enough,' Carol said.

'Rod Westlake? Never.' Nedra jogged her fat knees. 'Oh, I'll have to wrap him up a slice. He was a nice kid, Rod. Always a gent, which you know our Jim liked.'

Carol said: 'Bet he's still a pimp.' She drew Zuley into a look and the girl chewed her cheek.

'Oh shush, you' – her maminlaw's face, her voice, changing for Mac. 'Did Rod ever marry?'

Carol kept on: 'Does he still go around telling everyone he keeps a gun?'

Mac swallowed.

Nedra twisted the bundles of tinfoiled cake and left them by his mug.

'So, what have these two got planned for the day?' Mac said to her son.

'You tell him,' Kelly said.

Zuley sipped from his tea. 'Got it all sorted, haven't we? Gunna go for a walk round Styal, after we see about getting him a job. Then we're going pictures in Gatley to watch that *Starman*.'

'Ay, lad. There's probably a bit of work for you with us in town if you want it?'

Carol scoffed.

'Doing what?' her son said.

'You driving yet?' Mac said.

'Yeah but I've no car.'

'Can fix that.'

From inside his suit jacket Mac unclipped a wad of fives, maybe a hundred pound or more, and slid it folded across the table to her son. 'It's work I'm offering. Have a think, anyroad. We can have a proper chat if you're a grafter. And if not then this'll sort you till you find summat to keep you out of bother.'

Kelly took it and unfolded it and stared at Mac. 'Ta,' he said, stuffing it down his dressing-gown pocket.

Zuley brought Kelly's plate and mug to the sink, thanked Nedra and said to Mac: 'Don't worry, mate, there's no chance he'll waste it on me.'

'He has the look of your Jim now. More than your Sefton. Don't you reckon, Nedra?'

Carol stared at the table, saying nowt.

Mac embarrassed and Nedra peeved and Kelly wondering and Zuley wanting to help but unsure how.

Mac said to her son: 'I best be going. I've gotta look up a few rum buggers before I get back to Rod's. Tell you what: come with, lad. We'll have us a ride out, if you want—'

'That's enough,' she said.

'I wanna see to it that he can pay his way,' Mac said. 'But it's up to you, Carol. Ee-ah, lad. Come if you wanna meet a few faces.'

Carol left her chair out.

In Kelly's room the baby slept content. Warm-smelling and salt-smelling and one of his legs twitched under the stiff blanket as Death's shadow brushed him –

Vern Jenkins', checking the radiator. He raised the temperature and pushed at the window to be sure it was shut.

'There a draught in here or is it just me?'

'You *are* naked,' she said.

'Well, who's to blame for that?'

'I don't know. What you doing out in the day? Come away from the window.'

Vern turned, waving to nobody. 'Neighbours ought to be impressed. First yesterday's do. And now for some culture.' Vern swung towards her, full-mast.

'Can't you cover up?'

'What with?'

The baby coughed awake and grinned and Carol picked him up and he smiled at Vern who admired him over her shoulder.

'He's the best-looking one yet. And this family's produced some lookers. What's his name again?'

'Told you, love. He's not got a name yet.'

'Carol. He's minutes from walking. Soon to start his classics degree.'

'Hold him a minute. He'll just sleep.'

'Can you hear that? He's singing sonnets.'

'He's your blood.'

'Mine? Me bloody grandson. And I don't look a day over thirty, I'm told.'

'Make it go down,' she said.

'Only you can do that and even then not for long.' Vern shrugged and stared quietly and she felt his expression not wanting or willing anything from her but a smile.

'Does it go when you're not here, with *me*?'

'Where do I go when I'm not here? Stockport Library? I've nowt to read but *you*.'

He nosed her temple, her bunned hair. Back in her arms the baby's dreams sang to them.

Vern held her waist by the cot and whispered: 'Listen to that song.' She winced when his soft daughterly hands left her and Death's shadow moved to the window again. She hadn't dared look at him straight on for longer than a glance.

Yellowed linen and a ripped mattress protector and mildewed towels were wadded beneath the radiator and Vern shook them out and fashioned a toga from the best sheet and twirled. Beside her again he breathed along her cheekbone, whispering: 'I dare you, Carol Dodds, to get dressed and leave this house before the Macintosh Munster carts you off to his crypt.'

'He wasn't bad in bed.'

'Quick. Find your shoes.'

'I dare you to go, too, if I go.'

'To leave you?' he said.

Carol set the baby down.

Vern was scratching his elbow, not coy not proud not punishing her, just reading their grandson's song.

'Right,' she said. 'I'll go now, shall I?'

'For a walk.'

'Round Wythenshawe Park. How long's it been?'

'Why not?'

To the window: 'Smashing weather.'

'Shame nobody'll watch the baby except you.'

'Take him with. Do him some good.'

'Vern, love, where did they bury you?' Carol went sick and heavy with a happiness. On seeing Vern limned by sunshine after sixteen years. She knelt next to the cot, her legs about to give.

Half-clothed at the window there was only gleam where Vern's lovely nose and mouth should have been. He lifted another mucked towel off the floor and revealed a box of Sugar Puffs overturned. Vern maraca'd the box, scooped a handful of stale cereal to offer it her, but she didn't respond, wanting only to listen to him crunch and the pleasure it gave her stopped her saying:

I must know where they buried you, love. He's the only man left who can tell us.

Instead Carol said: 'Do you miss your books?' – remembering Vern Jenkins was lovely and daft and hers.

'*Clever* is rightly a Northern pejorative,' he said. '"Oi, teach me big words," you said to us once. When? I forget. "So I can sound as useless as you and sign on."' He pulled the waistband of her stirrup leggings – tugging her away from the cot. Her thighs and crotch were chapped from sop water. As he inspected her she looked up at him, loving with her bones. 'Where's your knickers, love?' he said.

'No clean pairs. I'm as bad as Minnie, aren't I? Do you remember her? Dead now. She never wore none alive. Nedra used to call her Lucifer's concubine.'

'That would make Jim Lord Lucifer.'

'That's right. It would.'

She wept and giggled and woke the baby and lifted him: giggling too and grabbing for her nose, tickled by her tears.

'I'll marry him. Mac. If he's back to ask me. I'd marry him just to know.'

Vern nodded, accepting her pain. Dried her grin with thumbs softer than her own ever were.

Then Mac entered the room to speak to her alone – brave, for him – while her son waited for him downstairs by the door. Carol heard Kelly fobbing off Zuley. Who only shouted mock-cheerfully up the stairs: *Ta-ra then* before escaping Carol's house, quick and easy, and all by herself.

ONE OCTOBER SABBATH JIM swept her to the howling moors for two nights, having sorted, he said, a black stone cottage with a fire and a great big kitchen, overstocked courtesy of Minnie McGowan. That woman who only spoke arch or blue, who even cheeked Jim, and whose barren body was sinful standing, sitting or waddling. Aged thirty-five by then, but denying gravity; still Mac's twenty-one-year-old bride.

That Sunday Jim returned from the Woodpecker at two and sprang it on her. Told her to forget his bloody dinner, neat's tongue, already dished up having scented the house before he'd left. They were going on their holidays and going now. He wouldn't say where, which was romantic. Her Jim told her like her Jim: calm, firm, and then went out and sat in his cramped Triumph bibbing the horn while she packed fast as she could, packing for him too without knowing what to take or how much, which was romantic.

Nedra Dodds was fifty then and working. She, the most beloved dinnerlady in Wythenshawe, let alone St Christopher's Infant School, feeling guilty that October for having more time off and guiltier for not feeling guilty enough. It'd been eight days since she lost the miracle and still she bled constant. For the first few she was punch-drunk with pain so intense she couldn't stir a pot on the new stove fast enough to keep the stews from burning on the bottom and so found herself bobbing in the wake of Jim's wrath come teatime. Twittering sorry twenty times to his feet and twenty more to Our Lady.

Our son gets his self home, back home from that blinking place, and here's you, here, bringing us down. Make us wanna be back inside meself. Jim talked these truths to her Friday. Mary speaking through Jim so she'd listen. And Nedra tried and tried yet found herself in tears just gossiping with the streets' women after Mass about nowt more than those hairdos you only see in the wicked magazines they bring out for young girls, who knew bloody better round this way. Nedra, wet-cheeked, reassured the old aunts and new mothers, until two went past up Dunkery Road, bare legs and dyed dos, like foreign harlots, both girls unidentifiable through her tears, but surely spoilt and truanting. But truth was, if her Jim wasn't in, Nedra turned no child away, no matter whose, no matter what. Fed every stray who found her table – absconding lads from Rose Hill reformatory, with those glints of fear and shame shining through even the unruliest buggers; lasses rouged and disowned and with hardly a stitch of skirt (for this was 1969 and man had decided Heaven wasn't high enough so built rockets to fly beyond it) – she fed them and fed them seconds. Nedra spoke of each, in kitchens, front rooms and Sunday pews, settling her suspicions and reproof in saints' prayer.

Days ago: the tears came while explaining to a new neighbour how to balance ingredients in some recipe or other when you were short, like back during rations. Tears washing her doorstep. Anything could set her off. Anything what had stolen her mind from the pain long enough for her to realise it'd momentarily gone which meant the miracle would soon be truly gone as the cruel spells of mess and pain shortened and the physical marks went and then the physical memory went too and finally it would be like the miracle never came upon her at all. So at fifty Nedra prayed the hurt kept, and was grateful that week, and grateful even after the stay at the moorside cottage, for each minute it did. Knowing soon there would not be enough pain to believe in. . .

For years, after the miracle and the pain of its leaving had left her, almost up until her Jim and her Sefton were taken, she often woke herself of a night having salted the pillows. She wept them through, pretending she was an oyster diver like in the pictures they used to show before the one you wanted to see, at Tatton Cinema, during the war. Nedra would trap the sound of her swimming inside her pillow for fear of waking Jim and causing another to-do.

Nedra returned to church and baked plum cakes to raise pennies for the tots keen for shoes. And if she was fit for church she was fit for work; but her Jim understood once he'd been fed, told her not to mither just yet and give it more time.

See how you feel, our lass. Just mind how you go.

Feeling so out of things, so suddenly aware of herself that she feared she would splinter. Her bleeding mind from her bleeding body. Maybe there was no Heaven for her. Maybe there was no Heaven. No miracles. Only a harlot moon.

Nedra banished these thoughts; confessed her shame and her precious pain.

That October Sabbath, the stone cottage mid hill and sky –

the moors, pitiless home to lost graves. A Devil's garden planted of angels. Those Manchester horrors: tabloid headlines Nedra still wouldn't read. But that day the moors were –

for her resting; Jim's treat.

Miracle blood.

Innocent blood.

She bled.

When they got up there, as well as an open fire and a stocked pantry, she found indoor plumbing and a cellar full of what looked like her old linen, knotted, and several spades and shovels. Upstairs were three draughty blue-ceilinged bedrooms. Mac was there too, with his Minnie.

'Your face,' Minnie said, sauntering towards her like Cleopatra in her silk stockings, her teeth lit with excitement. Mac was behind her, his shoes off and all, but still having to duck the painted beams.

Jim stared down Nedra's shock, warning her to keep it buttoned, and so Nedra just said – having been told nowt, and knowing it best not to ask – *Oh hello*. Even as Minnie hugged her warmly and took her smallest case from her and hauled it to the biggest bedroom before Mac grabbed the rest.

When they returned Sefton had arrived, driving somebody's green Morris Minor up the gated mud lane. It matched the moors' green through the cottage window but minutes later when Nedra looked again, it didn't.

So it was a family holiday.

What with her son here, fresh out of prison. What with her Jim knowing she needed it, having come unthreaded. A change of room and air. The landscape a humbling display of the Lord's hand. Thanks to Jim, they had rallied.

Sefton stepped in sullen and prickly, without his Carol or bag even, or change of clothes. But Nedra pressed him as mothers can and learned that Carol was back with him already, as was little Kelly. Nedra had her grandson again. Things had been put right and she kissed his face, everso glad.

Minnie said: 'Ay, this means you and Carol are new again. And all new couples do is each other.'

Sefton's bleak smile as Jim roared.

Minnie went: 'Why've you not brought them along, love? The more the messier.'

'Kelly's caught a bug,' Sefton said, picking knuckle scabs.

'Poor lad,' Nedra said.

'Fix us a brew, Mam. Am gasping.'

And she did.

Then the menfolk went for a ramble on the moors before last light, leaving her with ageless Minnie, who ran a bath and stripped off in front of the fire. Took her tea with three sugars and no milk into the tub and read *Reveille* magazine. Nedra briefly forgetting her miracle and her pain while she prepped supper for five – all Dodds men and women, regardless of what it once had said on their ration cards.

With the last vegetables chopped, she heard Minnie emerge from the tub and stoke the fire.

'How we doing, Nedra, love?'

Working. Bowed at the pew: 'Long as this stove stays lit we'll get there.'

'Been everso quiet, you. You're not right in yourself. And we all know *someone* has to give us a dressing-down when I get gobby, and if it's not you, well. . . Our Mac won't do it. Will he 'eck. God, this fire's toasting me tits. A good dressing-down is what I need regular, otherwise there's trouble. From not having a mother, that is, Mac reckons. But you know I've meself to blame there. This fire. This place. Feel like a fucking duchess, don't you? Sorry. Ay, shall we have a drink? Brought Babycham for us and bottle of Navy for your Jim.'

Over her shoulder, Nedra saw a steaming white body bent before the fire, gold-beaded with bathwater.

'Good God, you'll catch your bloody death, girl—'

Minnie laughed, straightened, turned. 'If our boys don't catch us first.'

The sittingroom and fireplace were divided from the kitchen by an oriental rug in need of a beating and Nedra left the black stove to drag the heavy curtains. Sent dust into the reach of firelight backshaping Minnie. The rooms became a glowing pit and Mac's wife a glittering cut-out limned against the coals, her beauty blasphemous, her hipped stance wide, her waist a child's, her eyes rubbed out. Minnie seemed to be prancing skyclad like a Pendle witch above the fire, but never moved more than her head to follow Nedra crossing the rug to dark the cottage.

Again Minnie laughed at her. 'They'll be a bit yet, don't worry. It's just us girls.' A satanic-sweet giggle coating the words – only around Nedra. A tool which any other vulgar tart with fantasies would no doubt overwield. Plenty flocked after Nedra's men. With coarser soaps and thinner stockings and cheaper rosewater perfumes than Minnie's. Sawdust on their worn-down heels. Lasses in pencil- or mini-skirts, hanging off the ends of war stories and good tailoring, while stuffed inside corner booths at the Woodpecker, supping heads off her men's Watneys Red Barrel. Nowadays Nedra didn't frequent pubs with her husband. Jezebels posed no threat. Though Carol had once been one of them. And by the Devil she'd done well, having snared Sefton to be accepted, had Nedra's first and final grandson, only to take him and run off at the first sign of bother. Now Carol was back, to be forgiven and embraced once more. Carol she saw through. But not Minnie. None like Minnie. Who could talk nude under a cottage roof on a strange hinterland in autumn afternoon without her flesh goosepimpling, without her lashes, breath or bones quivering, without breaking into shards of shame.

The big light was on now and Minnie took a folded towel from the settee arm and patted herself without modesty. The snowtops of her thighs wore delicate blue veins. A fresh outfit for evening laid over the moss cushions though Nedra never saw her lay it. Minnie rolled on a clean stocking:

'You've always been a mother to me. And he's like me little brother, is your Sefton. Even if it was just daft business. He had us going – thinking he might do real time, you know? No idea why we worry. Glad he's out, though, ay? And back with his Carol. There's plenty worse about. Aren't you glad it's sorted? They've all fixed it.'

'*Fixed* it?' Nedra said.

Minnie, eyes reckless, insinuating, welled with some colour of sympathy. Nedra hadn't noticed her put on the pearl brassiere. Minnie wandered into the kitchen, her crisp plum dress folded over one arm. She spooned the broth on the back burner, sampling it greedily. The cold-carved whiteness of her: like a provocation from those French picture pamphlets that Jim's lads once left a box full of in the Triumph's boot.

Nedra tried: 'You forget your drawers in a hurry?'

Minnie seasoned Nedra's broth, chuckling, then offered the spoon for approval.

But the hurt reclaimed Nedra who winced and stepped backwards across the oriental rug till she caught the settee arm as a crutch. More of the miracle was leaving her. Could she make it to her room before the lavatory?

'Nedra?'

A vision of a lipsticked teacup left on a sopping bathroom tile.

'You know, I've lost all mine. Three. Or four. Dunno whether to count the last.' The broth spoon down. Counting on painted fingers.

'That's right. One last year. Then there was another two just after we got married. And then the time I'm not too sure about, over the summer. Our Mac always makes like he don't know what's the matter. *Women's business*, they call everything, don't they?'

'. . .'

'Men can't think what to say, can they? Not men like ours. Don't care how many fights they have; we know, don't we? We bleed better than *them*.'

'You never said.'

'No, I know. . . But what with you. . . I mean at *your* age. When you've a couple grown already. Must be different for you.'

'Minnie. I am sorry for you. I'll say a prayer for you before bed.'

The giggle not gone: 'Why? It's you I'm worrying about here. Don't feel blue about *me*.'

'Did our Jim tell you?'

'Told our Mac what a right shock it was. You at your age up the duff. Can't blame him. He didn't know *what* to do. Course, neither did our Mac. Course, me, I must've said the right thing *somehow*.'

Nedra unclutched her belly, watched her and winced. '*Sorry?*'

'What you keep saying sorry for? T'isn't your doing.' Minnie came closer, cupping Nedra's elbows, and Nedra had never felt such naked warmth from a grown woman. Both of them brewing tears.

'Our Mac's fifty now and not bothered now. Reckons it's down to his *shortcomings*. Honest to God. He's good; he's like that; it's way he thinks. It's him what was after some babies. Only what can you do?'

'Pray. Our Lady will listen.'

Minnie lit the dry saucepan of garden peas and hiked the flame. 'Don't worry; I'm not burning them. I get the pan dead hot, right, then I pour the hot water in. I like seeing the peas dance. Taste sweeter this way, I'm telling you. Can blame me if they don't.'

'Minnie,' she whispered.

'Said a quick prayer *for you*. Soon as I heard you'd lost it, I said one.' A wet wink. 'We do some kneeling, don't we, me and you, ay?' Old Shuck lit Nedra inside Minnie's irises with his unholy flame. 'Nedra, love, you can kneel to please, but' – the saucepan spitting – 'I wouldn't swap my little cunt for the world.'

Nedra gasped, saw Minnie in the flesh once more and was afraid. Minnie wriggled into her plum frock away from the stove seconds before the cottage door blew open. Dodds men returned with splattered wellies, jackets and shovels but without voices till after the meal was had and Minnie fetched the drink.

Jim said the broth was her best ever but them peas were a touch too sweet. Nedra just cleared the plates.

Right before night tipped to morning Nedra woke herself. Bad with the pain. Cheeks smarting and sticky from her oyster dives. Beside her Jim breathed shallow, muttered but didn't wake. She reached for her rosaries and found only dead space and remembered where she wasn't. She waited for sight, then claimed the rosaries on the wicker bedtable, lower than hers at home, scratching them into her fist –

her Jim slept deeper.

A Dodds man, hilled peacefully under a quilted spread, even after she peeled a corner to sit up. Saltwater had spilled across their pillows and darkened his bedshirt collar. Further south were spots where she'd lost her miracle through to the mattress – leaving her worst for five days.

Nedra trembled in sweats and bit her rosary fist.

By night the floorboards' dust had somehow grown into dank fur and the sharp chill cramped her foot, but she'd forgotten to pack her tattered moccasins and Jim's house slippers were too big to borrow silently.

Time was suspended in the bathroom behind the plank door, dealing with the mess by moonlight, ashamed to turn on the light. Such awful business, and on the first night away, made her meek and feverish and queered her faith. At some point Nedra woke on the lavatory when she upset Minnie's teacup on the floor tile. It clattered; then the silence burst her ears and her toes were splashed with icy dregs. By the moor's moon she saw a frantic spider in the bathtub, flinching under the tap drips.

Crossing the L-shaped hall before dawn Nedra felt the air shake with metal falling on cellar stone. She knew the shovelhead sound and knew not to go to it but still went and started the cellar stairs and paused, listening and peeping in a daze, only to retreat in a clumsy hurry and find her son tranced in the livingroom dark listening with her. He was completely dressed; the texture of him told her. His breath showed and again she trembled. The braced oak door to outside squeaked ajar with the draught smelling of dew and wilderness. Sefton raised his fists slowly like an automaton. She went and latched the door and shut out the moors, catching him gently at the wrists and walked him to the kitchen sink where his silhouette became red flesh. She couldn't get his wedding band off for the swelling. His mangled hands were frozen. She rinsed his blood and cleaned out ticks of grit, grass and soil under his fractured nails, then bathed his knuckles in a pan. She'd done this countless times, mothering one local warrior or other, but most often her son, prefacing the Saxa sprinkles with: *This'll make your teeth whistle*. But tonight she was dumb. Sefton didn't struggle or swear or clown, so she pressed an ear to his chest to hear his heart thump.

'. . .Mam?'

'. . .Yes, love?'

His fists dribbled. One broken for certain. Nedra twittered her prayers like tremens. He'd been hitting walls and earth outside. He was not right in himself. In this, he took after his mam.

She heard herself go: 'You've been cooped up for twelve month. That's why. Needed to stretch your legs again. Lucky you didn't get lost. Daft devil.'

'Mam, you not seen them down there?' A flattened whisper. 'D'you not hear them?' Her son's lips didn't move.

Her ears tuned to the cellar.

Nedra wrapped his balloon hand in soaked teatowels and walked him to bed like some noctambulist marionette. Then got back in hers.

Jim returned from the cellar soon after, rosewater-scented. Warmer than the bed he'd left. He fell right asleep beside her on a dried ocean pillow.

Morning the moors breezed, the ground frosted, the clear sky empty sun.

'Have you no scarf?' Mac's eyelids crinkled to the wind, were studded with moles and blended bumps.

Near him Nedra tightened the headscarf knot under her chin, afraid of losing hers as the wind whipped Minnie's hair loose, then forwards. She screamed for the thrill of it and tugged down her skirt. Nubs of long grass in murmuration for miles about. Rolls of lowland rising with ripples of violet. Once the wind died Minnie picked flowers and they stayed long enough for her to French kiss Mac with them in her hair.

'Like bloody kids these two' – Jim smirking and tutting, pointing with his arm round Nedra; their son off ahead on his own.

Small at a distance, Sefton stepped so straight and steady into the sun so as to never be moving farther or nearer, only the wind filling his sports jacket in random animation like a scarecrow pitched in a gale. Stiff-backed, taunting and unreachable like a mirage.

Pushed by the weather, Nedra raised her knees to stride the taller grass without slowing. Each pace they climbed: the moorland unspooling unnoticed into grand region, the incline felt in her lungs, her legs, as she pursued Sefton to higher ground. Her fabric scarf under the plastic hood fluttered; the wind deafening one ear until she adjusted the knot so the wrap squeezed her cheeks into her eyes, trapping sweat.

'Like bloody kids,' said Jim.

'Or just man and wife having their holidays,' Minnie sang, beside him, garters emergent whenever her coat and skirt inflated. Shrieking and falling about, cat-rubs against two men. That milk complexion powdered, her forehead turned by albescent rays into a second sun. Nedra stared blinded until the wind or bonelight made her tear. Her leaking body knotted tighter in horror. Each step Nedra took became automatic. Mounting steps. Mounting sickness. Doubt the decades she'd given him. A life spent keeping house with and without him. Doubt words spoken to silence local nattering, rumour and dissent, whenever he got put away. Doubt his loving arm now warming and curling her thick waist while he kidded her and Mac and Minnie; at ease unlike yesterday, handsome at fifty-nine but younger that morning, even without a shave. The anger in Nedra's belly wouldn't light. To be like them creatures she twice saw on her way to Civic, battling on their roads in broad day, clawing each other bare in front of neighbour and child, over one working man. Doubt Jim's greatest blessing: a brain which belied his schooling – think of the things he could read and retain. Doubt the miracle of which she was unworthy. Doubt the saints even.

But no.

That morning Nedra had risen last, gone nine, having been awake much of the night. She hadn't drunk a drop after supper, afraid it might steal her pain. Minnie rose first, they said, despite drinking herself sick, and having been up in the night too. Minnie claimed the kitchen to cook more breakfast than they could hope to walk off. Nedra smelled it, and heard them all, while she knelt to pray. The ruined linen went into a cobwebbed wicker box. Then with effort Nedra flipped the stained mattress, appealing to no saints to lift it through her.

When she came out dressed only Mac at the table looked up. 'Morning.'

'Knew you needed a lie-in,' said Minnie, twisting at the sink. A pyramid of pots. A chequered pinny pinched short and still longer than the hemline beneath.

Mac finished his plate and stopped reading yesterday's *News of the World* to pull out the heavy chair between him and her husband; and Nedra said *ta* and sat across from her son who was scoffing toast. Thirty-one in January and he still left the crusts. His left hand bandaged from a first-aid tin in the boiler cupboard. Right fingers ringed with gruesome plasters.

Nobody sat where they'd sat the night before.

Jim had finished his plate too and yesterday's *Manchester Guardian*, which he shut to kiss Nedra's cheek, then opened again.

'Sleep well?' Mac said.

'Not while *you* did,' Minnie said before she could speak. 'This one were snoring the second he climbed in. Go anywhere and he's out like *that*, once he's had his drop of Lamb's and a bit of nookie. Bloody

Count Bartelli here. Broke the bed.' Jim's laugh crumpled the paper. 'Reckon we could be mithering you and Jim tonight. The four of us having to top-and-tails it like sardines. Imagine?'

'. . .Twelve eggs?' Nedra saw the open cartons empty on the sideboard.

'*This* lot.' Minnie accused left and right. 'Your Jim had three. Anyone'd think you don't feed him.'

Jim tattooed his belly, reading.

'I kept two for us.'

Nedra let her serve her and they ate together last. Facing. She felt herself between Minnie's teeth. Minnie ate like she talked like she dressed like she moved: with a sheer lubricity. A taunting behind the put-on, able to conjure Nedra's worst fears, of desecration and devaluation; to be kinless, unDodded, ungodly, unwanted, sulphurous and alone. No kiddies or men to dish for. No saint to thank or beseech, no Holy Father or Mother to forgive her sins, no blood to make her world beat. Aberrant thoughts these. But soon she'd be *right as rain, right as rain*. Even when –

Minnie sang summat wordless and gay and beckoning – as she swung on Mac's arm after breakfast, on their walk, and did a skip-step to keep up with his long strides. By noon they were a good way from the cottage and the wind gone. And though they saw two chalk-and-slate mountain hares big as dogs, the birds never sang with Minnie. A red grouse got chased off by a magpie beaking moths off the thistles, ripping them to dust. Then the clouds arrived black. It was pouring when they turned around, when Sefton marched through them like a living statue and skimmed his father without apology, and led the four again.

'Bloody hell. Good job they was no picnic, ay?' Minnie said as Sefton passed her, lifting her face to him and the weather, and releasing Mac's hand to cup her mouth and shout: 'Sefton, love! Slow down, you moody sod! Only bit of water.' Her makeup soon washed and she looked at Nedra, glinting and giddy: 'Plus your poor mam's only got wee sausage legs!'

When Jim jogged after him Minnie said: 'Oh just leave him then,' and snatched Nedra's waist where he'd held it. 'What's he expect, that lad of yours? He could've brung his Carol. It's his own fault. She might've enjoyed herself. Got the neighbours to mind Kelly, then come flattened some grass up here before it pissed it down.'

'Watch how you go here, Nedra,' Mac said.

The moors slipped to mud. Her wellingtons turned and sank.

Minnie kept her straight. 'Sefton's not had nowt for months, has he? I'll bet that's how he duffed his hand last night, beating out one too many confessions.'

With her other arm, Minnie reined Mac closer. A beast of burden. Slanted into the rain, he looked like a ceremonial shire horse with his drenched Crombie and black parting pasted flat to his temples like blinkers. Minnie kept him slightly in front, breaking the worst of the weather with his body, and sparing Nedra the most.

The rain-wind noisy. The cottage nowhere. Her garb a soaked weight. Its plastic sweaty, her legs chilly. She was near exhausted, hurting. Ahead her husband and son. Talking maybe. Sefton still farthest. It was so hard to see.

'Oi, this isn't right, this,' Minnie giggled. 'Where are we?'

Mac, pointing at an empty road across a hazy peak, the winding track a garden worm at this distance.

In the other direction waited her Sefton and Jim.

They arrived at a slick rocky bluff where lay a six-by-two scrap of fresh-turned and patted earth. Crescent shovel slices, waterlogged.

Minnie danced across the free soil to reach a final rock where she let nature insideout her skirts and take her bald rubber soles to the rock's lip. Her hair raised and separated like scored ribbon.

Nedra was about to charge her off into the short drop – maybe enough to dash her or twist her neck. But Mac left first and reclaimed his wife, at the last moment, after she was off the stone, kited and airborne.

He folded her into his arms with her giggling the same unfaltering notes, only muffled by the kisses she fed him. Then Minnie's eyes rolled onto Sefton, onto Jim, onto Nedra. The giggles spent. And the Heavens shut. Minnie stroked Sefton's battered hair as Mac carried her past him. Nedra untied her headscarf – dry enough under the plastic – and tied it round Minnie's alabaster cheeks.

Within an hour they were all thawed by the cottage fire, silent with chipped cups of scalding tea. Outside, another wave of rain. Drops so heavy they hit and bounced on the drive like little dancing men. Nedra watched them dance. A catechism recited, reaffirmed, till she was right as rain and believed it.

THIS GIRL, JAN DODDS –

put upon then shat upon all Thursday from morning bell. Even by *Alice*. Gormless Alice. Who Jan had maimed for robbed for took the rap for. But by ten to ten that night Jan had acquired a throbbing blackeye and a bellyful of lads and arrived finally at Mr Somerville's bedsit, exultant, having cadged her way to Gatley from Civic, after spurning his offer to pick her up after school, by the new Kwik Save, once she'd gone home and changed. She'd told him, for Alice's sake: *Not tonight*, while corkscrewing his ear behind the science mobiles. On patrol with his borrowed PE whistle lassoed over his blue serge suit, freshly drycleaned because of Jan. There to flush out the smokers who flushed save Jan –

exhaling smoke well after his whistle blow. She had a taste of him, but then knocked him back. See, Alice was lovesick and bad with it. Worse than she'd thought.

When first bell pealed Alice threw up with longing. Jan bent in the bogstall, stroking the pills of her Poundswick jumper since Alice had no hair to hold back. The walls gloried Jan in Magic Marker with exploits and diagrams, taunts and vows over nabbed conquests. Even the ones claiming she'd been up the duff couldn't puncture her pride. That Sharon, in their year, was her only competition.

'. . .but Jan. . . I love him. . .' – Alice, spewing colourful break-fast, suicidal over that no-mark lad from next door who she'd just seen in the corridor before registration. Jan never noticed. Too busy noticing Mr Somerville. Twenty-five he was and subbing English for Mrs Baxdale while that fat hen fucked off on maternity. Miss could've been carrying triplets year-round, though appeared to Jan physically unshaggable: her double-decker arse required a special chair too wide to tuck under her desk. Jan had once placed a single rusty tack before Miss came clucking into the classroom after a gravy dinner, apparent on a blossom-pink crochet cardi which wouldn't button. Sitting convent-straight and prim behind her back-row desk, Jan said: 'Enjoy your dinner for two today, Miss?' The bitch ignored her to note the tense frequency of the room's hush. Instead of sitting she stared down the classroom, past Jan, to the wall, slack-gobbed, and saw the top left corner of the bleached atlas curl, a tack missing. Jan watched it curl with her until Miss, lurching to Jan's desk, struck Jan straight across her face which only made Jan laugh with the shock of it, royally impressed. The longer Miss stood there the wilder grew the class's amazement. *Oohs* and *ahhs*. Lads drumming their desks. Miss fled the classroom defeated; her arse unpricked but knocking pens and exercise books to the floor on its way out. No letter home came. Not even another EWO about Jan's truanting. For a night or two she almost worried. But Mr Somerville arrived at Poundswick the following week to replace Mrs Baxdale and improve Jan's attendance.

All that day Alice adrift. Agonising over her own daft shyness – losing her breakfast, tears, shop money to the same toilet bowl, like it was some foul wishing well. Alice was behind the science mobiles at break – not answering Jan's smutty stage-whispers about a new member of their nicotine club who'd joined uninvited and offered Alice his red lighter. He was a marcid beanpole of a lad from the year below; and Alice seemed to see him, but Jan couldn't be sure even when those kohled eyes fell on the Zippo he pushed under her nose. He was more of a looker than that no-mark she was after, but it made no difference. Jan saw he feared gentle Alice: all chest and piercings; crimped knots gone to a laddish grade four. He scarpered like the others when Somerville showed up again with his whistle. Alice too. Jan kept a scoop of Somerville's honeyed earwax under her tongue and was still chewing it when she found Alice shaking in the corridor alone, and then chased her into the bogs. After seeing what Alice saw: by the pigeonholes, courting looks –

. the no-mark lad Alice was mad for, stitched at the gob with that Sharon.

'Fuck you gawping at, slag?' That Sharon, lips agleam.

Jan had nutted front teeth grey, had scalped ponytails for their scrunchies and slit earlobes by plucking out hoops. But Jan stayed stone-quiet in the corridor and let herself be out-stared. In the bogs she coaxed her way into Alice's stinking cubicle and coaxed her back out. At dinnerhour they skipped dinner but stayed on school grounds because Alice was scared of seeing them at the shops. And so Jan taxed a Marathon bar off a first-year Billy No-Mates roaming the playground borders. *Ta.* His voice broke swearing at her. By the time she'd teethed open the wrapper and bit into the bar he sounded two-foot taller. His manhood he owed Jan, like the rest. But Jan's day was thankless. She wanted to go halves with Alice on the Marathon even though it was her first meal of the day – and so saved the rest, tucking it in Alice's satchel, from which it would fall out, later, under the changing-room bench, alongside green coppers and loose tampons and broken hairbrushes. They had netball last thing. In the emptying changing room Jan waited for Alice to find her kit. Poor Alice, moving like a pissed snail. Days-old Ringo crumbs freckled her outgrown bra. Stooping and pouting in odd socks and hockey pleats she looked ridiculous, like a pinup in mourning. The underwire had given her a weird rash. Spokes of kohl ran to her nose. Miss jogged back into the changing room to hurry them out:

'You won't lose weight gabbing, girls. Get out there or you'll make the time after the bloody bell and I mean it. And Willows, take out those teardrop earrings. Leave them all on me desk in the office for your mam to come collect next week.'

Alice benched herself half-changed and wept. Jan held her fiercely, too mithered to gloat up at Miss. Just tending to Alice as she had done all day.

'Dodds. *Jan.*'

She looked up at last.

'What's the matter with Willows?'

'She best go home, Miss.'

Miss looked at Jan like she'd just pulled a knife.

When school let out, Jan walked to Civic to blow a pinched quid in the Oxfam – swapping price stickers till she left with an oxblood scarf and a 7-inch of 'Playground Twist'.

Susie-Ann was skipping between the odd slanted poles holding up the big Co-op entrance, her cheeks domed with sweets. Some game. There were smaller kids in uniforms waiting their turn. Knowing Susie would freeze at the sight of her, Jan charged, slapped her first and the girl went flying, spitting sweets. She picked herself up, vibrating. Trying so hard not to cry.

'Bet you had me dinner today,' Jan said.

The girl stood her ground. 'Ay, Missus Dodds says your mam's got a boyfriend.'

'A boyfriend? Me mam?'

'Your uncle Mac.'

'Who the fuck's that?'

'He come today seeing your Kelly and now he's gunna marry your mam.'

Jan dressed the scarf round Susie-Ann's throat. 'You mean he wants to take her out.'

'Yeah. For her tea.'

'When?'

'Dunno. Your mam said no.'

Jan groaned, and snatched the scarf.

She didn't go home with Susie-Ann to eat and change but went straight to Alice's. Bev answered the door holding Alice's denim jacket bundled and nesting a little tin of needle and thread.

'Ee-ah, girl. Giz a cuddle.'

'If you give us a fag.'

Bev laughed her giant laugh and swallowed her into a short slushy frock covered in little daisy print. It was new to Jan but the cotton worn thin, the daisy yellows faint, and it clung to her flab like the old shifts Jan's mam always wore of a night, though Bev was twice her mam's size. Bev called her own thighs her skullcrushers. She smelled cidery and lotioned. Sometimes Jan wished Bev were her mam. That it was *her* denim jacket on which Bev was stitching shite band patches, with its Bully-chewed collar mended.

'Been shopping, have you?'

'She upstairs?'

Bev had a quick glance round, checking the landing. A heaped ashtray smoked on the phone table. Then with a chuffed nod she shut the door and brought Jan into the cramped hall.

Mouthing at her: 'Have a guess who's up there with my little girl?'

'. . .'

Alice's jacket, better than new. 'I've got our Bully in there with them, making sure they don't get up to owt they shouldn't. S'alright. Go on up.'

'. . .'

'Don't worry. They'll be decent. S'only next door's lad. He's a keeper.' Bev laughed big and shuffled to the foot of the stairs. 'Alice, love! It's Jan!'

While Jan put the scarf and the single on the phone table and left.

She sprinted down the entry and boosted the Willows' back fence to lob a milk bottle over it. Aiming for Alice's bedroom she missed and rattled the guttering. Shattered glass rained on the slabs, playing notes. Decent music for once. Alice opened her window. Jan ducked and ran off.

On a wooded mound in a shaded cranny of Wythenshawe Park floored with bluebells and silverweed she had three blond brothers from St Paul's RC, and their mate, fatter and uniformed, who answered to Paki Jon and worked, so he said, on the indoor market flogging Betamax with his uncle, though Jan had never seen him before. He'd given her two fags when she'd asked for one; she chained them. His Sergio Tacchini was missing buttons and he stood the same height as her, same age about, but said he was seventeen which made her laugh. In the shade these four lads watched each other and timed each other by Jon's Casio watch. Jan used both hands. Jan used her gob twice to shorten the odds. While kneeling inside their circle she heard a football being smacked across the park; a Mr Whippy's jingle start and fade.

Inside this circle she was wanted; they were dead easy to amaze. She felt the oldest, the cleverest. They began talking at once and didn't mind her talking back. Then afterwards they went shy again and the circle broke and they looked away. But Jan rescued them and soon had them pissing about and wanting her again. The three losers clubbed together and bought her saveloy and chips, biking her to Wendover Road for it, on the overgrown side of Baguley Brook.

Jan ate with them at the park gate, the blond brothers doing wheelies for her; sunset trees purpled behind them, the air dandelioned and heavy-sweet. She had a right laugh till she mithered them for another ciggie and one of the brothers threw a chip at her instead. When she lobbed one back, Jon spat on her and she spat too and he pushed her and she tore her Poundswick jumper on the top of the gate rail. They rode off leaving her with the thrown chips and *News of the World* tumbleweeds on the pavement lit.

From there Jan trudged back to Civic. Went right up to Tony Kinsella, who stood smoking dope against a ruby car beneath Violet Court, blasting Piccadilly Radio, surrounded by rum lads she'd had. That evening they smelled like animals. Whiffier than the St Paul's lot. They reshaped around her. Clocking Tony's older cousin Cid was there, Jan grinned hard at Tony: 'Can I cadge a lift off you in this then, or what?' Her palm, to be seen, slipping down his keks. He eyed Cid to smoke, then she brought his smoke into her mouth.

*

Jan cracked her window to let her hair fly. 'This car robbed?'

'Nah. It's our Cid's.'

'Ay, *he's* doing well. Looks brand new.'

While he drove, she tucked a greasy strand behind a cauliflower ear before he ticked her hand away. Tony's widow's peak was so low it joined his brow. He looked like Felix the Cat.

'It's next left here,' she said. 'Ta. You're dead good.'

Stub fingers wrenched the gearstick; joint ash bloomed like a sparkler and dusted their thighs. 'So who you visiting round here, then?'

'Me nana.'

'Thought she lived w'you?'

'I'm kidding. It's me new feller. He's coloured, you know.'

'He the daddy then is he?'

'Here'll do.' She rolled up her window.

He dibbed his joint in the ashtray. 'Bet it was ugly what came out that fanny.'

'Oi, at least he could find me fanny.' Jan knew better but was glad to have said it, as he pulled into the leafy silent street. Tony braked so sharp she tagged her eyebrow on the dashboard. They bounced up the kerb; the engine cut. His seatbelt buckle whacked her funnybone. He waited. Sat and sucked air. Jan held her stinging eye while her curses grew into laughter. Tony stammered summat, shaking, but laughter took her and tightened her body until her own words couldn't fly: 'I'm gunna. . . piss meself. . . Honest, Tone. . . I think I've—' Then, on the backseat, he continued what he'd begun that cold February. A cartoon cat's face above her. Her laughter mad. She listened to herself, spinning, trying to watch him through her good eye. Saw herself thrashing under him in the cramped space, turning until she could smush her running nose and mouth into the seat joins – till his weight left her and he panted: 'Jan Dodds, you're a mad bint.' He kept her spinning. A numb bliss she felt without flesh without sensation: the freedom to leave her body and see it take, and take from, these lads, gifting her the power to age and crown and kin them. Jan Dodds of Woodhouse Park, Wythie: winged above them all, seeing what was what and what was not.

Jan climbed back into her body –

made no noise now except for the floss of his hair stuck between her teeth. Her flooded eye stung shut. The other watched him hunched, panting and zipping.

'When's your Kelly getting out?' Tony said.

'Yesterday,' she said.

He coughed.

'Wait'll he sees what you done to me face,' she said. 'Driving like that. '*And* you've got me new feller to worry about.'

Tony helped her out the car, kissed her, then tore off.

Left her to finish dressing on the warm moony street with full trees and ten or so houses old and new cut up into bedsits. She skipped up the steps to the entrance console and poked the buttons until somebody buzzed her in.

Jan wandered unsupervised with the milky brew he'd made her in his teacher's mug. A navy towel for her on the bed. Pale curtains sealed, the big light blown, a reading lamp on his desk spotting a pile of bottle-green exercise books to be marked. She counted the stapled spines: just hers missing. Behind her, gold light leaked from the bathroom with soothing thunder. Blasting taps to cocoon her, keep out the slights, the wrongs, the backstabbers; wash off the whole day. Her head already good as empty. Only her blackeye talked. (Somerville had said nowt yet, just winced.) For her to be welcomed and have him ask of her so little, before brewing up, just for her, and remembering how she took it; then running her a bath. . .

She heard him in the bathroom while she rooted in his cupboards and drawers, flipped through tatty paperbacks for any photos he kept in them; sniffing his laundry pile, checking the brands he wore and contents of his fridge: Findus Lean Cuisine. Takeaway cartons. Lamb steaks going off. Meals for one. But on the bedtable was a painted fruit bowl which since her last week's visit he'd turned into an ashtray. Elsewhere other things which weren't his. A useless vase too short and thin for flowers. Last time Jan found two snaps in his wallet, fished out of a puddle of clothes while he slept. He wasn't married;

Jan knew that. She was older than him: thirty-odd, wore red lippy and thick round specs. Bronze cheeks, bronze perm. He wouldn't say her name or why she had left but her stink was still on his pillowcase, in the pits of his shirts.

Jan finished the brew, picked up the daft vase and used it to putt the stack of exercise books. They fanned neatly across his desk where she left his mug. She carried the vase to his bedtable and dropped it trying to set it down. The carpet saved it and she footed it under the bed. Jan found a blue pair of knickers. She sneezed whipping the dust off them and again giving them a sniff. Tony had finished off the elastic in her own. She shed them and left them under his bed, ready to go home wearing these instead. But re-hid them for now and went in the bathroom, towelled, just as the taps went off.

'Try that,' he said. 'Shouldn't be too hot.'

'I want it too hot.'

They were both squinting under the bare bulb. 'Right. In you get.' He nudged the bath mat neat with his foot. She stepped on it and curtsied. Proud to be alone with him but a bit afraid. Not of him, and not of her saying or doing summat to ruin it, which she no doubt would, but afraid of the quiet. He held her towel waist to pass her as he went out.

Jan stayed on the mat – cinching the navy towel with both hands and glancing from the shut door to her mad reflection in the cabinet mirror and back again. He returned with a bag of frozen veg for her eye. And a torn box of tealights; a lighter between his teeth.

She got into the bath finally, shy almost – soaking while he placed candles along the lip of the tub and lit them. Then he switched off the gold bulb and sat on the toilet seat in the flickering gloom. They watched each other. Candles scrolled water shadows up the tiles to the low ceiling.

'That better?'

Jan nodded, speechless.

He held the iced bag on her face for a minute, wincing again, till it burned her eye open.

She'd gone to him knowing he wouldn't ask. He expected her to show up with blackeyes or blue knuckles or scrap-torn clothes. She knew she didn't need to explain it to him since to him and those like him it explained her. She was far beyond her reputation now and living up to his idea of her, which pre-existed her and his interest.

'I know I can't stay,' she said.

'I know you know.'

'Can I kip here an hour? One hour. Promise.' Jan soaped herself unselfconsciously. 'Didn't sleep last night. See, our Kelly's back – you know, me brother? He come home from Strangeways and he's took me bed.'

'What's wrong with his?'

'Mam sold it, didn't she? Pawned everything in his room.'

'Does she work, your mother?'

'Not now. Used to be at the Mr Kipling factory.'

'But she had to give her notice?'

'Got any shampoo?'

'And then there's your nana, who's a childminder?' He had a bottle out the cabinet and she approved the label because it was his, not because she knew it. Then he squirted a cold dollop straight onto her crown and rubbed it in and she couldn't stop grinning. 'So your Kelly has to be the new breadwinner, does he?'

'He's a man now. Only three years younger than you.'

'Where does he think you are – right now?'

'He don't care. None of them bother with *me*. Nana says I'm just a tabby what comes and goes.'

'You not close to your mother?'

'She's not said two words to us this week. But she can be like that, me mam. She lives in her head.'

'She pretty?'

'Who? Me mam? Got a face on her like a smacked arse. I'm telling you. *And* she's going fat. She wasn't bad when she was younger, though.'

He swirled his hands in the bathwater to rinse them, then stood and raised the bog lid to piss. Jan kept his shampoo out of her eye.

She said: 'Oi, why can't blokes ever make it go straight?'

'We're all deviants.'

'Deviants! I know what that means. Just don't ask us to spell it.'

'Jan, you're not thick.'

'Words are worse than sums. Once you know how to read that should be it. They shouldn't give you books.'

'Have you ever read a whole book, Jan?'

'Kelly used to. When he was younger. Used to read them me.'

'If I give you a book will you read it?'

'You give us enough homework.'

'Since when do you do your homework? Do you have anywhere at home to read? Somewhere you can get a bit of peace for half hour?'

'No. I'd have to come here.'

He kissed her, with slow heat. Sleeve-rolled arms and cleft chin on the lip of the tub with the tealight flames. It seemed like he was rehearsing his next words and when he finally spoke them his voice changed: 'Jan, who knows about this?'

She tried kissing him the way he'd kissed her but his mouth wouldn't give.

'Have you told Alice Willows?' he said.

'Don't say that name. She's dead to me that girl.'

'What about Kelly?'

'Look, are you getting in here with us or what? It's going cold.'

He put his specs on the cistern.

He climbed over her and got in dressed and hugged her slipperiness. Shot waves up the side of the tub drenching his mat and snuffing the tealights.

Jan shrieked with happiness, rolling with his body in dark water after her day of ungrateful giving: to be carried to his bed for an hour's kip before he drove her some of the way home.

'I CAN'T BE DOING with it today, me,' said Bev Willows, lewd large loud, clocking on after Carol, trying to shield her from that morning's skens, which came before a shift, from the other factory girls, who, unlike Bev, were long resigned to Carol's frost and bruises. Those factory girls of December '76, on the last shift of the festive week, with their upturned noses catching a bad smell. Claiming to know her business so thoroughly that among them it could no longer be over-sold as gossip. Finding her solemn as a Benedictine nun. Wary of her married name. Talking out of their plucked-chicken gobs: *Well, you can't help them what don't help themselves, can you now?* They tutted and left her to it, unpitied. All except Bev bloody Willows: trying to distract her from their ritual scornful apathy. Bev made out she hadn't noticed the brutal colours that marred Carol's wrists – colours worn without pride or shame but as banal news reprinted weekly on her body to be read and then folded up inside her factory-floor coat so that she could go and sit for seven hours on a production line, quality-checking Battenbergs, French Fancies or gluing Viennese Whirls while her maminlaw minded the kids. Her Jan and her Kelly, steadily bewitched by their nana's careful slips and home cooking: sweets and cakes nicer than any industrial-estate confectionery Carol brought home by the boxload to bargain for love. See, Nedra was still, from time to time, accident-prone herself. Stove burns and bath falls; tumid cheeks and sudden limps due to bad knees, advancing age. Carol had often enjoyed teatime round her inlaws over the years. Nedra, serving

Jim his heaped plate first, ignoring his 'What the bloody hell's *this*?' He'd wait till they all had their meals served before throwing his at the ever-changing wallpaper. Then Nedra would twitter, uncontrollably, fetch dustpan and brush, with Jim demanding Carol and Sefton start without them. Which Carol would, almost untroubled, as Nedra cleared the mess. Like Carol, Nedra didn't hide bruises with tutty, but unlike Carol, she had the purity of a lifer; living her lies not as lies but as faith – summat to believe in for herself, hoping to convert others. Which was how Carol's two – her lad soft at fourteen, and his six-year-old sister who soiled the beds whenever their dad came home off remand – got taught to despise their mam. Both Carol and Nedra had lived each day since Vern Jenkins' murder seven years ago in mutual assurance. They relied on each other to maintain their martyrdom, as one battered wife scorns and saves another.

As she slotted her punch card into the wall – while the factory girls slit their eyes; while Bev bloody Willows crowded her, gabbing on and on – Carol wondered why it was Sefton let her work. He said they needed the drip of clean cash to keep the dibble off their doorstep, not that it did. He said it kept her occupied whenever he was inside, which was often. And she was grateful to him for both. A few of the girls there knew what it was like being married to a crook, to have wed into a proud clan of English thieves or Irish hellraisers; but none had fell to a Dodds man.

This, the day before her husband died. He was taking her out tomorrow: Christmas Eve with Jim, Nedra, Minnie and Mac, as was tradition, for a tipple at the Woodpecker or the Cock of the North, where the Burtonwood came in plastic cups. Each year, Carol wore an old frock and pattern stockings and three squirts of a discontinued Charles of the Ritz that due to association or alchemy only suited her once it mingled with clouds of Minnie's rosewater scent. Sefton would always drop Carol off home by half ten and take his mam to midnight Mass, then drain the rest of the estate pubs with his father till dawn, before going on to town in the Triumph to breakfast in a Moss Side brothel, and return to Wythie at dinnertime, tinselled, bladdered and reeking. In a hum of dope, yoni and scotch bonnet. Still have bellyroom for his mam's glazed ham, local turkey and sherry pud. At her inlaws' last New Year's, Minnie had grabbed her on the landing, squeezed her into the water closet and drew these details for Carol with *Never-guess-what* eyebrows and titters. Some Christmases Mac stayed home with Minnie after the pubs, but some he not only ferried father and son to and from town in their Triumph, he also. . . *Wet his wick! Having a bloody whale of it, they were. Our husbands, Carol. Playing* Tarzan of the Apes *with two to a bed*. Minnie was proud. She never thought Mac had it in him – to step out even once a year, so rare did he step in. So she said. And Carol knew when she saw Minnie tomorrow for Christmas Eve at the Cornishman, Minnie would still be heartless and childless and free from envy. At forty-two uneaten by age: practically a Pendle Hill spell that was to be severed finally on Christmas Day, once news of the accident reached her. After dropping her home from the pub tomorrow Carol would spend late Christmas Eve with Vern – who was ageless like Minnie – testing the fold limits of time and mattress springs. This cuckoldry had continued after his murder, regardless of whether her husband lay in the bed leaking fears from his dreams or resting sound in a cell bunk, and regardless of whether her husband had beat her blue that night or called her Minnie as he shot his own muck into her, fantasising he was his father, and she his father's mistress. Whatever Sefton did to her, Carol could erase it with Vern, his daft jokes shared inside her, flushing her husband out.

Contrary to factory whispers she now had no mystery to her. She was numb to friendship and motherhood and affairs worldly or local, having let life alone so that all that existed for her was Vern's horizontal stand-up. Their chatter spiralling into and out of delightful rubbish until Carol would be too spent not to sleep, even knowing when she woke he'd be gone. On fag breaks she would bob in the staff toilets and scratch her itch. Biting down on her free wrist. The thirty-four-year-old lawful battered wife not-yet-widow to Sefton Conan Dodds, swimming from owt that stopped her from reliving the night in the day. And had managed all right until Bev Willows started full-time and wanted to know her. She'd worked there too long to hear the machinery, feel its blast bounce off the concertina roofing and ping to the floor as an undiminished echo made and remade on the eternal belt of cakes. Too long to even smell what they made or to crave it, except when she was on. Vern had told her only that week she now permanently tasted of Bramley apple filling:

'Factory – or homemade?' Carol worried.

'If you're lucky enough to have lived in Paris as a young feller, then wherever you go, it stays with you, for Paris is a moveable feast.'

She wrestled under him, winning. 'Oh-aye? Even if he never got to Paris, but had digs behind Sharston Baths, floor-to-ceiling with books? Took in somebody's wife and kiddie, the daft sod. Died on his own doorstep.'

'I was Last of the Jenkins, I'll have you know. The buck stopped here.'

'You dunno how lucky you are. . .'

Now a telephone was ringing in the factory office. From the corridor Carol saw through the empty window, the office unstaffed except for saucy schoolgirls and topless nurses staple-gunned to the walls and tinsel-framed. Sweet names, upturned noses and nipples: Mary and Madeline looked down at her sisterly. Mary wasn't climbing out of her clawfoot bathtub to answer any telephone. . . It kept ringing. A tiny red-haired office girl, not much older than her son, rushed in with a hot drink, which she drizzled over her typewriter, lunging for the receiver. Carol turned unhurried. They had minutes before their lines went live but Bev dogged her all the way down like some barmy chaperone:

'. . .and it's bloody Christmas, near enough. So I say let's have us a merry last shift, *ay*?' Fag ash glowed in Bev's crooked hairnet like a rubied tiara. She slowed to flash Carol a hipflask before nesting it back inside a colossal lavender bra. Old girls bustled past, cackled. Bev danced a sort of reverse burlesque where she restudded her factory coat. It took the talk off Carol and was meant to.

Since starting that spring Bev was like a toad after a kiss, having quickly wooed the other factory girls, the technicians and apprentices, the foreman and the packers, with a half-dozen blue gags and frank tales too detailed to be fibs. Each had a filthy boast and a sting at her own expense, to put her in a harmless light, which allowed her to get away with blue murder on the clock. She was single mam to a little lass who went to St Thomas' RC with Jan. Estranged wife to a Trafford Park warehouse manager who had broken furniture on her back. The night he left her, she let him stay gone.

Carol knew Bev wasn't daft, wasn't trying to get close to her for the challenge. Bev thought them the same – wanting only to treat her like she were just another factory girl, and Bev would continue to, unless Carol did summat and soon. So stubborn Bev was with her sympathy – expressed under all that noise – that she could withstand Carol's indifference. Bev's volume hid patience. She could clown and gab till pay day on one breath.

'Ay, I do everything better after a few. Honest to God. Is it same for *you*? Cos I can –' Bev was pouring words over her, but an old bint ahead of them answered instead:

'Pissed?'

'Not saying *pissed*. But just, you know. . .'

'You still are. Time you get in last night?'

'Now, now. Don't be jealous cos I do as I please. Stephie, love, I *am* sorry, but if you stay with that bossy wee feller of yours, you'll never live to be as old as you look.'

'Cheek!'

The corridor grew small with tickled women.

'But listen: working, singing, dancing, shagging, you name it. Should see me needlework after six ciders. Bloody straight as a die.'

'What about your driving?'

'Who's got a bloody car round here that *you* know?'

'Our Terry just got himself a Reliant. Brand new, it is.'

'Oh, he has, aye. Plenty of room in it as well. Even had Maeve in the back, didn't he? Must've been Grab a Granny Night at the Ritz. Hope he got the stains out.' Bev got louder by the word to compete with the laughs. 'But it were *me* he had it off with in the Reliant *first*, to christen it.'

One went: 'Poor Terry spent the night in a cell cos of that.'

Another: 'Bet you nearly died.'

'Don't see why it shouldn't count as indoors and in privacy, long as there's roof over you both. But no. You get a bobby come a-knocking on your fog window.'

'What did he say?'

'"You again?"'

How they laughed.

'Poor Terry.'

'You won't be getting any of *this* in a bit.' Bev jiggled to remind them she was wearing gin.

'Best give us a tipple *now*,' an old girl said.

'All in good time, gorgeous. All in good time.'

'Ay, Bev, me dad used to say he always drove best after four Mackesons.'

'Like them Jamaicans I met in town, the other night. They like to smoke that stuff, Jamaicans, don't they? Like the Red Indians. Every day, they do. So I ask one why and he goes: it clears their heads. Well, I'm the same. Only with the drink.'

'So, you let one of them drive you home after you'd had a dance, did you?'

'Did I buggery. Never mind one bobby; we'd have the whole bloody constabulary after us, thinking I'd been abducted.'

'Ay, Bev, who minds your little Alice?'

'Next door. They've got a young lad. They're dead good. Ay, why don't we all go town Christmas Eve instead of the Garter, if any of yous fancies it?'

'You're alright.'

'Suit yourselves. Nowt wrong with chicken in a basket.'

'Ay, Bev, do they get Christmas in Jamaica?'

'I should hope so, love. Mind you, we don't even get it here, do we? The miserable gets.'

'We'll get the chop if they catch us, Bev. I'm telling you now.'

'See what I mean? Look, the brass can join in, can't they? Fucking hell – it's only once a year. Carol, love, tell them.'

'Why not?' Carol said.

This was the first she'd said to Bev, to anybody, in days. It halted the other factory girls' feet and gobs, left Bev's fat face open with childish amazement.

Carol split the plastic curtains and they filed onto the factory floor, taking their places on the line. Bev climbed the stepladder and blessed the mixing vat with a sprinkle of gin, then sent the flask along the line from girl to girl all morning till it was empty. Each time Carol got passed the gin she knocked it back and the whole line of blue-coated women – bowed and remote now – juggled their duties and their swigs with choreographed precision. Carol swapped out misshapen Fancies, missing none. While Bev – whose voice, alone among them, could compete with the machines – kept schtum. Instead she and Carol traded smirks without looking up.

Before dinnertime three girls were stone-drunk. Of the three, Frances Hewitt, fifty-odd, wasn't the worst but was dismissed, despite Frances being well-liked and a good grafter and married to a crippled Pomona docker. With Carol she had worked there off and on since the site opened in '62, through two changes of hands. Knowing nobody would grass on who smuggled in the booze, the foreman and duty manager had ceased production so they could hear themselves yell – show off their bushy tashes thick with wasted spittle. There Carol stood with the girls, around Frances, watching this cowed and sunken-faced woman slowly unstud her factory plastic, then put on her own coat and headscarf, which the office girl had been sent to fetch from the locker room. As Frances walked, the girl leaned out the office and called to her. Frances stopped and saw Carol and the rest, then the young girl beckoning her. She went to her dazed, as if wondering if it had all been a wind-up. But the typist just gave her a cut brown envelope and flew back into the office to answer the telephone.

At dinnertime Carol sat in a ladies' cubicle and listened like a priest to Bev suffer through the partition wall. They finished their half hour hearing one weep and the other come. Carol made sure.

When they left their stalls to complete their extended shift, another fleshy factory girl rushed in for the sink. Bev blew her nose with bog tissue, waiting sullenly for her to finish, then said to Carol in a broken whisper:

'We seeing you Christmas Eve?'

'Her husband always takes her out,' this other woman said for her, into the mirror, having likely been told this by another who'd been there longer. Maybe Frances.

Bev blinked to show she understood. Her blotch cheeks and throat and chest –

still rashed when all the girls got out at four, with their docked wages.

'Happy Christmas,' they told themselves, for gallows' comfort, lingering in the locker room in their woolly hats and gloves, like penned cattle afraid of the open gate.

Off home first: 'Ta-ra,' Carol said.

***

Nine years widowed and now:

Friday again he came for Kelly. Grey-suited and brogued and widowed also. Towering over her apologetically in the tight hallway like some ancient packhorse whipped into the wrong station. Terrified of her, he'd asked her again to dinner. *Alright*, she said, nodding, corralled between greyed laundry drip-drying on a mangled rack and radiator. Mac didn't look at her again or speak to her again, maybe in case she saw summat in him that changed her mind quick. But there was nought new for her to see or to feel – so little left he could keep from her. After he took Kelly for another ride out Carol lingered in the hall and caught her own morning reflection: fat and dishevelled and grimly imperious inside the picture glass of Jim's studio portrait; a glossy black-and-white that had him looking like a B-movie mobster – taken well before she knew him.

THREE MAYS GONE NEDRA took seven hellsoaked scrubbed-up kids to Heaton Park to see His Holiness Pope John Paul II. This was only one May after the Holy Father had survived an assassin's bullet; but the day before their trip, which would cut thirteen miles north through town, Nedra reminded her chosen seven in her kitchen why the Bishop of Rome was fit to honour them so soon: because Lord Jesus had turned the filthy Turk's bullet into smoke. Joey Harvey was four then and loved miracles so on hearing this his eyes held a private mellow joy when he raised them at her from under Susie-Ann's kitchen chair. Sunday teatimes Joey was Blackbeard's pet monkey, below deck, caged by the chair's legs and Susie-Ann's cotton-string calves. He climbed onto Susie's lap and let her finger-comb his hair while he ate one of her chips, holding it up for her to blow on. He forgot to chew, so wonderstruck he was by –

the Miracle of the Assassin's Bullet.

Kevin and Roger Burton had questions on their stained lips. Questions seven- and eight-year-old lads knew better than to ask in case their legs got slapped later by their mams. But Nedra answered daft questions about Adolf Hitler or Captain Scarlet or Sinbad the Sailor or the Six Million Dollar Man. Sometimes her answers satisfied; sometimes they sparked new questions, and so could leave her tangled in lore, mixing cowboys and catechism, as she scrubbed her chip pan. And so she told Kevin and Roger not to talk but to listen.

'Now, get that et.' Nedra pointed at their eggs and ham. 'Then go home and fetch your best shoes and I'll give them a good brush for tomorrow.'

'Tomorrow,' Joey repeated, climbing Susie-Ann.

Joey's big brother Gene mopped his plate with a round of buttered bread. He was thirteen and so deaf to miracles, his stuffed cheeks hived with fear of Nedra's granddaughter, who was sly and rabbit-eared when it came to wickedness. Jan ate at the crowded table and kept reaching under it to thump Gene's thigh if it grazed hers. Acid looks. Lips growing fat and feminine – a horror to behold in a child's face – that pulled in disgust at all in this world except for their Kelly. Jan had been that way for weeks – since she came downstairs one morning with a stained sheet and a body too grown by half for twelve. It was Nedra who took her to Lewis's for her first fitting since Carol couldn't be mithered. Nedra who had to suffer that Ladies' Department junior assistant whose mouth ran longer than her measuring tape: *Dunno how you managed so long doing PE.* Jan answered with star jumps just to mortify Nedra. Then pinched lippy bullets from the sales display while her nana was at the till bleeding a week's pension on women's garments for a thieving grandchild in a body almost ripe for ruin. And Jan denied this theft – denied what Nedra witnessed under God – only to laugh it off later, window-seated on the bus home, when Nedra turned out the girl's pockets and found nothing.

'Where a'they, then?' Jan had said like a slattern Bo Peep, the bus window doubling her grin.

Nedra looked hard at her granddaughter, all of her: the painted nails; the plumping legs sprouting wayward from a small turquoise skirt – once too big, that Nedra had never got round to taking in. Jan breathed and Nedra read the broken line of the girl's chest and from which the girl extracted an assassin's bullet. Using the bus glass to paint her mouth. No need for pockets now.

Nedra went to scoop out the rest and Jan squealed so the whole bottom deck turned and saw her nana pinching Jan's butterflesh, the new brassiere cradling them both like a butcher-shop scales. Nedra couldn't free her fingers unless they withdrew empty.

Jan squealing: 'Seen this, you lot? I'm being interfered with!'

If Nedra had been home she could've downed a shot of vinegar at the cooker and let it burn, but there she could only mutter *Enough's enough* and she rose before the next stop and resat opposite, beside an elderly coloured lady – smart in a fur-trim coat, browline specs and mohair cap – quietly rocking to the bus's motion. Every new passenger the bus welcomed could smell Nedra's shame. Passing her with their weekly shopping, Nedra bore their judgement, and the next day she begged Father Culler to forgive her. The things she held in.

The following week word came of Jan flogging lipsticks round school. Nedra said nowt – not wanting to waste a prayer – but in the kitchen come Friday Nedra found her own bag undone, purse filled with coin from the sales. She didn't count it, only tipped the lot in the collection box noisily after Mass.

True, Jan kept the Devil's shade for herself. Had the cheek to wear it to Heaton Park, to apply it in front of her, on another bus, with a steady hand. Another bullet meant for the Holy Father. Their Kelly was sat with her, having been swayed by little Joey to come see miracles. And where Kelly went Jan followed while she could. Jan got him to say whatever she wanted to hear while she still could – since Kelly was then a gorgeous lad of nineteen growing less sweet by the day. Starting to top up his giro by way of mischief or local enterprise, and only beginning to play out the wish of what others thought he should be. All this Nedra had seen, had known. Jan kissed the bus window scarlet, kissed her big brother's cheek scarlet, shuffled round and threatened to kiss Joey scarlet, who in horror hid his face in Susie-Ann's First Communion dress.

The night before – that crowded teatime – Kelly had sat on the counter facing them to eat Sunday roast scraps since there wasn't table room. When he heard Carol coming in:

'Ee-ah, Mam?'

But Carol tramped straight upstairs.

He leaned to put his plate in the sink and dig out some banknotes folded small from his denims. Then he slid off the counter and left the money where he'd warmed. Twisting on his trainers, laced.

Nedra opened the oven and took its heat – smelling charcoal but nowt was burned. 'Your giro's not in for another week.'

'The Lord He giveth and He twoc'eth away.'

Jan snickered over her tea, stopping only to thump Gene's leg.

Nedra shut the oven and boxed Kelly's ears with her oven mitten but he dodged round the kitchen like Brian London.

'You'll be getting a good hiding, and none of this pud.'

'Then good job I'm going out.' He rushed her with his chin out, windmilling his fist, then surprised her with a soft peck on the other cheek. His own shadowed, coarse, not yet lipsticked. Then he pecked Jan's. Then at the other end of the table he messed Joey's hair before claiming the striped windbreaker off Susie-Ann's chairback, his housekeys jangling in the pocket. 'Right. In a bit.'

'Best be up tomorrow, Kelly. This is history, this. Give yourself enough time for a proper shave.'

To Joey, he said: 'Wouldn't miss it, lad. Would we?'

'When's history?' Joey said.

'History was yesterday,' Kelly said.

'It's tomorrow,' Nedra said. 'Take no notice.'

She dished up – chipped bowls and scratched spoons – and divvied frugal, but with plenty custard. She took Joey off Susie-Ann's lap to let her eat and set him on her own hip. 'If you get a good night's sleep, Joey, love, then tomorrow comes quicker. Isn't that right, Kelly? Tell him, love.'

'Aye, but you don't end up kipping through tomorrow into next week.'

'No tomorrow,' Joey said.

'I'll box you,' Nedra said.

'I'm going,' Kelly said at the backdoor. 'Tell Mam.'

'Which pub you be in? I'll ring and send for you.'

'Not going pub, going pictures.'

'Who bloody with?'

'Right rum sods, Nana. From Trinidad. You'd like them.'

'I'm coming,' Jan said and stood.

'You're bloody not,' Nedra said.

Gene scraped his spoon across his teeth. Jan pushed her bowl and Roger and Kevin abandoned theirs to claim it. They ate like factory looms.

'You're too young to be going anywhere of a Sunday night,' Nedra said.

'*Why?* We've no school tomorrow.'

'Tomorrow.' Joey twisted Nedra's arm fat, monkey-gripping her sides with his feet. She put him down.

Jan said: 'Think the Pope's gunna catch us yawning?'

Kelly had the backdoor wide and Jan kicked the pyramid of shoes hiding the mat to surface her own pair, lingering on a buckled ruby sandal of Susie-Ann's which had once been hers.

Nedra glanced at the table and saw the dishes had already been cleared away. Kevin and Roger had run home for their smart shoes, their places empty. Susie-Ann was reading her book about well-to-do Cheshire children meeting Merlin. They'd all gone.

Nedra said to nobody: 'I'll keep Kelly's covered in case he fancies it when he gets in.'

But the table was spotless and the smart shoes polished and the stove cool and the kitchen silent and alone now at the table it seemed everso big with her feeling like Queen Victoria taking her supper – a mug of Ovaltine hours cold – long after Carol came down to brew up and eat leftovers, looking more tired than she'd ever seen a woman look, and she'd seen tired, known tired; but Carol couldn't fill the table again even with that accusing silence of hers or with that insistent hum of sexual satisfaction about her which was the only thing about her daughterinlaw which was frank and indisputable even though she knew Carol hadn't been touched in years, had courted not once since Sefton died. Carol wasn't mithered where in the dark her only daughter and son were or weren't. And of the seven sinners that Nedra was shepherdessing tomorrow to worship under the Holy Father Himself, only *her* two weren't home in their beds.

Nedra left the light on for them.

Under a brass-necklace sun they caught the bus from Civic. That brass-necklace sun scored the orange and white paint and Nedra shooed ahead some of her seven to keep the bus from going without her. Monday's queue of queerfolk – bark-skinned elders dressed for sea or snow: ancient matriarchs of other denominations; unwashed bovver boys of precious hairdos and jewellery. . . the queue was shrinking faster than her toddle. A quickstep at sixty-two and fat as fruit. She was only breathless once she sat down. With her flock seated and counted for. Eight commemorative return tickets to Heaton Park for the papal visit. She shut her purse.

Susie-Ann watched her – sweetly beside her with Joey on her knee, creasing her First Communion dress. Nedra took him and pulled smooth Susie-Ann's frock.

After climbing Princess Road to town:

'Look!' Roger said, two benches in front with Kevin.

Nedra squinted at the grubby window: a helicopter low under cleanest high Heaven. It looked like a dangerous insect. Kevin, Roger and Joey followed it with their fingers to the glass. She blinked at it and caught sunspots.

'It was *Him*,' Kevin said.

They'd heard on Piccadilly Radio that the Pope would travel by helicopter and for a moment she wondered.

'Was it Jesus?' Joey whispered.

'Don't talk daft.'

'The Pope knows Jesus,' Susie-Ann said.

'He's. . . Jesus's dad,' Roger said.

'That's Joseph,' Kevin said.

'That's God,' Nedra said.

'Who's the Pope's dad?' asked Susie-Ann.

'He's not got one,' Nedra said.

Joey tipped to see her, tom-tom-ing her gammon arm which barred him like a seatbelt. 'Like Kelly and Jan.'

'Like *you* and your Gene now and all,' Jan said, then sat round. But Kelly touched her with a look and Jan turned, to him, then to Joey, then spoke again, softer:

'Oi, mate – don't be getting upset. Yours'll be home before you know it. Ours won't.'

'He's with Jesus.'

'That's right, love.' Nedra matched his whisper.

Joey pushed to the window, chasing Heaven or helicopters, crawling over Susie-Ann for purchase. Nedra retrieved him and jogged him on her knees but he wouldn't be still until a kick juddered the back of their seat.

'Now be *good*,' Gene Harvey said, twitching behind them, sat by himself. A torrential nosebleed spotting his blue collar shirt and his dad's tie.

The shock of him.

All she could do was pass Joey up to Kelly and root in her handbag for tissues.

An hour before, Gene's shirt still crisp and spotless, the breeze lifted his tie; his expression drawn as he stood farthest right, lined up at the privets with the rest, to have his picture taken in front of her house. Waiting on Jan.

'Kevin, don't fidget,' Nedra said.

Linda Harvey stood with her, off the kerb in white curlers, a bloke's dressing gown and slippers, winding a disposable camera. Her eyes were small and shot from kipless nights spent worrying on a husband calendared for sentencing that week at Crown Court. Linda's duty was to see him off, to spend tears like he spent his wages. He was and would be 'working away', as far as Joey knew. But Nedra wondered, what with Gene, Linda's eldest, now at big school, where you couldn't hide them from owt. Joseph Senior had lost another pay packet on the dogs, and his pride in the Happy Man, and smashed up Cornishway bookies, demanding his money back. To get it he crossed the counter to have words with the bookie's middle daughter – a brainy lass fair and slim with darkened freckles – who worked Saturdays. Nedra had fed her through primary school and always got waved at by her round Civic. She'd even passed the senior entrance exam for Withington's Girls' School. Dead keen on sums. Having robbed the till, Joseph had stopped battering her to stab the father twice through the neck with his betting pencil. Left the poor girl wearing his blood. Yet she managed to ring for the ambulance that saved him. And saved Joseph too. The *Evening News* said it looked like Dracula's den. BOOKMAKER AND DAUGHTER ALIVE AGAINST THE ODDS. But by the time the papers printed half the story Joseph Senior had turned himself in at Benchill Police Station – brought those crooked bobbies the money and a full confession. He brought Father Culler along too, for courage, meaning Father Culler had really brought *him*. The good Father postponing Mass to be at the station, ensuring a local man got treated just or at least met his cell walking. Nedra pictured the scene at the bookies after Joe had scarpered: all the blood and prayer. Nedra was careful what she said to poor Linda on that jewelled morning, who was doing better than Nedra had expected. Linda was grateful to her for taking her Gene and Joey for the day. . .

'This lot don't half scrub up well, d'they?' Linda said, winding on the camera.

'I've stitched tags in their clothes in case God forbid. . .'

'Bless you. Our little Joey'll be dead good. It's your Kelly you'll have to watch don't get lost.'

Kelly had surfaced, hungover but cat-washed and shaved. And hearing his name he cringed at them through the morning's gold. Joey, Kevin, Roger were spotless for the minute; their shoes blazed on the pavestones. Susie-Ann pigtailed and frocked and hop-scotching now from one end of the restless line to the other, looking like a vision of Whitsun past. Two Harveys, two Burtons, one Dodds (one still dressing) and one Stone. Nedra's necklaces clattered as she spun to read her Sunday wristwatch without glare. Not late enough to leave without Jan. Only Joey seemed as keen to go, the others just glad of a Monday off school.

Linda wasted a picture: everybody was slouched in doing, looking somewhere different.

Kelly cupped his yawn, which left Roger boxing into one palm. 'Ballies,' Kelly shouted, dodging low blows.

'Right. Someone go fetch our Jan.' Her wristwatch ticked but hadn't moved.

'Speak the Devil,' Linda said.

'Our kid!' Their Jan, calling from the top window, damp-haired, in her bloody bra, to drop a pack of Sterling which bounced out of

Kelly's hands with the glare, so he had to catch it twice, but it didn't touch the slabs.

He sparked up like his granddad and said *Ta* through his teeth even though Jan had shut the window. Then he offered a fag to Linda who scuttled over in her slippers. He lit it for her and dropped another few down the torn gape of her husband's dressing-gown pocket which had her blushing. Seeing through the camera, Linda shuffled backwards into the road to get them all in, just as Jan came out and locked up, Carol having already left for work. Jan cat-stepped along the privets in front of six lambs before joining the photo at Gene's end, not Kelly's.

'Them are more bloody hole than tights,' Nedra said. 'Go in and put on a decent pair.'

'There's no time,' Linda said out the corner of her mouth, smoking hands-free. 'You'll miss your bus.'

Nedra read her wristwatch and saw the Devil's tricks on its face.

Linda said: 'Gene, *squeeze in* a bit, love.'

Gene did. Jan didn't thump him. All seven young sinners quieted, and almost all of them smart in their Sunday best on a Holy Monday. But their smiles began to strain. The moment sieving away. . .

'What you waiting for?' Nedra said.

Linda lowered the camera, then gave it to Nedra, then held her knees to sob. She went in quick. Nedra took the photo instead. It captured a gravity befitting the day. And despite all, it got framed and joined her lifeblood on the mantelpiece for Carol to dust.

Other buses corked Oxford Road and Princess Street, slowing their ascent to Heaton Park. Nedra read her wristwatch, read the window. Heights of Manchester brick. *Used-to-bes*, she called them. Gloomy picturehouses, grand hotels, warehouses, palaces, hippodromes and public baths, loose-knitted together for survival.

Kelly and Jan had swapped seats and he smoked with his temple to the glass as he ticked ash into the tray behind Roger's seat. Nedra leaned into the aisle to check on Gene, behind her – shutting her out to study the street at his window. His nosebleed had finished off her tissues. His jacket fastened to hide his spattered shirt and tie. Even Jan had the gumption not to say owt.

Meanwhile Joey fretted at the bus's crawl, sensing they ought to be closer by now, while Kevin wrestled Roger, Susie-Ann scissoring her cotton legs to control her excitement.

When Joey began to cry Nedra told him an old story. 'You know, love, when I was your age *my* mam's mam met the Sultan of Zanzibar on *his* royal visit to Manchester. He seen her through the crowds, through *all* them people, and sent his grand chief to tell her he wanted to meet her. Now, she wasn't much more than a girl then, me granny, and didn't know *what* to say to a sultan. But she went, thinking she might as well.'

'Was he wanting to marry her?' Susie-Ann said, her legs falling still.

'Listen. Here's the rest: the Sultan give her a perfect white rose from his garden in the desert across the sea, and he pinned it to her hair like a princess and she curtsied, which is what y'have to do whenever you meet a sultan.'

'And the Queen,' Susie-Ann said.

'And the Pope,' Joey said.

'And the sultan asked to marry her. But of course she never. Since she was already engaged to be wed to me granddad, you see? And you can't be having two husbands, can you?'

'Was the sultan sad?' Susie-Ann said.

'Was he mad?' Kevin said.

'Yes, but Sinbad helped him find a new wife. The Queen of Sheba.'

Kelly was snoring; Jan held his fag, low, out of sight; Nedra snapped her fingers and Jan waited, head cocked, before stubbing it out.

'But me granny kept his white rose.'

Joey: 'Will the Pope want a flower?'

'We could've brought him a few of your mam's freesias. Ah well.'

The bus crawled to a halt for a blue fancy car overtaking. She saw into it and thought of her Jim's Triumph, of those with Conservative Club dads; of those who'd worship closer to the Holy Father in Heaton Park that morning than she and her fold.

The bus doors split for a mithered lass who'd sooner walk to the next stop instead of waiting for the traffic to uncork.

Gene flew from his seat –

and bolted to the front of the bus. He was outside, with the window between them, before Nedra could scream.

Kelly jerked awake as the scream came out of her like a hand making a wild grab for a wayward child too wayward to catch in time –

the bus doors clapped.

Nedra stood and all of them stood shouting and patting the glass.

GENE HARVEY 13 Y.O.
292 FELLSIDE RD
WOODHOUSE PARK
WYTHENSHAWE
RC CHURCH ✟

And Gene sprinting through shoppers to round the corner of *was it Whitworth or Fairfield*? She twittered a prayer that she hadn't heard herself recite since girlhood and couldn't place – not even with the pontiff in town.

And Gene gone. The shame.

She sent Kelly after him. The bus driver swore at her when neither returned after a couple of minutes. Off the bus, on a noisy scrum of pavement, she counted what was left of her flock, trying to fit them inside one stretch of sight while they hassled and jostled, questioned and strayed. It was then she remembered her bag on the seat: her purse and commemorative tickets, her rosaries and bible and house-keys, the eight tinfoiled butties for dinner.

She saw Kelly smoking at fifty yards, but didn't know if she could make it to the end of the marching street without rest.

'I know where Gene's gone,' Nedra said to her lipsticked grand-daughter, but her swelled tongue wouldn't give edges to the words. Jan only nodded before her eyes set on little Joey, like they both agreed she'd gone mad.

Four shallow steps weathered and graced with rubbish. They took her to Gene. This was once the front entrance to Minshull Crown Court. Back before the city dug up its tramlines. Now the stone arch was sealed and shaded. Discreet yet grander than any Wythie church's. He was panting and white as a cross-country runner. He smelled like lads his age smelled.

Nedra sighed for mercy and crossed herself. The doorway hid them from the street. She gripped his arm and lowered herself onto the cool dry dirty step, taking him down with her. 'You get in round that corner, you daft thing. Shut today, anyroad.'

Nedra read her wristwatch and saw the Devil had cheated her again. 'Can't be running off. Your mam's enough on her mind, hasn't she, without me losing you.'

'I just wanted to see me dad, before. That's it.'

Nedra cuffed him round the head. He let out a scraping sound, like a knife buttering burnt toast. Then shrank from her into the corner of the doorway to rub his hot hair. Then as quick as he'd fled off the bus –

he hugged her.

A dampness on her dress front, shining on her coat collar. Not noseblood.

'Your dad's tie still looks smart. Keep that shirt covered and they'll never know.'

They nodded at each other –

while a young woman with bunned hair passing them in loud heels and an electric blue suit sprinkled coins on the steps, between their feet, and carried on. Nedra tried to stand but her knees locked. She rocked onto her backside, choking: 'They take us for bloody beggars.'

Roger and Kevin blew into the doorway in a rush to collect the coins. The rest were there, waiting at the kerb with joined hands, as if posed for another snap. Kelly was ashing their shadows – looking the spit of his young grandfather. Only what she saw wasn't the ghost of the bad-tempered bugger that her Jim could be, but some germ of propitiation. And she did not know whether it was for her to witness or bring to pass.

Roger claimed a new twenty-pence piece; she slapped the coin out of his palm, dragging three lads from the dark doorway onto the baked street.

'Maybe he'll wait,' Jan said with her mam's sarcastic air and one of Kelly's fags on her breath.

They got off a Bee Line bus and hit the day's heat. Quickly each was sweating, nowty with hunger and thirst; all eight of them dragging or carrying somebody smaller.

The hazy stretch of path and meadow before them littered with torn flags, chucked banners, picnic rubbish. Thinning crowds dotted about, sun-stupid and blessed. A tall policeman with what looked like birdseed down his roomy uniform approached them after the Middleton Road gate.

'We're here to see the Pope,' Nedra said but knew.

He was baby-faced with a tash. Sweat dripped from under his hat. 'Afraid you missed him, love. He's gone.'

She read her wristwatch. It'd stopped.

'In his helicopter?' Roger said.

Nedra's ping-pong eyes clocked the carefree and gabbing. The idle curious. Shirtless pink-backed lads. Cheap young lasses. Skiving mites off the local estate who'd climbed a fence to see what the fuss was about.

Nedra gripped her grandson's arm tight. By the time Kelly let go the bobby was nowhere and the two of them were sat on a bench in a different slice of the park, a little further in. Steaming trees behind metal platforms with concert equipment and manned stations flogging frozen lollies and fizzy drinks. Trampled flowers lay on the smooth dusty path. A fallen flyer in the latticed shade beneath her was for an under-twelves C of E choir in Rochdale. Nedra read it in amazement, just fine without glasses – the bench paint tacky under her stout thighs.

'Ee-ah,' Kelly said, people-watching with her, while lapping raspberry sauce off a 99.

'Where'd you find spends for that?' she said.

He offered a choc-ice. 'Our kid just found a tenner in her bra.'

Nedra split the blue wrapper with her good fillings, cracked the thin chocolate and spilled liquid ice-cream.

'Our Jan. Sorted out the lot of them. Whatever they wanted.'

'That girl. You daren't ask. Where they now?'

Kelly pointed and she looked and counted six: ducked at a section of park fence nearby. Roger was talking excitedly but she couldn't make out what was said. She got up with her choc-ice and started for them. Kelly caught up and she slipped her arm through his.

Joey was sat in the dry earth where grass and park finished – protecting a lumpy bin bag.

'The Pope chucked it out his helicopter,' Roger said, cupping his eyes to see her against the sun.

Joey's sleeves and hands one rust-coloured stain.

'Come away from that,' Nedra said.

Jan leaned at the fence, chewing a lolly stick, her lips another colour again. Gene was squatting and squinting farthest along the fence – his jacket and shirt arms pushed up, stained like Joey's.

Nedra pointed to the fence. 'Joey! Get out of it.'

He widened the top of the bin bag to show her a litter of brown dead pups, tiny and swollen and greasy with shared blood.

Nedra threw her choc-ice at the bag in horror. A slap of brown and white. Brooks of ice-cream spreading.

'Baby Jesus mended this one, see?' he whispered. 'A miracle.'

Kelly crouched with him as Joey lost his whole arm into the bag and scooped out a white squirming dog pup from the dark still pile. Rolling and matted in filth. Giving his cuffs fresh stains.

Kelly scrunched the bag shut. 'Listen, mate. Some right wicked knobhead's gone and done this.'

'It was Lord Jesus,' Nedra announced –

as another helicopter chugged overhead.

She stared at it, against the high blue.

Before it had passed over, Joey began feeding the pup drips of ice-cream.

Roger and Kevin sat on the grass, grinning in silence.

Susie-Ann swished her frock and inched nearer.

Even Jan wanted to see.

***

Heaton Park dissolved into her own kitchen, three years later, the same young'uns with her, half-grown half-thanks to her feeding and minding. This was teatime Friday, when the wall clock ticked ten after five. . .

132

'Get washed up, loves,' Nedra said as some ran in through the backdoor. She'd sent Kevin, Roger, Joey, Susie-Ann to pick blackberries after school, then called to Linda over the fence to send Gene to fetch them for their tea. Snowy, little Joey's white staffie, trotted in too like a monster from a Sinbad film and lay under the table, hoping for scraps. His chops were purple; the kids had tried feeding him berries.

Roger raised their sandcastle bucket filled with dark pickings. They talked at her at once, waggled their dyed fingers. Only Joey's hands were clean but she ran them under the tap the same and wiped his grubby specs on a warm teatowel.

'Where's your Kelly?' he said, letting her adjust his specs.

'Where'd you think, love? Off out courting with—'

'*Zoo-lee.*'

'Don't be learning names like that. Do you no good.'

'She's eighteen and a half and I'm seven. Her bestest colour is red and mine's red.'

She gave him his cheddar butty. 'Yours is blue. City blue. And besides, your Snowy don't like her, or that great big scar she's down her face.'

He ate standing, flitting about while she rinsed the berries.

'We'll make crumble, ay? Then pie for Father Culler. How's that?'

Joey dropped half his butty.

'What's matter?'

Snowy lapped at the mess, pushing it along the green lino.

Gene dawdled shy now at the backdoor, asking after Jan without asking, having heard no doubt that she'd come in last night with a blackeye. She'd be with Bev Willows' scramble-brained girl, Alice. Trust Jan to knock about with a lass whose mam drank pubs dry and had broken four Wythenshawe marriages and counting, aborting the sons and daughters of good women's husbands like their souls were hers to damn.

Creaking and puffing, Nedra dried the lino with a rag under her foot, then scrubbed her own chapped hands at the sink. As she served the table Jan came in, shoved through Gene, who didn't dare look twice, just went home.

That blackeye swelled shut. The same shade of berry. Jan sat where she sat, picked up knife and fork, and stared with her good eye at Susie-Ann, at the chest of her threadbare playing-out jumper, specked in berry juice. Susie-Ann was wise enough at nearly twelve to say nowt. Knew better than to meet her eye, especially with Jan's face how it was.

'Hm,' Jan said. 'Time *you* got yourself a bra.'

AS JAN ATE HER tea on Friday, her fat square of a nana deflated beside her until her corners were curves and she was stooped over Jan, a pink arm tent-poled on the table as she cupped Jan's chin, upturned Jan's face, less to inspect the eye than to tut at it. Jan chewed food patiently, gob open, inciting.

Around her the pack hushed. Pathetic strays whose own pisshead mams need never make hot dinners since there was always plenty scran for their broods at this table. *Need never* applied to her mam too, who came downstairs now with it kipping on her shoulder, lemon cardi patchworked with dribble. Her nana switched off the cooker which cued Mam's turn to paw Jan's face, stare into the black-eye and say fuck all.

'Was it Kelly?' her nana said, soaking the chip pan.

'Was it 'eck.'

'*See*,' her nana gloated.

Jan went to move her chin away, but her mam kept it.

'Tryna eat me bloody tea here,' Jan said.

'Let the girl eat,' her nana said.

Jan cast her good eye around the kitchen:

Joey hopped on the spot with his butty as he repeated Kelly's name like it was a magic word; the Burton lads' forks couldn't find their gobs; Susie-Ann, the altar girl, cut food to chase it round her plate without ever catching it – her chest showing beneath a pilled-to-tissue forest-green pullover that was sticky with blackberry mush and had once been Jan's and before hers Kelly's.

Being older Jan had nowt to do with them but had begun to feel like another teatime stray.

She matched her mam's cold surety until the thing in her mam's arm hiccupped and by then she'd had enough and swatted her mam's fingers off her face so hard her mam nearly dropped the thing and for this Jan got skelped which made her blackeye weep and she shot up, taking Susie-Ann with her by the wrist, maybe only because the altar girl was in reach, and towed her out the kitchen and upstairs, both girls running. Susie-Ann still had her table knife in her fist when Jan footed the bedroom door to behind them and made the girl undress.

But first the quiet. Louder with their breathing. Conscious of it, Jan held her breath and Susie-Ann noticed and held hers too. Jan tried winking with her good eye but it wasn't enough to break the spell she had the girl under.

'Does *your* mam wallop *you*?' she said.

'. . .Loads,' Susie-Ann said, with a catch in her voice.

Jan could sense her excitement; her gulping the urge to escape. Jan wanted to smile but couldn't. She stepped from her, letting Susie-Ann see the small room: the lamp left on and the drapes quarter pulled, the unmade bed and stale after-smoke of a dozen Sterlings chained from its pillow. Ash-heaped breakfast bowl on the window ledge. All Kell's doing. Jan stalked backwards over his strewn garb till her knees bent and she was sitting on the end of the bed, not once taking her good eye off the girl.

'Reeks in here,' Jan said. 'Guess who stunk up the place?' She winged the bedspread smooth around her.

Susie-Ann tensed – maybe accepting Jan had brought her up here just to devil her.

'Thinks he's gunna be moving in with his bird but bet you she finishes with him quick now he's out. Mam won't care where he ends up. Will she fuck.'

Susie-Ann nodded but Jan knew the girl didn't know why she was nodding only that she should be and now couldn't stop until she shook off her blotched pullover and paused hiding her hands inside its reversed cuffs. Then she peeled them onto the floor, dropping the knife too.

'He's been taking me clubbing in town, you know,' Jan said, appraising the girl's body which wasn't stocky or slim but as moon-grey and indelicate as her own or Alice's; the blue blood mapped inside her, showing.

'Has he?' the girl said, so timid now there was more catch than voice.

Jan slid off the bed and groped underneath to retrieve an item long castoff, furry with dust. Reading its torn label which hung on a stitch: 'Ee-ah. Try this on.' She helped her with it, then guided her to the full mirror, preening and adjusting. Like Alice, that ungrateful backstabber, the younger girl seemed to fidget in slow-motion, but there was nowt sleepy or unreadable about her features which danced to Jan's pulse.

'You've got nice ones already.' Jan left her at the mirror and got changed – removing folds of school bog roll, re-tucking their pink inside a louder bra which showed beneath an off-white crochet waistcoat.

But Susie-Ann wouldn't look to compare. Instead the girl stood round-shouldered in the mirror, holding her hips as she swivelled left, right, her bellybutton outrageous. 'Hi-Yo, Silver,' Susie-Ann told herself in a Lone Ranger voice.

'Ay, Suze, I'm your fairy godmother, me. Like Cinderbloodyrella's *bra*, that is, I'm telling you. Whosoever tits it fits keeps it. She'll nab herself a dark prince what plays for City. Dead nice-looking.'

Just then, from the landing, little Joey Harvey began to murmur. Susie-Ann blinked at the sound and Jan hissed at the door. Little feet scampering away.

'Me mam says am not ready for one yet.' Susie-Ann spoke to the mirror.

'*She's* not the poor cow doing PE – *you* are.'

'Says I've to start wrapping them up till I'm older so I don't be giving lads ideas.'

'No wonder you good as *live* here.'

Susie-Ann caught Jan's reflection.

Jan said: 'But that's mams for you. Mams hate you just for having you, and just for being a girl. So they make you grow up round here, same way, sad as *them,* and then hate you even more once you do. But they don't put girls in Rose Hill, do they? They can't stop us from doing owt. They're not arsed enough.' While she wised her up, Jan exhumed her mini-boombox from under a mound of clothes and racked a cassette: 'Spend the Night' by the Cool Notes, Frankie Beverly's 'Back in Stride Again'. Stuff she'd taped off Piccadilly Radio for their Kell while he was inside. 'Now, dads are different, right? Dads'll fuck off down the Woodpecker or fuck off forever, and dead right I don't blame them. State of this place. Keeping a missus and sprogs. I mean, would *you*?'

Susie-Ann wagged her head.

Jan cranked it up, then pranced over, to share the mirror. 'Anyroad, forget mams and dads. It's dickhead lads you wanna worry about, now you've got summat on offer.'

The girl stared. 'Gene Harvey fancies you, Jan.' The catch in her voice was gone.

'Oh *well*. Bloody hell. He'll have to marry us, then, won't he?' Jan danced daft while she rooted under Kelly's clothes, cleared a shelf, emptied her satchel, gathering makeup to pile it at Susie-Ann's socked feet. 'Ee-ah.' She found Susie-Ann a Fruit of the Loom T-shirt scissored to rags at one sleeve and big enough to wear as a dress with laddered tights, which was how Alice had worn it, and how Jan made Susie-Ann. She relaxed her by untying her church plaits and mimed snipping them with two fingers. Susie-Ann seemed to take to the new order of things, accepting the impossible since it was there in the mirror.

'Question for you,' Jan said, teasing out her hair. 'What does me nana have you do at Sunday Mass?'

Susie-Ann looked at her blankly, as if Jan's voice were just part of the music. 'Bring out communion bowls, wear surplice, sometimes ring consecration bell. Once Father give us the thurible, just to hold.'

'Father Culler's a right bastard. And a poof. He'll be the reason that young Joey lad can't never keep still.'

Susie-Ann's face twitched in shock – convincing enough to fool her until the girl cut new dimples and a grin. 'If Missus Dodds heard you talk like that.' Then, chewing her cheek: 'Jan, how did you know you was. . .having a baby? And. . .how did it get coloured?'

'I never had no baby. Think that thing's mine downstairs? Is it fuck. Does it look like me?'

Susie-Ann wagged her head.

'*Well* then?'

Lightning lit the corners of her good eye and if the forks met Jan knew they'd spark a migraine. She frowned at them both in the mirror. She scratched her elbow from habit: a permanent faint rash from years of lying on the rough brown dog-stinking carpet in Alice's back bedroom while the pair of them defaced *NME*s and scranned fistfuls of pic-n-mix stolen from every cornershop between Ringway and Sharston and kept stashed inside ancient shortbread tins Bev had once used for thread and yarn and which the girls emptied of sugar faster than they could fill them when their cycles were coincident which were not the only days of the month they lay on the rough carpet together marking up pull-out posters but became the only times they lay together with the tins open and stuffed their gobs just in case one girl were to officially put more weight on than the other. But by September the tins had gone unsplit for months. Jan checked her elbows: only two days and the carpet rash had nearly left her but she was back –

in Alice's room, fourteen again, starting a new school year at Poundswick. Having too much of a laugh to notice. Too busy marching in place on Alice's single bed, nose-to-nose with her, not even pissed-up, as they held the swirl ceiling for no reason, pressed the ragged stipples and danced to KFM. Taught each other the words to songs but now Jan couldn't remember which; maybe 'Ghosts' by Japan. But for an afternoon it was all they truly loved. That same day they'd stripped off to that music to don stolen frocks and skirts which Bev had resewn for them in the box room by treadle. Bev came in after their fashion show asking if they wanted a brew and saw Jan half-undressed and said it. No note of surprise, accusation or disgust. Bev just said it. And it gave Alice permission to look at her too and then Alice looked at her mam, then looked again and said numbly: 'I thought you was going fat but I didn't dare say.' Bev sniggered but it was fine for another few heartbeats because so did Jan. Because they were both wrong. Then she saw herself strike Alice across the face, Alice's head snap back with the blow. Then Bev took Jan out the bedroom but it was no good; Jan was sobbing so hard it frightened her. Loose, Jan returned to the room where Alice was holding her slapped cheek but otherwise hadn't moved. Jan got no sense of how the girl saw her or felt. Alice refused to demand. Alice was like a black sheep in a dream whose wool turned out to be a cloud. Before she could hit her again Jan was sick on the carpet. Her sobs heavier and heavier, making her whole body do strange things and there was no way to ask for help. Bev made her scotch broth, made her put on Alice's old pyjamas, tried to soothe her with stories then mucky jokes then whispered advice from experience then gave her silence. But Jan couldn't stop. Even hours later. Finally bedded with Alice inside a weightless hug that she slipped out of gone midnight, forgetting the Willows' staffie would wake the whole street before she even made the stairs. . .

'If I had a black baby,' Jan said now to the terrified altar girl, 'be God Almighty what grassed and told me mam' – masking the memory of those tidal sobs and of the trapdoor to Hell. A wink from her good eye, refunded in the mirror.

Then she marked a clean canvas with a big sweep of kohl, erased it with a licked thumb and tried again.

'Am not allowed to wear tutty,' Susie-Ann said, tilting her face to better let Jan paint it.

'Why's that? Your mam waiting till you need a bra? You know you want your hair cutting as well.'

'Jan, she'll have a fit.'

Kohl stick dragging her lid: 'Oi, I can only see out one eye. Keep squirming and you'll be the same.'

Next the unplaited hair. Jan took bites out of it with card scissors. Jan cut it Alice-short to the girl's horror:

'Me mam told us mine came sooner cos I'd been misbehaving down there. Cos I'd confessed to Father Culler about what I'd dreamt.

And he told me mam. She said it's just as bad as interfering with your-self' – her voice catching again.

Jan stalled a second, taking this in. Her hands hovering over the shoulders of a younger girl whom she'd ignored for half her life; but now Jan's hands were ready to land, to comfort. They'd become kinned in ways primitive and profound. Ways distinct from the shared street and dinnertable, handmedowns, forgotten Sundays knelt at the same pew when Jan was small, before Jan knew any better, before Jan did as she pleased. But here was a girl who didn't know better, joining her prematurely in womanhood by mistake. To be judged, cheated, punished, pariah'd, pursued, as she. To be taunted by playground songs. Sneering remarks from form teacher crones and baby-faced wankers and bus-stop jackals and cocky sons of *Open Sunday-*cornershop-keepers who would stop whenever they sighted her and change the tune of their whistle. Those summertime pub-garden-benched no-marks sinking *Special Brew*, no worse than the briefcased and necktied or the dog-collared. Or gorgeous Longsight heartbreak-ers who made you levitate with love.

This girl would soon be like her in others' eyes, only without Jan's gob or Alice's fog to help survive Wythenshawe's finest – stop the bastards from clipping her bee wings.

But Jan stopped her trembling hands from resting on the girl's shoulders. Ten-inch cuttings fell to the floor. Then Jan turned her, to finish without the mirror. Shiny hairs covered her slashed T-shirt like she'd fought a stray cat.

'Jan, *was* it your Kelly what give you that blackeye?'

'Tony Kinsella done it.'

'Did he? Why?'

'Cos. . .' How best to explain. 'Cos his older cousin Cid wouldn't need to.'

Susie-Ann seemed to understand, even though she didn't know who or what the Kinsella cousins were; or about copping off or copping a feel, or doing dares and favours sometimes just for fags you'd never finish, after shags too quick to warm you or the seats of twoc'd motors parked across Sunbank Lane.

Done.

'Hi-Yo, Silver,' Jan sang to their reflections.

Susie-Ann sang it too and they both got giddy and fell on the floor that was all Kelly's new clothes, which stank so much of lad they decided to fill his pockets with hair, then fling his garb across her room.

Day-blue evening. Good sun not set but powdered through the entry that cut adjacent to the semis. She cupped her good eye to see up into Alice's grubby window. She pointed for Susie-Ann who followed her finger along to the next bare window where two bodies appeared smoky and colourless through the bright glass.

'Jan, what's he doing to her?'

'Nowt special.'

Jan had them balanced on rainsoft ashbins to sken over the rotted fence. Standing tiptoe, dancing out cramp, the girl's teeth shining:

'Easter Monday, Shrove Tuesday, Ash Wednesday, Sheer Thursday, Good Friday. Does it matter what you have for tea on Ash Wednesday? I mean if –'

Jan pressed her pointing finger to Susie-Ann's lips. They hiccupped. Susie-Ann had stitched her a bracelet out of red liquorice and now bit it gently, on Jan's wrist, chewing her closer so the bins wobbled.

She had Susie-Ann pissed-up on four swallows of discount Babycham that were traded for love on the cool weed-split slabs behind Simonsway offie with the stock-take lad on his fag break. Susie-Ann had sat knees tight, ringside, on a pallet by the open backdoor. Gesturing while the lad tried his luck, Jan mouthed to her but the girl was too absorbed in education to sneak in and grab the good stuff, like she'd been told.

Now the drunk bottle slipped through Susie-Ann's hands and bounced off the bin lid. The din as it rolled away had them both bobbing behind the fence. They hid and waited with the cobbles and dandelions and flat tins of super lager. Rubbish shivered when a sharp gust shot through the entry and left their legs chilly and pushed the bottle on. Susie-Ann retrieved it with exaggerated care, plucking a long dandelion which she fed inside – its flowerhead big enough to rest over the mouth of the bottle. Then she re-climbed the bin with her new vase.

Wait.

Jan held her. They heard the top window squeak wide – seeping black music, summat Jan didn't know but liked.

She whispered: 'Bev must be down the Happy Man for them to be at it with their kit off.'

'Are they in love?'

'A'they fuck.'

'*Looks* like love,' Susie-Ann said, scared.

'And you'd know, would you?'

'Does she help herself to his chips at dinner?'

'She did *today*. Greedy cow.'

'And does they hold hands walking home? Cos then that means they love each other.' Susie-Ann, glazed and hiccupping.

'It's you what should be teaching *me*.' Jan rested her chin along the fence again. 'She's mad, though. He'll be done with her by next week.'

'Jan, have *you* been in love?' Susie-Ann was too short to chin the fence but tried anyway.

'Once. But we never said owt cos we would've felt daft. I never see him, even though I know where he lives and what bus he gets.'

Susie-Ann, waiting with her dandelion vase for more. When Jan didn't give it Susie-Ann twirled the stem and put her ear to Alice's fence as if to better hear what she couldn't see. She plucked a petal.

'Piss-the-beds,' the girl hiccupped.

'There's an idea.' Jan took the bottle, hitched her skirt and squatted. 'Holy water,' she said, blessing it.

Having kept the dandelion, Susie-Ann crossed herself, her eyes spooked and round:

'Jan?'

'What?'

'Have you ever laughed till you was sick?'

'Me and Alice did. Once, in her front room. Her dog ate mine. Dogs are disgusting.' Jan tossed the refilled bottle over the Willows' fence.

It Catherine-wheeled over the birdshat kennel, bleached and broken gnomes, and washing-line slack, to tag the shared brickwork between Alice's bedroom and the lad's bedroom.

Glass exploded –

and piss washed Alice's side of the guttering.

Susie-Ann hopped quicker and higher to see what happened next. But this tipped the ash bins and they both fell off. Jan touched the entry's earth foot-first and went with her weight. She stumbled to a stop along the fence.

When she turned Susie-Ann was lying down. Posed like a chalked body outline and with a stretched shadow that fit between the capsized bins and dark enough to be road tar. On her: Jan's laddered tights, burst skin at the knee. They each saw the blood at the same time and the shock kept Susie-Ann there, too afraid to move.

'Jan. . .? Get Missus Dodds. . . *pleeeese*.' All creeping panic.

Daylight was skimming the entry. By now her nana would be in the pew for Friday Mass.

'If you tell me nana or your mam or anyone what I done to your hair, I'll do more than batter you.'

The words seemed a comfort to the younger girl, who lay gazing up at her against the sun. Shiny makeup. Bra lines. Joan of Arc hairdo. Breaths slowing to even.

Jan sensed then Susie-Ann really was another Alice and would always know things Jan didn't and wouldn't. '. . .You're fine. Now fuck off.'

She gozzed on the cobble by her face and waited for Susie-Ann to pick herself up and limp out the entry. Jan turned the other way, went without seeing the girl at her kitchen table again.

'Whose are them?' Zuley asked with her foot dropping out of bed to sift the twists of clothes and hair and buried junk that could half-cripple if you misstrod, like Jan did on her way to the bed, to sit there slack-gobbed and tingling, after finding Zuley alone in her house in her room in her bed in the dusk. Jan had a rush of daunting happiness; she went giddy and young. Zuley seemed deracinated from somewhere magical but nearby that Jan had never found. But there Zuley was, and keen to talk to her and keener to listen, at least while their Kelly had his bath. It was a year and a bit since Jan had last seen her, but Zuley was the same: piss-funny, gorgeous and wise; doing everything and nowt; just teaching her how to be.

Until Zuley's foot, having dived into the midden, had surfaced with the knickers from Mr Somerville's flat hooped blue on her big toe: 'Oi, Kell! Your uncle Mac already got you another bird, has he?'

And Jan swung her head as Kell came in, shirtless, rubbing his pits with Jan's clean towel.

'You what. . .?' he said.

The toe twitched; blue fabric swayed.

'. . .Bit saucy, them are.'

'Glad you like em.'

'Cost a penny, I bet. Sure they not yours?'

'Guess again, Kell.'

'Couldn't tell you.'

'Well, I've got a few ideas, me.'

'What's that mean?'

'They're mine,' Jan said.

'Bollocks,' they both said.

Kelly flung the towel over her – knocking down cassette cases bricked by the stereo that was now on the window ledge. Songs rained on the bed. She could hear them. . .

When Jan had got home after seeing off Susie-Ann, she'd come in through the front door for no other reason than it was shut which was unusual before nine. It opened, was just on the latch. She rubbed off her manky-white tennis shoes while she climbed the stairs and flipped one over the stairwall before reaching the landing. She didn't see it drop but heard it bomb a passing young head in the hall. A yelp. Then a slap as the shoe got chucked back.

'Missed!'

Evelyn Champagne King's 'Love Come Down' sweated through her bedroom door.

Jan paused, hand on wood.

The bog flushed at the end of the landing. A line of light under that door split by feet. The bath taps thundered.

Jan peeped inside her bedroom, clocked Zuley's hair wedged big on her pillow. She waited for the song to finish and Zuley to notice her. Zuley lit up and sat up and called her closer with both arms. Jan stabbed her foot on summat sharp while crossing the room.

'Hey you.'

'Iya.'

Dressing quick, in bed: 'That prick said you're never in.'

'I'm not. . . I can go.'

'Let's just pretend I'm decent.'

Jan felt this older light from her so warm and good that she hop-scotched the rest of the way and found herself hugging Zuley for too long and was so embarrassed that she went to the end of the bed where she could only hug herself – her boombox behind her, Cheryl Lynn starting 'Instant Love'.

'Feel bad about us pinching your room like this on a Friday night.'

'You're alright.'

Zuley listened with her whole face for answers before asking Jan any questions. 'So. . .?' she started.

'So what?'

'So what you been doing?'

Before she could stop, Jan had told her about Alice and that no-mark wet leaf of a lad she'd fallen for. It dawned on Jan that she could never get with Gene Harvey, even if she got bladdered, since then she'd only be copying Alice, collecting her own lad-next-door.

'*That* won't last,' Zuley said.

'But he must've said summat to her cos now she don't wanna know me.'

'She'll skin her knees crawling back to you, tryna be best mates. What's he got against you anyway, this lad?'

'How should I know? Bet you he's seen me having a laugh with some lads what took his dinner money. Honest to God, Zuley, he's nowt.'

'Aren't they all. I've got mates telling us to chuck your Kell.'

'Them's right, though.'

146

Zuley grinned. 'You'll have to start coming out with us, Jan. Club it in town, ay?'

'Yeah?'

'D'you like to dance?'

'If it's to summat like this.'

Zuley's eyes drifted to the midden. Kell's and hers and Jan's. 'You've grown up, you know? Can I say that? Or do I sound like your uncle Mac?'

'Who's me uncle Mac?'

'Don't ask.' Zuley shuffled down the bed to reach the boombox on the window ledge. She flipped the tape and pushed play. 'Your Kell can be a right knob, can't he?'

'About the best you'll get round here.'

'He was dead keen to move in with me, you know? It was sorted. You were gunna get your room back. But this was before Uncle Mac shows out the blue and says there's a job going. Now all of a sudden he's not so sure.'

'What job?'

'Don't ask, Jan; I'm not.'

Jan notched up the stereo.

Zuley notched it one more. 'Kell wants you to say who give you that blackeye, so he can—'

'Shake his hand?'

'You two had a scrap after he come home, but he said most the bruises were ones *you* gave *him*.'

'Tell you what, I'll say about me eye if you say about your scar.'

Zuley stayed close, sat lotus, rolling her head with Melba Moore. 'This? Just after Kelly got sent down some skinhead lobbed a tangerine with a razorblade as I got off the bus on Withington Road.'

'Fuckers.'

'He ran off, right, but these lads I was with caught him. I mean, they *really* battered him.'

'Good.'

Zuley traced her thin silver scar from cheek almost to corner lip, slowly, maybe recalling the marks those lads had made on him in reply to hers.

The girls swayed for a chorus.

'What?' Jan said.

'You mean *who*?' Zuley said.

'"Who"?'

'*Who* give you that shiner?'

Jan smiled and prised the tuttied blackeye with her filthy thumbs but saw only water with it.

Zuley took her hand and kept it. 'Kell's hoping it was the father. So he can kill two birds with one stone.'

Jan went cold. Jan saw a dozen dandelions on a kitchen table in a vase full of piss. Jan slumped to the window, to the music. It was her blood that had stopped swilling round and made her bedroom cold.

Zuley turned the music down and rubbed Jan's arms with hot hands but Jan wouldn't warm. Too cold for that older light that reached her only as a faint glow. Jan jerked back and said with a Dodds man's swagger:

'I was at me English teacher's flat yesterday. Been seeing him a month nearly.'

'Jan, what's his name?'

Zuley looked at the boombox but didn't turn it off. Waiting and waiting.

'Mr Somerville,' Jan said.

'Likes em young, does he, Mr Somerville? And he likes it rough?'

'Swear you won't say owt?'

Zuley just listened to the music and swayed softly, watching her. But then Zuley had gone and found the blue knickers.

And then Kell had come in towelled from his bath.

After Jan told half the truth and wasn't believed she said: 'Who's our uncle Mac?'

'Ask Mam.'

'Did he ask her out?'

But he was rooting for his fags.

Zuley, up out of bed – fastening a lemon rah-rah skirt, then fixing her hair in the window reflection instead of the mirror. It was full-dark out.

Kell jumped into his 501s under the big light and chose a grey T-shirt from the heap but it was pasted in Susie-Ann's hair. He tried another shirt, sniffed it, pulled it on. 'Mac's picking us up at ten for a drink.'

'Since when?' Zuley said.

'You can either come with or get dropped off.'

'Nah, Kell. You're alright. Rather make me own way.'

'Gone dark.'

'Don't worry; I won't be smiling at anyone.' She nodded ta-ra to Jan, then crossed the room without stabbing her feet.

'Oi, well done, knobhead,' Jan said.

'Whose is this hair?' He came near but it was only to spy Zuley from the window, shutting the gate on her way out. He kept on the glass, even after she'd gone, maybe fancying himself, fresh out the bath; maybe seeing only the street. He said: 'You're just miffed, our kid, cos you thought you had your room back.'

Jan said: 'You know she's took your cigs, don't you?'

AS LIVING GHOST OF her vacated house Carol slept undead till the baby called to her in a song sweet enough to reach her.

Carol woke, knees drawn, sexually sore, bathed in netted light, the whole bed hers. She knew what day it was – Saturday – having agreed to leave the house that evening with Mac.

Yes, tonight Carol would tart herself up for Ira 'Mac' McGowan, if she remembered how to, if she exhumed a frock that about fit her. *Yes Mac I'll go with you tomorrow and every day after no matter when or if you carry out your jewellers job with my criminal son under your wing my soft son who was once so in danger of forgetting his name he threw himself in Strangeways to find it before you came to teach him its true meaning but since you are more Dodds man than he and as a Dodds man in all but name and with an eye now on a dead Dodds man's wife and another on a dead Dodds man's son you can claim us both and save us from ourselves and so it is a yes to you and Kelly and Rodney Westlake and whoever else you've dredged up from Manchester's sorry canals filled only with loyal luckless blood and it's a yes if you get away with armed robbery and a yes if you get pinched and sent down which at your age with your record could leave you forever at Her Majesty's pleasure and it is a yes without needing you to rob me a diamond engagement ring because if you kept it I shall wear your Minnie's rock instead like a trophy and toddle out of Wythie for good like a past-it glamour puss of the North, the last of her kind. Yes I will love you Mac McGowan. Yes come take me and take my name*

*and give me yours. Yes so long as tonight you say where you dug my
tender Vern's grave.*

Because to learn his burial ground meant escape for all things
trapped in her house by accident, consequence or design. Dodds
women were women of inflexible devotion. She had carried gentle
Vern with her through time, having locked him, with her, between
life and death, in a purgatory he did not deserve – a shared cell too
good for her yet too much for her to bear. To let Vern rest she would
forsake ten thousand sweet fucks without which her wounds could
not remain open, or her guilt be nightly renewed. Scarred instead she
would abscond from a life lived to be forgotten, in a place vast and
proud and half-abandoned by the present and half-ruined by false
promises made to it in the past, made before Carol was thought of,
made to her own house-proud Wythenshawe mam and the house-
proud Wythenshawe mams her mam knew: lies whose legacy had left
Carol as set and sad and defeated as she ought to be; lies which had
helped her pay small penance she could otherwise scarcely afford.
To let Vern rest she would forsake more than Vern and no less than
Vern: her maminlaw, son, daughter and daughter's son. She would
escape this zoo and its rolling menagerie of boisterous, unwashed,
unfed, unloved kiddies on the cadge, filling her house and keeping
her cupboards empty, and her scrubbing endless – and for which her
maminlaw scarcely charged the neighbours enough to break even.
Tonight Carol would gladly make like Eunice and fly the broken
nest. To be with the womanshy older thief, the late guvnor's loyal
muscle and cuckold. They had enough in common. Both cowards
both widowed both killers. Their better halves monsters slain without
swords.

So, Carol left bed Saturday, peeled her shift, its egg-blue seams
and trims navy with unguent and grime. From behind the door she
unhooked a scratchy towel dressing gown so shell-dry it couldn't mop
the nightstain from her thighs – proudly jellied from hugging Vern.

Downstairs she lit the stove to brew up and warm some powdered
milk. In what was once her son's room she changed and fed the baby
then licked his nose to bring back his light. Nameless and officially
undeclared, unvisited by state or health visitor. He looked up at

her with inscrutable happiness. Wriggling bunflesh refusing to be swaddled. He gave her a stream of excited chatter and babble in the metre of speech – sharing his dreams with her this way before he tired and dreamt some more. Carol looked over the cot for Vern. When she looked down the baby was sucking her fingertip content – more watchful of her than she was of him. Carol checked over her shoulder, as if she might find Vern by the porridge woodchip wall, his ridiculous prick bobbing while he told her daft things to shield her from his useless cleverness and instead impress his unwavering and contented light so that it might kindle her own. A soft light and warm; she hated that it couldn't burn her. His light neither forgiving nor unforgiving since Vern didn't recognise or confer forgiveness. Alive Vern had said to her it was funny to be living. The joke wasn't that he was dead. One night in bed Carol reminded him of this while he pretended to magic an endless hankie out of her bellybutton, a hankie that was really her snazziest black cotton briefs (snazzy meant by some miracle their elastic hadn't gone). Mid-trick, Vern kept gesturing naked that there was nowt up his sleeves; and at first he hadn't remembered what or why, because the dead forget quick, but then he'd said:

'Do not mourn the living, Carol, my love, they don't know what they're doing.'

And she'd laughed herself awake to find him still in her bed and her bed still a catafalque, his girlish hands shushing her. He had her knickers in his gob; and he gulped like in a *Tom and Jerry* cartoon. Mimed amazement. Fish-hooked himself to show her they were gone. *Bloody blinking magic.* Then he rolled off her to banter with Sefton – her wedding photo framed on her bedtable –claiming Sefton knew how the trick was done and had threatened to tell out of spite.

'Tell who?' Carol said.

'A certain regional ruling body.'

'Mine.'

Vern raised his chin. 'You always get *one*, don't you? Sees the rest enjoying themselves and ruins their bit of clean fun.'

She'd turned her husband's picture to spare him and woken without her black cotton briefs, beside her maminlaw who slept like a walrus, sinking the double bed. Carol had looked for the pair on washday and was relieved to never find them again.

Was that the joke? That her dead men didn't give threats or answers or forgiveness or mither with or recall even the dull petty graft of living. *Funny Living* as Vern had called it, being in love with life because he saw it for what it was: a Sharston to Piccadilly double-decker, on which the two of them had found themselves strangers sharing a bench, not so much fated to sit together but had done so anyway, and got off together instead of where they were supposed to, knowing from then on they couldn't go anyplace without the other.

But the dead could steal your life while you lived it which was itself the answer, the threat and the punishment: all of which you could count in old pence like the small currency of forgiveness.

But Saturday morning in the backroom with the baby, Carol saw only motes and heard only a quiet odder than the one that had preceded Kelly's do. Neither of her kids had come home last night. They'd left separately, would return separately. And with Nedra churching early (Carol had come downstairs to a cold stove, counters dusted with flour, a pie bird drowning in a rusty pool in the blocked sink) those who weren't strictly of this house were yet to invade. Nedra had likely got next door's eldest to carry her dishes: weekend dinners and pudding for her priest – full-haired, bow-legged, sixty-odd – who made fewer social calls since October, but still bobbed in to drink whatever Nedra stocked for him and poured from an old decanter into the surviving tumbler. Between regal sips he would glance at Carol in her kitchen the way brutal men, home after last orders, ageing in their frontroom chairs, stared at water bowls under gas fires. Men hollowed. Wedded to women of battered bodies and mocking faces. On his regular visits Nedra's priest wouldn't ask Carol owt other than a clenched *Well?* to which she'd reply by the same word or now and then with a sigh, after which he would laugh weakly and steal his glances.

Carol shouldered the baby now and took him from Kelly's old room into Jan's, which had become Kelly's too, since the baby had taken his. It was fag-stale, the single bed unmade – the floor a jumble sale. Slagheaps of robbed clothes. Sun diamonds spotted the floor via the mirror. Carol waded into one and warmed her gleaming perfect feet. A skinny orange Bic lighter stood on a shelf with bottles and palettes of tutty. Tea rings, stacked coppers, costume jewellery. Torn pages from schoolbooks leafed the tiny dresser: doodles scratched right through the paper.

'Has Strangeways changed him?' Vern had asked her in the night.

'Changed him how?'

'Made him more of *this* or less of *that*.'

'I wouldn't know. I don't know me kids. Times I forget they're there.'

'I don't believe you. They're both too *there* to ignore.'

'But *I'm* not all there, am I?'

'Some of you is. Which means you can be there for them some of the time. And that's all you can ever be.'

'Give us the punchline.'

'I'm not there at all. But we make do.'

Now she put the baby down on the sheeted mattress and banked him with pillows.

Shhhhhhhh. . .

Without waking, he hushed her like he was in on it; his sibilant breath telling her to hold her nerve: let Jan get home and fight somebody else for her own room.

Carol scooped Kelly's ashtray bowl off the inside windowsill and went back downstairs where she managed to spark up with maybe Jan's, maybe Zuley's, orange lighter. She binned it after it gave her a flame and took up her housework, foursquare on the speck-green lino, cig between her lips: wiping dark sticky fingermarks off doorframes and cupboards. Cloudy marbles, a ruby hairslide and squished berries filled her dustpan; even a duffed charm of St Jude, helper and keeper of the hopeless, and a broken crystal chaplet and devotional medal, each Nedra's, each of which Carol had been accused of pawning, last week maybe or last year. Found beneath a fresh warp in the lino, at the skirting that ran to the backdoor. Under the table was what looked like a cold drumstick but what she swept up was a plastic baby doll leg, webbed in dog dribble and toothmarked. Though she didn't let in next door's staffie she knew Nedra fed it on the sly whenever Carol was mithered elsewhere.

Carol kept the ashtray moving –
on the lino with her
as she cleaned from the floor up, the opposite
of how it was done.

No less perverse for her than knowing what day it was.

The nicotine technicoloured her memory, regrew the divides between moments lived, shaping her inner world with solid edges. She hadn't smoked since before Jan was born. Not since she had caught her sisterinlaw Eunice in the chilly WC at her inlaws. Eunice, sat there under the flat spongy cobwebs, wearing a straw pillbox hat after Mass, holding a just-lit fag when Carol pulled the splintered door. The lit match in the tight space gave Eunice a fugitive glow. She looked up at Carol and then down again and smiled, quick, without teeth, and Carol joined her without knowing why. Eunice, maybe twenty-one then, fat as a duck, a shy office girl – who no one knew was even courting, never mind weeks from mixed matrimony, elopement and emigration – passed Carol the cigarette, already lippy-stained, but not as a bribe. Then she lit another from a packet of Embassy inside her Sunday purse. By then Carol had been four years in the family and knew next to nowt about Eunice, just that the girl typed Monday to Thursday, took no milk in her Lyons instant coffee, lived at home and more than enjoyed her mam's cooking. There Carol sensed for the first time not hidden depth exactly but muddy shallows, an unexplored sadness in the girl, like some mystery scab in a reachable blind spot: ready to pick. Not that Carol wanted any female communion. She was after summat from this girl, but what, she couldn't decide so might have called it *fun*. Locked in together they puffed the water closet into a tepee, waiting to see who'd speak first.

'Is it sore?' Eunice whispered, seeing her rub at her jaw.

Carol wondered then if she could make one of them cry. 'You're best not asking.'

Eunice's posture rounded; she glanced behind her at the Izal. Both knees jogged with the chill. When Carol and Sefton called round, Eunice always forgot to cross her knees after taking her usual perch on the green three-seater, end furthest from the fire, in that maple-veneer front room. Nedra would notice and tell her daughter to mind herself. But on the toilet Eunice smoked with bolted knees. Carol took a drag and another and cupped the ash: 'Your brother, he batters me about once a fortnight. Does it if I please him. And if I don't.'

'. . .'

'Ay, least it's not in front of our Kelly.'

Without warning, Eunice half stood to lift the toilet lid and ashed the bowl and resat and smoked what was left. 'Wasn't your Kelly good as gold today? Don't know how you keep him so clean. When's he turn four?'

Carol remembered telling her and remembered Eunice had flushed their stubs, and shivering, taken off her hat to fan the smoke out the dirty latch window but the hat had slipped out of her fingers – into the toilet bowl.

'*Fuck*,' Eunice whispered, covering her mouth too late. At that time in that place that word from that girl: it froze them. She saw her pinch the hat rim and lift it, wringing.

Carol talked into the splish of the bowl: 'We're daft apeths, ain't we? Me and you.'

'. . .'

'It'll dry. I shan't breathe a word. . .'

Now, crawling on her kitchen floor, Carol heard her street echo and she put on the telly not to watch it but to snuff the playing-out shrieks. Mike Read, patronising Five Star on *Saturday Superstore*, a pop group she only knew because Vern had once told her that Jan liked them. When Carol had asked how Vern knew, he danced a *Top of the Pops* routine full-mast. She'd cackled, sat up in bed, applauding. He'd bowed and put an ear to the wall between her room and Jan's. *See, the dead can only listen. . .*

Carol hoovered her front room. The TV's square picture settled. Kelly's girl, Zuley, had a look of one of the sisters in the group, but under a pound of tutty she couldn't be sure. Carol wiped new dust off the telly top with her dressing-gown sleeve, planted the ashtray bowl and balanced her dog-end. Carol jogged her baggy pockets: lippy bullets, applicators, vials and pots from her daughter's shop-lifted makeup hoard. They clacked together like a bag of marbles. Her sleeve fell down her arm and passed over the painted singers being live-interviewed on her telly, answering daft questions. Static lifted her hairs, tingled.

As she went back to her housework short shapes appeared in the mottled glass of the front door. But the shapes soon ran off, impatient. Carol outwaited them – spying from the kitchen through the hall. There, Carol sucked the unsmokable cig right to the filter, dropped it into her dustpan and poured another brew.

Her floor drying spotless.

She stared at it into October last: when Vern had woken her with kisses so that she would have to listen and leave his arms and go downstairs, none of which she would've done voluntarily –

to find their fourteen-year-old daughter in the kitchen having come down in the night to break a full glass of water before taking a sip, her own waters already broken.

Jan gave birth upright, backed and squatted against the cooker, while Carol swept glass and Nedra midwifed, without asking the good St Gerard for help. Jan didn't scream but panted the same as when Carol had found her there – moonlit feet bleeding on broken glass – in just a rancid sweatshirt of Kelly's that Jan had kept out the wash and worn for bed ever since his conviction. Only once Jan howled blue murder, when she first noticed Carol in the kitchen dark with her. Carol had stiffened and her daughter recoiled and Nedra found them with the big light off – the bulb gone when Nedra tried the switch; the fuse blown – the crescent moon in the window cutting wide between net curtains which normally met. At that point, Carol and Jan had peered over their noses at each other, like they were both about to sneeze. Then Nedra rushed forward –

Jan sinking

and no sooner had it slipped out of her.

A tiny mess of recremental blood finding it had a voice and with it began the unwanted task of living as it entered their kitchen song-first.

Nedra took it beaming and tut-tutted into its noise. Then she gave it Carol to change the bloodwater in the pot-wash tub which she set on the lino beside Jan, right where the afterbirth had slapped like a dropped pie. Redding a new dish cloth, Nedra said to Carol: 'This is like in the old days.' Her voice had lost that sharp flutter; it even carried a trace of sleep.

Out of moon's reach, Carol knelt and held the corded baby. Drenched in glop, passable as a clump of clay and about as real to her, it was surely too slight and unwelcome to stay but its song said otherwise.

Not once did Carol see Jan look at it. Jan's tears fixed higher, her crown resting on the oven door. The moon caught her daughter down one side, showed her hair sweated flat, her resting features greased and florid, her lifted shin dirty, bruised like a lad's. Fluid pearled her thighs, between which Jan groped absently almost, tame with exhaustion.

Nedra took the baby again. At sixty-five Nedra was claiming she would soon be unable to genuflect before the tabernacle. Carol watched carefully. No wince or strain or hissed prayer; not while she was bent-kneed under Jan; and this miracle went unrecognised. Nedra had caught her only granddaughter parturient, and it'd cured her aches on sight. Left her oxblooded. Nedra's acceptance of the situation seemed instant, like the surprise was none, the event minor, and only proving she had been right about the girl. Nedra and Carol had raised her without love but with enough basic thankless upkeep to stamp their pain on her which by virtue of her blood Jan provoked.

For Carol, Jan's thereness was best ignored, like everyone else's. She might look too deeply into Jan over breakfast one morning and find Vern in there, then split her daughter open with a bread-knife to free him, and have him to herself. Carol knew Nedra had always treated Jan different to the kids she saw to school, who ran riot, who gave as much cheek and caused as much grief and still Nedra fed them love. Bitterly, Nedra had accepted that Jan was Sefton's daughter and Nedra could not entertain otherwise. Especially when Jan became her *dead* son's daughter. Carol had brought about Jan's ruin by abandoning her to Nedra's forecasting of it. Carol knew that Jan's fall would redecorate their martyrdom. Knew her maminlaw was keen to greet this great-grandchild and picture scandal.

Lucky then there was more –

and that Nedra had saved her sign of the cross for when – washing the baby – she learned its stubborn skin. 'Nigger brown. Carol. Look. Them wicked buggers. Look. God help her. Nigger brown.'

And from then on Nedra shunned it just like its own mam. Which left Carol caring for it. Having to jack in work. They had little to live off without Kelly's thieving and were left with a single giro, a pension and a few tenners a week from Nedra's childminding. Nedra claimed Jim had been wily and thoughtful enough to put away some brass, so nobody would go short after he was gone. Nedra kept this lie alive. But the fatter Carol grew – living off reheated leftovers and Vern – the surer she was that nobody round here starved. Mouths you never knew you had, you could feed best.

A month Carol had known her daughter was pregnant and said nowt; she'd not even told Vern. Bev Willows had rung the house before work, sounding more legless than hungover. She promised to keep it out of the factory girls' ears and for a time – gobshite or not – she did. Nobody shopped the Dodds women. Sat on the bottom stair on the phone Carol shook with bottled laughter and thanked Bev, sensing that thanks were wanted or maybe required, and thanks were simpler than questions. Before Carol could ring off Bev asked her to clock in for her, and if she couldn't, then tell the foreman she'd be in by nine so not to dock half her pay. While Bev waited on the line for an answer Carol heard hope. And hope was always pregnant. Carol moved her mouth from the receiver to laugh – rolling and twisting like she did at Vern's jokes. . .

Nigger brown. Carol, look.

Carol looked again in her kitchen by October moonlight and wanted to rush upstairs and shout Vern, then she remembered he was dead.

'Gorgeous. Must take after his daddy, whoever that is.'

Carol looked at Jan.

No words for or from.

The last time Carol had had words for her that mattered was on the maternity ward when nursing with a painful latch a shallot face in shade and shape. Carol hissed that she would swap this life of minutes for ten more with Vern if she could. Him being dead and buried before they'd known they'd made her. . .

Carol bedded Jan's baby in a wrecked Easter basket, tucked it under moth-bitten shawls that her maminlaw had been saving for the rag-and-bone man since the year of Carol's wedding. When she came to bed she found not Nedra sleeping but Vern waiting. He had folded the corners of the sheets, like he was setting places for ghosts, which he was. Odder still, he was wearing summat: a pair of sixties clubmasters. A twist of Sellotape replaced a lost screw. Through them he stalked her bedroom reading a snapped paperback and missed her undress: '"At first you think that you can bear only so much and then you will be free. Then you find out that you can bear anything, you really can and then it won't even matter."' He saw her, over his specs. 'Any cop?'

'You can write down owt and make it sound clever. Won't make it true.' Carol took his waist – his prick heating her belly. Behind her head she knew he was rereading the passage to himself, in agreement. She rubbed into him to try to take his smell but couldn't find it –

till he dropped the book on her bedtable, where by morning it wouldn't be. 'What about "a dead body revenges not injuries"?'

'Well, yours still looks in fine fettle – and to think now you're a granddad.' Carol laid on her bed, pointing thick white legs. 'I should've had the sense not to let meself go.'

His woman's hands: 'You're like a bloody Botticelli, you are.'

'Just get here.'

His lips reached her halfway through a joke, and he performed the rest inside her, and she waited until she could hardly see, then said:

'Vern Jenkins. . . a granddad.'

She reminded him of the day he took her and a sweet little boy to Belle Vue Zoo to watch animals do nowt. Kelly had cried when the big cats yawned but Vern put him on his shoulders and told him the cats were sharing stories to pass the time. Soon had Kelly giggling at nonsense about *Growltiger the Bravo Cat. . .*

Carol upset the bedtable – bruising her knuckles, tipping Sefton's bridegroom photo onto Vern's book.

He scooted up to straddle her. She took off his fogged specs and gave them her husband.

'Boy or girl?'

'Boy. Black as sin.'

'*No?* Sensational. How did Jan go on?' Vern stressed *hows*, like a factory girl, not *dids* like that German poet he took her to hear once in a mouldy Shudehill bookshop with no heating, rammed with students dressed in pulled threads, reeking of Bovril and dope. She could remember what she had on that day but not Vern – just that he'd smelled more of old books than the old books; and that smile he had worn for her when the poet stopped mid-line to fill a pipe he never smoked.

'Now it's out of her she won't be in a room with it. She hid him for the whole ride. Even from herself.'

He rolled Carol's body carefully and she shut her eyes and took his weight – even-spread. 'I feel bad for Jan,' Vern said.

'You bloody would, you mug. You know damn well what we women are.'

He tapped her skin thoughtfully. 'You're a public convenience.'

She tossed a pillow. 'If only.'

Vern straightened Sefton's picture, then said to her: 'Were *you* showing when you wedded?'

'Officially no. Course, that viper Minnie, she came up to me after the ceremony, making dead sure Nedra was in earshot before she went, "Carol, lovey, you can't hardly tell. Least not from the front." Minnie wore white too, you see? Reckoned if *I* bloody could, *she* might as well.'

Vern blew Sefton a kiss but she turned him away. 'So Nedra knew there was two inside that wedding gown?'

'She had to let it out then resew me into it. On the big day the thing was that clinging tight I couldn't eat, couldn't drink, so I spent the night dancing with all the rum villains Jim invited to the after-do at the Oaks. One got up on the bar with his little guitar for an Irish sing-song. They were teaching me. I can remember their sweaty hands being tighter than me wedding dress.'

'You had blood sitting in your bridal shoes.'

'That's right. Me poor little feets doubled with the swelling.'

'You fainted before midnight. You butted the corner of the bar on your way down.'

'That's right.'

'They fetched an ambulance and you spent your wedding night up Withington Hospital.'

'Tell us, how's it you remember what you weren't there for better than what you were? This was years before I met you.'

'Aye, but I read to retain and retain what I read.'

Reading her, Vern reached for the bridegroom photo, turned it again till they could see him and he could see them.

Carol had wedded spring '62 – on the day the A6 murderer hanged.

Carol was older now than Nedra was then.

Nedra forty-two; Jim fifty-two; Mac forty-two; Minnie twenty-seven; the groom a grand lad of twenty-three whose blushing bride was twenty and already a slut, seven months gone; and knowing this their shrunken whiskered priest read them an encyclical during the nuptial liturgy:

'"There is danger that those who before marriage sought in all things what is theirs, who indulged even their impure desires, will be in the married state what they were before, that they will reap that which they have sown; indeed, within the home there will be sadness, lamentation, mutual contempt, strifes, estrangements, weariness of common life, and, worst of all, such parties will find themselves left alone with their own unconquered passions. Let them, those who are about to enter on married life, approach that state well-disposed and well-prepared. It will also help them, if they behave towards their cherished offspring as God wills: that is, that the father be truly a father, and the mother truly a mother; through their devout love and unwearying care, the home may become for the children in its own way a foretaste of that paradise of delight in which the Creator placed the first men of the human race. Thus will they be able to bring up their children as perfect men and perfect Christians. . .'"

Carol closed and reopened herself. Pinning Vern to wrap him up –

her ankles and wrists
crossed so tight
she cinched
his breath
as
he read her
from
    cover
         to
             cover:

Carol's mam arrived at the church late and alone in a loose egg-blue suit and knitted snood on sale that month at Lewis's. She joined a packed middle pew. It was the perfect improper vantage from which a mysterious mother-of-the-bride could witness the ceremony, be declared prematurely a no-show and, when later discovered, be raised by the groom's lot into the canon of *stuck-up cows* and *queer fish*, and evermore thought of as harmless, if not a full shilling.

Vern
turned
back
a
page
and
reread
it:

A cold, slabbed aisle to aggravate the pinch of Carol's scalloped bridal heels and each step they took for her cut her feet as the aisle stretched endless. On both sides she saw a leering jungle of stranger-guests twisting to her ascent. Starved wolves. Twin packs of curled lips. She clocked her mam among them. A mother could recognise the agony Carol's smiling stride concealed.

Carol passed another pew and another and looked dead ahead, grinning wider, until finally she got two steps beyond her mam's row and tasted salt: her face wet.

See Carol's mam was a waif and a Methodist widow who ate less than she spoke and only spoke when others intruded far enough down her own mental canals which could not be drained. She knew Carol was courting as soon as Carol knew. She didn't caution her daughter or weight her with expectation or offer aphorisms of instruction or any peculiarly Northern counsel, and instead left the business of sex to open shop – just not under her roof. And she took the news of a Catholic marriage with cold bemusement bordering on disinterest. Sefton met her the once, so they could announce the engagement. Carol saw her mam look him over while he ate her cooking (beef bourguignon; jam and custard for afters) and through her mam's eyes Carol saw him put such effort into his manners that his fingers locked in spasm and he ruined her new damask. A crude lad contesting his place in this world. Through her she saw Sefton Dodds as needy and savage and not as handsome as they said and unable to step into let alone out of his father's shadow; and that she had fallen for his smouldering hurt and misunderstood it by thinking there was summat there to understand and that it could be coaxed into the light by her, then soothed better. Meeting this lad again for the first time, through her mam's sight, made Carol sick with pride that it was by him she'd finally *got caught*.

After the wedding Carol's mam stayed an hour at the do, then snatched her hands to say ta-ra in a grim quiet voice, her eyes damp but not humourless and not anything like Carol's own, whose might've taken after her dad's, but her mam had kept no pictures to confirm it. There in the Oaks Carol was finally rid of this silent hipless woman who had birthed her and raised her without men and had never bothered to defend a life without them and so Carol had had to go out and find brutal male contest just to know if it existed and see if it were to her liking and, if not, acquire a taste. She found that easy enough and only later knew why: her mam had been teaching her from day nought how to live without life. She seemed to have moved through Carol's childhood and adolescence like she was rehearsing a play. She had interests; she seemed about happy; she remained house-proud, was a Portway shopkeeper's assistant through the week; she knew most of her Delwood neighbours; but by forty she was so prematurely withered her hair was too porous to hold a colour – not even grey.

After saying her ta-ras in the Oaks Carol saw her ask Jim to fetch her a cab. And Jim left his top villains crooning at the bar while he flagged one down and overpaid for it. But she returned the money a fortnight later in a scented envelope posted to her daughter's new address, marked *F.A.O. Mr Dodds the Senior*. Her husband had drowned at Dunkirk. Maybe there was the dream from which she had never fully woken and so Carol grew up as contained as she and left home as witted and doomed as she, having been raised less by a female presence than by a male absence.

After the wedding Carol saw her mam only twice. A quick visit after Kelly's birth, before she dropped dead at forty-one.

Vern stopped
reading her
to scribble
in her margins:

'Oh, we can't forget that great ox, can we? Poor Mac. Can you see him there on your big day, back at the church, right at the front, next to his missus, Minnie. Ancoats' own Veronica Lake! Now, he might have all that at home, but. . . well, there you are, swanning up the aisle, numinous in that tight white dress – and all he bloody well wants is you. Can you blame the bugger?'

Ahead of the final blessing Carol laid before the Immaculate Virgin violets and busy lizzies to appease her maminlaw. As she knelt to leave them there was an enthused sob behind her. Whispers travelled the front row for a dry hankie. When Carol glanced round it was Minnie foxing her, sniffling into the silk from Jim's pocket, not Mac's. Minnie always said: *We're only here the once. See what you can get away with.* The groom stuck his arm out for the bride but forgot to help her stand. Carol began to fall on her way up, then somehow found herself already a married woman, dizzy at her own after-do:

Mrs Sefton Dodds.

Sharston slut and mother-to-be.

'It's high bloody time our Sefton had a firm hand on his tiller,' said broken-nosed men who squeezed her arse.

No longer could she feel her blistered toes. Faint with the noise Carol stood at the wall, her breathing tough and shallow in that mousetrap frock, while the man of the hour gave his fat sister Eunice giddy dance after dance, and left Carol free to be felled by Minnie's third strike:

'There you are! Let me look at you. Absolute *stunning*.'

Carol got cornered not long after her mam went home.

'. . .A right good do, this, Carol. Ay, have you had a boogie yet? Not with me you've not. Come on.' A party-sweat on her exposed chest and forehead carried Minnie's rosewater scent farther. Her witch mouth tickled the folds of Carol's ear: 'I would've give you a couple of goers in like I did when we *first* met, only I'd get done for murder, now, wouldn't I? Anyhow, I slipped summat in your Sefton's toasting glass instead. You're in for a treat tonight, love. So, thank *me*. That said, I've a mind to pity a poor delicate thing like you once that strapping new husband of yours gets you home. . . Oh, I'm kidding you. Picked yourself a fine brute, there, love. Oh, very nice. Sefton sodding Dodds. . .'

All the while Minnie jigged her about, leading like a man.

'. . .Bit of advice though, love: never refuse them. Never. Well, unless you don't mind going without. Steady now. Stay with me. Don't you be fainting before I've had any cake. Where was I? Oh aye, yes: Let him have his wicked way with you little and often. Mind you, you've nowt new to offer him, have you. That's the trouble, see? They're all the same. After what they can't have. Take your Sefton. You know well as I do the years he's been sniffing round me. Then finally, right – God, this was just last month, this – your Sefton, he works himself up into such a bloody state he chases us into the cellar of the Three Coins. Poor lad must've thought, *Right, there's old Mac's wife again, that saucy bitch wagging her arse under me nose. Well, tonight's the night. It's shit or bust.* Course, Carol, he came on too strong for his own good. Didn't even get it in before he popped like a Roman candle! I had to bloody laugh. Course, then he whipped up his pants and kicked over a great big bloody keg. Flooded that cellar, he did. Oh, Carol, it *was* funny. But I did have to have a word with our Mac, who then had to have a word with our Jim. And you know Jim's not one to spare the rod. He didn't half belt your Sefton after I showed him what he'd done to me silk skirt. But Jim wasn't too rough in the end – not wanting no black-eyes or broken teeth in your wedding pictures. . . Beg pardon!'

Carol twirled into Minnie's belch; it smelled of Babycham and semen. Enough to send her skull to the bar, but Minnie grabbed her waist and straightened her in time. Minnie danced them from one end to the other, spilling pint heads and batting off half a dozen sand-paper faces trying to land kisses on each of them:

'. . .Sefton's not your first though, is he? Oh, right. I see. Beg pardon *again*. Well, you've still time to put it about a bit. Be quick though, love. Once you pop it'll be all over. A-way these bastards'll go. Only kidding you. We have to laugh, us girls, don't we? Listen, all I'm saying, love, is it doesn't have to stop now you're spoken for. No, does it 'eck. In fact, it makes you a more desirable *cut*. Just think: our Mac, bless him. Still be soggy in the head for you. . . Tis it, love? Do you need a sit down? Be a shock if you can in *that* frock. Let's have us one more dance!'

Mac appeared behind his wife, heads above her. His skin was sparking bright. He was reaching for Carol, but kept growing brighter and taller until he was too tall to pick her off the floor where Carol was dancing away by herself in the dark. . .

Here

Vern

shut

Carol's

b

o

o

k

and returned her to Saturday morning – her telly playing to itself in the front room. A fire had broken out in a football stadium in Bradford mid-match. They went there live but Carol bounded upstairs to dig out her wedding shoes.

The shoebox contained dead spiders and twists of newspaper but no damp. Both heels were intact in their coffin after twenty-three years, preserved in dust paste – nowt a good brush and polish wouldn't fix. Only her blood, which blacked the inner toes, showed they'd been worn. She pushed her hands in first and wore them like hooves. She tried them on again, this time with unswollen feet.

Stalking the house experimentally until she was sure her old blood didn't flow fresh.

Yes, Carol would wear them tonight for Mac.

SIT YOURSELF DOWN, NEDRA, love, and get right. I'll brew up. You keep sugar in here, don't you?'

'I'm bad with me heart this afternoon, Linda.'

'Give over. You're in better bloody nick than *me*.'

'Our Jan was out all night, you know? Left an hour after Kelly went. And neither's come home.'

'Don't worry.'

'I've told Father Culler. About me heart.'

'Have you? What'dee say?'

'. . .'

'Get to doctor's after weekend. I'll take you. Ee-ah, love. Fancy a drop of brandy in yours? I've a bottle of decent stuff next door; won't be a tick.'

'We've some in the back of that cupboard there. Don't you be going to any trouble for me.'

'Give over.'

'Time's it, love?'

'. . .Ten past two.'

Then the air hit Nedra's faded housedress – rippling – as the backdoor swung and the kiddies burst in and ran rings around Linda, halting her soiled bare feet as she lifted two slopping brews, the neck of the brandy bottle in her armpit; but Roger and Kevin and Joey took no notice, singing:

'. . .Rattle me bones, tickle me toes, scratch me belly and let me go. . . Rattle me bones. . .'

And from her thronelike kitchen chair Nedra chased the song as the kids ran out again.

'Good God, I've not heard that one in donkey's. Our Sefton and Eunice used to sing it at Ashcott when *they* was little.'

'What, love?' Linda was sweaty, garish, half her face made up for nowt – purple lips and eyes, ghoulish powder, a single roller. She was tracking garden soil across the lino. Nedra leaned to stare under the table and it made her notice.

'It's them lot. I'll fetch our Gene in a bit with the mop.' Linda lashed Nedra's brew with brandy, then her own; then her own again.

'Linda? Did you forget you've nowt on?'

'"Nowt on"?'

'Under that?'

'Under what? *This?*'

'You've come over in your nightie again.'

Linda glanced down to check, then cupped her loose breast and cringed and moaned. She pawed her unfinished tutty, drawing and jabbing at her cheeks like she was made of clay and wanted to begin again.

Nedra moved her chair. 'What is it, love?'

'I don't know. I don't know.'

'. . .'

'What a bloody pair we are.'

'Aye.'

'Me face feels like a chip pan.'

'Mine does.'

'But I *know* I got dressed today.'

'You did. I saw you looking nice in your ra-ra dress what you got from C&A.'

'We have to laugh, us girls, don't we?'

'You *have* to. We've got no tears left.'

'I'm going as loopy as your Carol.'

Her tightening heart. Her backteeth hurt. '. . .Well, good job your Gene weren't in.'

'God, yeah.'

'. . .Ay, put that bottle away quick and let's drink up. It's alright. It'll be alright. Ee-ah. There's a clean tissue.'

'Ta.'

They reached across the table and held each other at the wrists.

'There,' they said. 'There.'

'SEEN THAT VIEW?' – HIS bum chin a day unshaved, pointing at the moors unpeopled, untamed.

Jan cupped her brow in the same dead direction and cracked her chewing gum.

Mr Somerville dropped her hand. She went jellykneed and cold. They were high up or it seemed so to her – touching broken cloud, where the sunbeams began – having left his car somewhere off the Isle of Skye road, where the sheep were, hidden only a mile or so by slow dip and crest.

He kept tramping the invisible trail in his olive kagool without her until she went *Oi*. The wind carried her shout. Heathers leaned to her, like classroom iron shavings near a magnet.

'We flattening some grass or what?' Jan said.

He came back and they did.

And soon Jan felt the peat jolt beneath them, then quake. A ghost had left his grave to help her, to make certain that she didn't fall again. He was touch-close, but however she turned she couldn't bring him out from the corner of her sight and so she said nowt and her blood quickened and her breaths found a pattern that had nowt to do with her jointed body which was now corded to time, history's curled ribbon taking vein after vein. A weird calm took her, even as Somerville rushed her, weighted her, rammed and sank her into restive earth with his clumsy elbows and ink-stamp kisses. Again Jan tried to glimpse this ghost watching – no – reading her. Perhaps she knew his blood and love, as *Ghosts of all things that are, some shade of thee*. Jan heard this as a voice inside her head and shut her eyes tight to listen to its aftersound. It left her with that rare peace felt on the drift down into a safe kip, the kind she knew as a kid, after being read to sleep by her brother. Some shade of thee. When the ghost called her name it reached her as more echo than voice. She counted four hands. One clean pair dragging her bits; the other rigid and gentle and caked in peat. Fatherly but feminine. Breaching earth to console her. Love had come for her before, once, in a different way, and had done mad things to her then, impossible things, and this was only the same. Her insides did what the peat-soaked hands asked of them and began to churn and ache before Somerville got it done. He could have been shagging himself through all this. But he wasn't; he was shagging Jan; and Jan remembered and was glad. She knew the ghost knew she was glad. And the hands seemed to both mind and not mind. In the same way Somerville's prick could be perfect and nowt special, when it was her he was inside.

After, when the ghost's hands were gone –

and the earth calm

and their clothes pushed to their pits and ankles, Jan clung to Somerville taking his heat. He was shock-white, goosefleshed, his chest thumping through her. Crisp hairs made her nipples itch and she rashed wherever he'd squeezed for too long. Sweat cooled her again once it caught the breeze.

'Think I swallowed me chuddy,' she said.

She saw this tickled him, but he pushed away.

Sun-split clouds separated over them. It went warm. The wind fell and they left their brightened bodies uncovered. Jan tittered quietly as he leaked from her but didn't dare look.

'What day is it again?'

'Saturday,' she said.

'How can there ever be another Monday?'

'Must be shit teaching us lot at Poundswick'

'What's *your* dream job?'

'*This*. I was a devout girl, me! Never missed Sunday Mass till I turned twelve.'

'Who corrupted you?'

Jan tried to think of a name or face but nothing came. It was like her mind's eye needed specs. 'I remember him saying I'd nice ones for me age.'

'Good god, Jan. That's a crime.'

She was teasing him. 'So's this.'

'We sully each other, don't we?'

'I'd let you murder me.' Jan wasn't even blinking. She had a snap vision, of here but not now: a sky of broken light gracing the turned earth of a fresh grave. The sliced signatures of shovels pooled with still rain. Across them she lay, then and now, each sealed cut open – these blood-tinted waterways, unvanquished lines. 'Not told nobody I'm here. Not even our Kell.'

'You think I'd get away with it?' he said.

'Here? Murder? God, yeah. Sheep don't *grass*, d'they?'

Bleats echoed.

'They *graze*,' he said.

'Div.'

To escape her mouth he aimed that cleft chin at the empty distance. 'We'll have a roast, if you fancy it? There's a pub round here. Weren't you saying you like lamb?' He spoke without looking at her, just like the blokes did to their birds in the old films that Bev loved watching hungover; tragic romances that her and Alice sometimes caught the middle of.

Jan said: 'I can't have lamb on me plate, can I? They're hopping about up here.'

This turned him; he got nose-to-nose, his blond stubble grating her chin. '*The Jungle* by Upton Sinclair. That could be your first book. It's about a vegetarian.'

'Is she dead rich and gorgeous?'

'He's an angry, desperate individual, putting the world to rights.'

'I'll leave it, ta.'

'There's hope yet for Jan Dodds.'

Peat fingermarks scored her arms and she slapped herself clean, picked soil from her hair. 'Cheeky fuck. I've changed me mind; I'm having lamb.' Behind her shoulders she had what looked like hand-prints. Twisting to see better, she pulled her skin and gapped her top. They covered her back in wing-shape stamps; the closed fingers pointed to her waist. 'Oi, seen this?'

But he was checking himself. He jumped up, scared and shy. 'Shit,' he said. 'Shit.' Spotless hands worrying his bloodied prick.

Jan said: 'But am not due on. Not for a fortnight.' She stood and stepped out of stirrup leggings to escape the blue knickers. She bled them as she did it. Reversed them to mop clots trickling her thighs, then snuck them browned and fetid into the pocket of his other kagool – hers for the day.

He patted his own. Licked a hankie to wipe.

Jan moved a crush of pink bog roll from her bra to pack her crotch. There wasn't enough. She dug for more squares but had lost them. All this made him sick. She wanted him repulsed at the smell and sight of her. She showed him her shame in case he thought she had none. But he was too busy hiding his from her, not knowing which way to stand as he scrubbed off her stain.

Jan decided then that she was his forever. He'd have to bury her on the moors if he wanted rid of her.

'Shit,' he said. 'Shit. Shit.'

Jan could corner grown men on hinterland. Laugh the wind strong. Her eyes ran as she danced her leggings half up; their faded chevrons had been her mam's once, or maybe Alice's.

For this Mr Somerville looked – her arse out when she pounced. Jan caught his neck to laugh into his damp white face and cat-rub his weekend stubble and to have him. . .

. . .hold doors for her on the way in. 'How's that brother of yours getting on?'

'Ta. Good, yeah. Our uncle Mac's sorted him a job.'

'Your "uncle Mac"?'

This was between mottled pub glass as he bought her a ten-pack of Embassy Regal from a clapped-out vendor that shook to life. Jan hadn't asked, hadn't waited to be asked – just gestured for the dearest brand:

'I've not met him yet but, *apparently*, right, he proper fancies me mam.'

Mr Somerville reached with her for the dropped pack, then shied from her blood-rusty fingers.

She daubed his hand. 'Can read *you* like a book, you know.'

This was true. But she had convinced herself that it wasn't. And being convinced that it wasn't was what allowed her to say it to him smiling like a threat.

Her reeking taking fingers. Jan looked up. He tried to arrange his face for her. But he could not get it right.

'Ta,' she said, louder.

In she stepped, skenning the busy pub. Stone floors, wooden beams; Tetley's mats and dead pint pots ran the nook where day showed the dust. On cream walls hung painted owls and hares. Jan clocked rucksacks, purses, handbags, which chairs and stools wore coats. The fruit machines were off. A tan sausage dog kipped leashed below a round table with a smoking ashtray.

'What's the job?' Somerville rustled behind her, jagging his kagool zip.

Old birds with cauliflower perms glanced at them, still gabbing at their bald husbands – necking bitter, spooning fruit crumble, pie and mash.

'The job? Oh, yeah. Think they're robbing some jewellers in town, but no one tells us *owt*. . . Back in a sec. Mine's cider.'

Hearing this fixed his zip.

Jan hovered by the bar hatch, then moved to grab a lady's brown bag from under her stool. Rhino-arse, kinked straw hair, a queen of the hill-top run to fat. This one nattered away, her shrapnel ready-stacked on the bar. A stool along, an old timer nursing a short-stem glass ate a tanger-ine from a tissue. An ancient barmaid, sweating in a raspberry smock, pulled pints. She reminded Jan of her Nana Dodds. Tits like punctured netballs. Even a thin gold crucifix with Lord Jesus on a garrotte chain.

Jan hopped for attention, miming desperate. The bag jangled inside her borrowed kagool.

The barmaid raised a boiled-beef arm.
Down bar, up step, first door on right.

Two tens and four fivers replaced her bra tissue, plus a real lighter –
gold and heavy, like her brother's. Her canvas shoe squeaked on
the bog-seat in the clean lit stall, the laces grass-dyed and mudded.
Having hitched one leg to insert a tampon she poked the bag for
spares and surfaced: keys, Ray-Bans, small tubs of tutty and fancy
creams, the dagger glint of a metal nail file and a scabby mint tin
keeping needle and thread. Jan footed the bag behind the U-bend
and flushed her mess. She scrubbed those hands pink under the taps,
then preened in front of the mirror tile – without wrecking, without
improving.

Somerville was gangling over the pub phone at the bar when she
came out, watching for her while he used it, twisted at the waist.
Over-smiling he waved her to an end table laid with two Aspalls, hers
a half. She went and waited, scraping the ashtray off the next one. He
whispered into the receiver, his eyes crumpled at Jan. She opened her
new pack, sparked up with her new lighter. Sometimes he nodded
instead of talking, as if whoever it was on the other end could see
him. Waxy, mithered. Sideburns sweated dark. More than a day since
he'd shaved and she could tell now he was one of those blokes whose
beards didn't match his head. He rang off and took the stool which
had his coat. His hideous weekend shirt (colour of sick; big enough
for two) she loved. It'd lost a middle button on the moor. Jan's mark.
Jan's doing. He was looking half-lost too, half-sly – like he might just
let her cop off with him, if she went for it; let her taste him deeper
than mouths reached, into odd places where time stopped like hearts.
Any moment they might put on a show for these sad bastards. Give
them a treat and a fright.

But then she felt daft when she tried holding his hand across the
table – hers raw and stainless now – his beyond reach.

'Lamb roast, I'm having,' she said at the menu chalk. 'You gunna be
taking me out again, then?'

'I'd like to. Do you want that?'

'*I* do, yeah.'

'You know, your eye's a bit better. . . It's good for *you*, this, to be able to get away, I mean. Isn't it?'

The phone rang.

Drilling elbows into the table he turned enough to see the phone which got left to ring. He scrambled his hair, relieved, and looked up again at the menu, blinking. 'Was that true before, about your brother?'

'Yeah, course. Why?'

'Why tell me?' He held her arm then, but it was more to keep her from smoking. 'You're not mithered if he gets himself locked up again? Or worse?'

'But that's how he is now.'

'What'd happen if I met him?'

Jan properly cackled. 'Oi, he'd *smell* us on you. You'd be buried in the morning.' Jan took quick pulls then talked the smoke: 'Me mam, right, she used to say when we was kids that our Kell was the only lad what had *female intuition*.'

'I don't understand.'

Jan raked ash with her dog-end. 'When he's not tryna get in trouble he's dead soft. He's *lovely*.'

'To you?'

'He *was*.'

'What was he in for then? Really.'

'You know the Kinsella cousins, what went Poundswick?'

'Before my time but yes. I'm aware of them. Local entrepreneurs.'

'Pigs found a brick of their gear round ours, in the airing cupboard.'

'So, your Kelly was holding for the Kinsellas.'

'I was knocking about with both cousins. Neither much cop, by the way. They'd given *me* the stuff to stash at home. Just a one off. Kell had nowt to do with it.'

'But he kept quiet; he took the rap. Who tipped off the police?'

'Fuck knows. . .'

'. . .Maybe your mother? Maybe she found it, thought she was saving him from himself.'

181

Jan wanted to be quiet, but more words wanted out; her voice cracked and she felt a shame, a fear, in her blood, at having fated her older brother, for having been the one to remind him he was a Dodds man. But the more Jan talked the easier it was to stay quiet, to stop this blood from showing.

Mr Somerville said: 'Who'll redeem him now, if not you?'

'Sound like me nana's priest.'

'Is he upset you didn't visit him?'

'Visit Kell? Me mam went loads. But me nana never let us see him in there.'

'Sounds like you'll have another chance to soon.' Somerville seemed to shrink the longer they sat there; his questioning and listening robotic. Jan realised she'd no clue if he was smug or scared or what; or how she felt about this brick wall, having missed it go up. But he had brought her there; they had spent a night and a day together (a record). She was eating his weekend whole and still he wasn't sick of her. Sharing a sit-down meal, plenty miles from Wythie, somewhere green and nice, and just for the fuck of it. When he glanced at her tits it made his words trip their feet on their way out the door. And Jan was happy again and went for his hand again and she got it and kept it. On the table.

He made the same *hmph* sound that did for a laugh when he was tired in front of the class by final lesson.

'His bird keeps finishing with him. *Zuley.* She's absolute gorgeous. I was there for it yesterday. He said to me after that he wasn't even bothered and he was going out robbing, but I reckon he went to *hers*, to sort it out.'

'Do you want him *out robbing*?'

Jan had gulped her cider before his second sip. She went for another fag but put it back.

'Is he a good little gangster then, your Kelly?'

'Kell? Nah, he's no good.'

'Why's that?'

'*Cos.* They were all shit, wasn't they? Me granddad, me dad, now our Kell. *They must've* been. They was always getting sent down. But then you get some round Wythie what are scared stiff, right?

Dead careful with their manners, like in case me dad's still about. Some reckon he *is*. And me nana, she proper loves that. *Good manners.*'

'Is it the same with your mother?'

'Are we having our dinner or what? Told you. She's not all there, me mam. She's just shit at life.' Jan grinned all this, full watt.

'I see.' Somerville blinked and sipped. 'You're a funny one, Jan.'

'Oh, I know. It's cos, right, I live in a fucking madhouse.'

'No. It's because you can explain yourself. Most of us can't do that. Can't or won't.'

'Fuck off.' Jan went short with hunger, then clapped her knees hard under the table. Wanting to bruise.

'So, it's your nana who likes a villain in the family?'

'That's what too much church'll do to you.'

'Do you remember much? Your dad and granddad?'

'Our Kell does. He was – hang on – fourteen, right, when it happened. I were six.'

'And that explains *him*.'

She mimicked his tired non-laugh.

'What would you like me to do? I want to help you, Jan, if I can. What do you want?'

'Told you. I want lamb.'

Again the pub's phone rang.

'Somebody best be getting home!' croaked the old barmaid.

'*You.*' Another lady's voice, another end of the pub. 'You pinched my bag.'

The words flew at Jan. Kinked straw hair flapped closer and closer until it shadowed their table and Jan smelled honey shampoo:

'What's that in your hand then?' Jan said, giving her words extra grain.

'You took it and left it in the toilets.'

'Did I *fuck*.'

'Don't you dare speak like that. That's my bloody lighter, that is.'

'Not touched it.'

'Common sort, aren't you, love? Ay, this thieving tart's a bit young for you, isn't she?'

'Have I took her bag? Tell her. Go on. Tell her.'

Mr Somerville stayed mute and only cringed at the table and their shadows.

A tide crashed on Jan's face. Blinded by the splash, she leapt up and coughed from shock. It washed cold – ice and orange. Her top clung to her. She still had on his spare kagool, unzipped. She screamed and kicked and spat and missed and his spotless hands held her away and yanked her outside.

Jan wound the passenger window down to blow-dry her hair. Stickiness whipped her face. Her split-ends tasted of vodka. 'I need me another bath,' she said.

'You think you can get away with anything, don't you?' Mr Somerville had to shout.

'Bit like you.'

He wedged his arm around her and she let him pull her close till he needed to reach the gearstick. Her skin was glue. But he let her stain him now as he drove them townward.

Soon roadside houses went from stone to brick. She tried the radio and without having to fiddle found summat good: Loose Ends' 'Magic Touch', a track Alice had loved as much as Kell, though both would have denied it for different reasons. But not her, not Jan.

His blonde lady was back. She looked even older than in the photos from his wallet. Bigger too. No red lippy, no round specs just a blue clip to keep her lank hair set – showing off a small square ear and its big square stud. The head turning as if from a bad smell as the eyes stayed on Jan. Her bronze cheeks were massive; the late afternoon peached her and sliced his bedsit, their mess. In stripy pastels the lady waited neatly on his unmade bed, a set of keys in a blood-threaded fist. When Jan didn't come any further into the room the lady stood to better see her. A pleated skirt and tucked blouse hung immaculate, not a crease. She ignored Mr Somerville even when he crossed the carpet to touch her arm and gently prised the flat keys from her. She let him, sooner than take her eyes off Jan.

'Go home,' he said, now standing with his blonde lady – not that she'd noticed. The lady was tranced by her. Too choked to talk or strike but her body coiled – maybe about to do summat with that fist before knowing it; her peached face blanching but not blank.

Jan tottered forward instead of back, then overcorrected herself. She palmed cool wall. Slowly her fingers travelled the wallpaper, towards the window, as if to crawl behind the curtains.

'Patrick, who is she?' – the lady's voice bright and mild.

'Patrick?' Jan whispered.

'Go home, Jan,' he said, stroking the lady's arm, soothing her out of her trance or maybe keeping her in it. '*Now.*'

'Jan?' the lady whispered, then turned her head fast to note him standing with her, holding her arm. 'Patrick, why is she crying? Why is *she* crying?'

Together they looked at Jan like they wanted the answer.

'You've been to bed, haven't you, with this little *girl*?'

Over and over Jan shook her head for no – which hurried her cleansing tears – 'He's give us extra lessons, that's all, so I didn't fall behind. Tell her. Go on' – fat childish tears she couldn't stop.

'He's lending us a book. A book about the jungle. Tell her!'

Mr Somerville spun and crouched by the other side of the bed and toppled a tower of books to take the one he wanted.

He came to Jan. He snatched her hand off the wall, pressed the book into it, into her.

A paperback orange and white. A waddling penguin on the cover.

'Penguins don't live in the jungle,' Kell said, petting her crusty hair. She stretched out on him, sharing her made bed (her room less of a tip; their mam had been in while they were out), Jan's horrid legs straight and bare inside his, her blobby nose under his square chin. She hoped his fag would drop ash on her tongue, her forehead.

'It's not about penguins,' Jan said, hoarse.

'Was kidding.'

'It's about a vegetarian.'

'What can they eat in the jungle?'

'Prick.'

'Slag.'

He lifted her sticky head off his chest to slide out from under her but didn't.

'Love you.'

'How'd you feel?'

'Got a banging headache.'

He rocked her tighter. Her tired bones, stinging.

She hushed: 'We both been dumped, haven't we?'

'*You* have. Got a shag last night, me. It's back on.'

'Knew it. That Zuley's too good for you, Kell.'

'I know.'

'Good.'

For the first hour he had asked her nowt much and understood more than Jan knew how to say, either to him or herself. This she knew. He was patient with her again, like when she'd been a tiny terror only he could appease.

On their street he had heard her trot, then seen her winded and burning, heading for their gate, where he was, and she had seen his arms unfolding to catch her and take her in the house. Their arrivals concurrent. He'd just been dropped off by some great big tashed bloke who peered at her through the big windshield. She cleaned her eyes on Kell's Lacoste to get a better look. The bloke old enough to be this Uncle Mac – wondering at her ugly sweaty gasping tears. He didn't get out, didn't ask her Kell what was up, just peered at them till Kell, clocking he hadn't gone, turned and waved him off; and then the bloke gave her one last hard stare before his car squealed and sped.

Ten minutes of attention and Kell stopped her bawling; he said *Look* and she looked, expecting him to speak, only for him to be at her room window. Jan kneed the bed, her elbows on the inner sill, too exhausted to stand with him. Out there was next door's Linda – Gene's and Joey's mam – stripping off prancing in the road, slathered with tutty, her rollers in. Soon their whole street and the next over were cheering her and her ancient once-white girdle. It was only their own mam who wasn't out; and Jan sensed her doings through the wall. Gene was down there, by a grey van open-doored opposite, which she mistook at first for the Marco Rea ice-cream van. He kept calling *Mam! Mam!* But Linda took no notice. Linda was living for herself. Not her audience. Two hopeless bearded fellers in coats holding out green blankets, skidded and dived to catch her. A Juliet Bravo waited with them in her cap and uniform, but no jam butty was parked on their street. Jan leaned to check farther down the kerb. Linda flashed and vamped good-as-naked whenever she got enough distance between them and her.

Kell sparked up and leaned over the sill, his fag tip nearly kissing the glass. Jan wondered where she'd left that packet of Embassys. He blew the first drag to the ceiling. 'Bloody hell. And we think *Mam's* off her rocker.'

Below them, behind the shared privets, Nana Dodds gripped little Joey.

Kell creaked the latch and the street talked:

'Bloody mad bint.'

'Think of her poor kiddies.'

'She's gone.'

'Shake them, love.'

'Show this smug lot what's what.'

The two blokes finally grabbed her and their van bundled her away. Neighbours booed, clapped, then stayed out discussing what they'd seen. Nana Dodds called Gene in and put Joey on her hip.

Jan heard them come inside. The front door shutting, then locking. . .

'So,' Kell said now, resting her. 'Who's this such-a-show what's finished with you? Which knobhead round here are we talking about?'

'Zuley didn't tell you?'

He rocked her again and she put an ear to his belly and imagined she were lost at sea or safe at the bottom of a well. 'Kell? Will you read to us for a bit? Go on.'

He stroked her head. He broke the back of Somerville's book and began in the middle. '"Naturally, the aspect of prison life was changed for. . . *Jurgis*. . . by the arrival of a cell mate. He could not turn his face to the wall and sulk, he had to speak when spoken to; nor could he. . ."'

When Jan woke it was still light out but the sun had gone over and she switched on her table lamp to feel less alone since there was no trace of her brother on her pillow – just orange-juice smell and makeup sweat. Then she crossed the landing to wash up and plugged the sink ready to shampoo her hair and while waiting for the bowl to fill she pissed and changed her tampon and returned to her room. She found Mr Somerville's book while searching the floor for summat clean to wear. Jan opened it on the first page.

For Patrick –

Upon receiving his new post at Poundswick High School: now their very necessary Mr Somerville.

Good luck, my love. I'll make sure you stay off the drink.

knickers & kisses

Malorie

Jan binned the book and went and stood at the top of the stairs and shouted Kell.

'He went back out,' her nana crowed from the kitchen. 'Are you having your tea or not? Be dry as a bone.'

Then, the thing giggled like a sprite from behind her mam's door; and her mam hushed it, pacing with it; Jan heard the floorboard clicks.

In a mad rush Jan washed her hair and came downstairs with it wet.

Gene and Joey were in the front room for Kenny Everett.

Nana sighed at her, then gloved a plate out the oven, then waited for Jan to sit at the vacant table before serving it. She was stooping and mithered, her brow spiky with thought.

Jan slapped the HP bottle to coat her warmed-over mash before ganneting the lot as Nana Dodds pulled a chair and heaved into it, fat knees turned to the radio, which was on so quiet Jan had taken the hymns to be kids playing out on the next street over – white noise carried in with the breeze. Her nana crossed her forehead with a flannel from her apron pocket, and tutted at this world. One of Aunty Eunice's old postcards from the mantel was picture-up on the table. Some river in America. Jan read the name of the city – Trenton – then coastered her brew with it until her nana saw the tea ring.

'What's gunna happen to Linda?' Jan asked, chewing.

Staring off, her nana wittered: 'What that poor woman's gone through, they've no idea.'

'Does this mean we're taking in Gene and Joey?'

'Aye. For now.'

Jan scraped knife and fork while her nana drifted, listening to her hymns.

'I met Uncle Mac today, Nana. Out there. Before Linda had her turn.'

'Your granddad loved Mac. Your dad did and all.'

Jan held her brew. 'Is our kid out with him tonight?'

'Think Kelly's out with his coloured lass again. Said he mightn't be home till *Monday*.' Now she was watching Jan drink. 'Why's *your* hair wet? Always bloody washing it and washing it.'

'Where's me uncle Mac live then?'

'Town. He's stopping with Rodney Westlake. Up on Monton Street, he said.'

'Rodney who?'

'Oh, your granddad did love Rodney. Notsamuch your dad, mind.' Her nana cupped one knee to stand. 'Where's your mam putting your towels?'

Jan stepped out through the backdoor, no coat, with a pinched quid and caught the bus to town.

'KEEPING WELL?'

'It's you,' Carol said. 'From the bleeding bus.'

'I know,' Vern said, softly. And his smile went to his eyes.

'You still think you're funny.' Carol preened, see-sawing her weight on a warm leatherette stool.

This was spring '69, in the function room of the Posthouse Hotel up Palatine Road. A filthy night to strand a preening tart not far from her own estate, with packs of Burton-suited jokers and louts who daren't speak her name. So, Carol bought her own drink at the bar and the next.

Black leafy trees roared opposite. A gale gave the flooded carpark a tide. There was no one with whom to share a cab or cadge a lift or catch a bus to brave town after a couple of rounds. This washout had cut them all off. The place was easy with itself, under a white spell which had them making do without fuss. Men watched her with a brief and regular intensity that burned the back of her neck. But the spell let them snub her. They could sooner prey on a regular bit than risk life and limb over Mrs Sefton Dodds. Therein, young Vern, nursing a bottle of milk stout like an Irish washerwoman, bought her a glass of Blue Nun with half a crown and let the dreary barmaid keep sixpence.

'Oi,' Carol said. 'Do I look as daft in here as you do?'

'Dafter, I should think.' His local accent bared, not leaned in to or sweetened. 'By that I mean there's no obvious reason for some-one like you to be here on her own. Unlike meself. And a mystery

191

like that can vex the average member of my sex. One relying on a daub of Brylcreem to get his leg over. Then again. There might well be summat going on here that I just don't know about. . .'

Tie-less, dainty and daft in a pilled-wool, elbow-patched suit. Clown-sized shoes of rained suede. Weak hands Carol wanted to trap inside hers, the fingertips quick with life, touching her bare arm so briefly so gently, while he worded her, that she couldn't focus until he'd kissed her.

Knowing plain proximity as vertigo.

Swaying blissfully on her stool, then heels.

Poor Vern, watching her watching him: 'You reckon I'm radio rental, don't you?'

Lucky Carol had enough calcium in her bones to walk him to a table while he carried their drinks and then asked her to dance to that Archies song, then Love Affair's new one, then 'The Israelites'.

If he'd just been a soft clod, a queer, a penny policy man. Instead he smelled and sounded like no feller she'd ever been near. At a glance his student's beard was trimmed but up close it went patchy and scruffy. Carol reached for it, cupped his cheek, which had another gobful of useless words. In vain she searched for hints of other men she had known.

They surfaced half an hour later, tangled up in the dimmest loud-est corner, more drinks untouched, themselves unjudged between seated trios of gabbing sylphs with matching fringes, all five years or so younger than Carol, who at twenty-seven felt of a different species, with her hemlines and T-straps stuck in '62.

By now the place swung and bounced and poured inside like out.

Unstitched at the gob Carol and Vern began to readjust to the room with a bacchanal calm, lazily wondering what had locked them in time again, returned them to this present to which they did not belong and were not above or below but simply outside, both their hearts blinking together and out of sync with the healthy – theirs just sick enough to make life rub harder. God drew lives on shifting tracing paper. These were two halves of an unjoinable circle. With God she saw this place; its night sea of proud souls sticking to one another with drink and sweat, and each swanning deific in finest gladrags. . .

'Must be a full moon,' Vern said.

'What we must look like.'

'Like royalty in exile. Carol, you a hard drinker or do you find it easy?'

The room had fogged with Woodbines and became a crazed miniature disco hall. Couples dancing to Clodagh Rodgers' 'Come Back and Shake Me' looked like Kings Hall wrestlers. Waltzer lights spiralled patterns across backsides and necklines and the closed air continued to thicken till it had the unforced feel of some secret den in town that Minnie might have dragged her to, those Jamaican all-nighters, where white lads were chased out or barred.

'I'm celebrating,' Carol said, finally.

'On your own?' Vern said.

'That's what I'm here to celebrate.'

'To Carol then, who's on her own. And *doomed to glow*.'

She was draped on him, wagging her head, giggling in disbelief, then kissing his talking mouth: 'Just shut up. It's you what's bloody doomed now, you daft sod, and it's thanks to me.'

'That was good of you.'

The music had changed.

The singer sings of a love-haunted house. . .

Carol picked at his loose button threads, bloodletting, sharing heat.

. . .of ghostfeet forever climbing the stairs.

'You should ask what's going rate for a room upstairs. Go on. You can have the young barmaid on me. I've plenty money.'

'Keep it. I'd still come up sodding short.'

'Let her be judge of that.'

'Will she go for me?'

'She might.'

'If she's a curious cat. A cat with a lovely coat – one that must have cost five of these suits. Be a shame to leave it on the bleeding bus because some blathering idiot was talking your head off. I mean, whoever heard of a self-skinning cat?'

Carol went weak, delight shaking her body like a wasted muscle. 'OK. OK.'

His light hid her and hid them together from others in sight and talk and thought. Unhurriedly beneath the table Carol misbehaved. Changing hands five times to stave off cramp (down to his size), Carol seized the power to shorten his breath, to speed his sickly rose of a heart; if only she could think of summat lewd enough to do to say to be, then he might run away, saved. Throughout this attention Vern finally went quiet and looked at her twice, innocently, the rest of the time his face aglow in profile, like he was in front of holy fire. She studied his mouth while it was bookmarked. His twitching lips were fuller than hers, wetted and coloured by hers. And *she* talked now, telling him. It took some telling. She knew he was listening but she did not let herself believe it until she had brought him over the line. This final rush of weakness. They tightened together. Panting gently. She sensed her hip hurting him, over-insisting. With it done, Carol proudly returned the dead drink glass to the table into which she had spent him. Poor Vern. His night made. His fate sealed. And still quiet. He hadn't finished listening.

'Don't be worrying,' Vern whispered. 'Worries only wake him.'

'We're dead.'

'Then we might as well live.'

'For God's sake.'

'Well, if you can't get rid of it, and you can't get rid of *me*, what's there to do?'

Sheer curtains had his bedroom dusky and lush. Through them day poured in like cider, onto his yellow books and green plants. The dense air smelled baked, fertile. There'd been a bushy red cat called Macavity but she had slipped out during Carol's second night over – months back now – leaving Vern, and his rooms above the sad cafe, for good.

'We're dead,' Carol whispered, so as not to wake Kelly – naked and crushed between them after his Wednesday bath. Combed hair grown out, a smidge damp on Vern's pillow. The milk of his eyes showed dreams. Happiness flowed through her when she touched his cherub belly, rising:

'They've put your husband away,' Vern whispered. 'He can't touch him. He can't touch *you*. And they'll always be putting him away. Which is good of them. Now. As for your inlaws –'

'I can't get round them,' she said. 'They'll soon get word of this.'

'Carol.'

'You've got no living left to do.'

'And there's nobody I'd rather not live it with than you.'

'We sound mad, don't we? I sound bloody wigged.'

Vern shushed her, checking on Kelly.

'Makes a bloody change, that. You telling me shush.' Carol touched her son's smooth skittle legs and rested her palm on that hot fed belly, rising, falling. 'We best be getting back. His nana has to see him. We've not been round for a fortnight and she knows I don't go confession no more. They don't like it. She rings up and I don't answer. They don't like it. You know what Sefton give his mam, don't you, before he got sent down? A key. A key to the house.'

'Stay,' Vern said.

'Stop asking,' she said.

'Then live here. I'll wash, you'll iron. We'll both make the bed.'

'God help us.'

'I'll quit the library gig, get me a job at Dunlop or Craven.'

'Would that be a few bob a week *more* or *less*?'

'I'll pawn these books.'

'Don't you dare.'

Kelly stirred. His happiness flowed through them both.

'OK,' Carol whispered. 'OK.'

'Our child.'

'Yes, love?'

'Vern, we won't have it baptised, will we?'

'Course not.'

They lay as one, folded in Vern's bathtub in steaming dark. From behind he rinsed off her makeup with his hands. Pruned fingers read her face, her thoughts – left trails of sensation down both. She was panting gently. She heard herself panting gently and counted breaths like a mad woman. She knew he was counting them too. He was listening to her go mad. He shaped himself around her. He clutched her breasts flat to keep her sick heart inside her chest. She was panting *Kelly. Kelly. Kelly. Kelly. Me little boy. They took him and they won't give him back. They'll keep him safe till Sefton gets out. They couldn't let another man raise his son. They knew this time I'd run. They waited for me to run.*

'Vern. . .?'

'I'm here.'

'Then help me.'

'I'm here.'

'I want to die.'

'I know.'

'Help me die.'

No panting. No tap drip. The bathwater even as ink.

'We'll get Kelly,' Vern said, 'and bring him here and raise him here and love him here. We'll do that, me and you. He's *yours*, isn't he? They're not allowed to just take him. They *can't* stop you.'

'Yes, they fucking well can.'

'There are laws, Carol.'

The law's no good to me. Laws won't stop our Jim or our Sefton or any of that lot. They do what they please. You see, I just bore them that son. Kelly's theirs not mine. And I'll never see me child again unless I run back to that old house and put on that old frock and wait for our Sefton to come home and. . . Vern, Vern, they was waiting there yesterday, you know? Bloody Nedra. She had the new priest with her. They was just there on me settee with a brew each when we got in. Father says to me, Mrs Dodds, what do you have to say for yourself? And I says, I've nowt to say to you, Father. Well, Nedra, she chucked that brew on the floor, didn't she? And she slapped me twice right across the face. That's one for her and one for her Sefton. She'd been upstairs and unpacked me bags. They tried taking Kelly there and then, but I wouldn't let her have him.

'Today' – Carol panting again – 'Today we was leaving Civic. Me and Kelly. I had him here, right? On this side, just here. He'd been

196

good as gold. He was tired but he wanted to walk. He was sucking toffees. About the only thing that stopped him singing that tiger song you taught him. And then. And then I see the car. It stops us on Simonsway. Broad day, this is. Dinnertime. Out steps Jim.'

'Was Mac there?' Vern asked.

'He drove. He didn't get out.'

'Tomorrow' – Vern's arms crossed her and rocked her – 'I want you to ring Mac from the call box. If you get Minne just keep ringing till he answers.'

'Our Sefton won't know about you. They won't tell him owt till they've seen you and found where you're living.'

Vern reached to top up the hot water but she stopped his hand. He was still listening to her head, still reading the words inside her. They lay silent.

Then Carol asked: '. . .Tell us what you did this evening in night school?'

He rocked her more, the tub lapping. 'I got there early tonight. There was a room change. Nobody told me; *I* wouldn't've. So, what did I do? Well, I sat where I normally sat, only this time I drew for an hour on draughtsman's paper with a compass and ruler. And this teacher with a Kaiser tash, whoever he was, came round and said I was *really* coming on. . .'

Her giggles splashed them cold.

Panting again ceilingward –

until Vern's floral bath tiles became readable top down in the pale dark, their grubby petals and stalks arranged for her like blasphemous verse.

On the Thursday she met Mac at the Posthouse Hotel up Palatine Road where no sooner had he entered the bar alone, gone noon, a half hour late, a rock mass in a broad pond-green suit, she emptied herself of all she had rehearsed, neglecting her careful greeting, and instead hid nowt. Without a ghost of pride Carol uncrossed her legs and spilled forward, rinsed of sex and colour, her lipstick dry, her whole body parcelled and perfumed and numb, and even before she was fully standing she had in blank sincerity asked him how he wanted her.

He reeked of drink. His mansion of speckled hair was just-combed and he had a *News of the World* trapped under his arm. He waited for her to sit again, then sank a leatherette. Mac looked to her like a sullen sculpture, chipped and pigeonshat, features worn off, eyes fixed low in dazed solemnity.

A tubby wax-skinned barman, about thirty-odd, quit polishing glasses and approached their table with a squeaky cake trolley. Mac's name caught in his throat like he hadn't spoken all morning. He was Irish. He circled them pouring black tea as he winked at Carol as he talked at Mac – masking obsequiousness in a fantasy of familiarity to which Mac never gave up an inch, refusing to look up until the Irishman, searching Carol's face for help and finding none, packed up the trolley and left.

'Does Jim know you're here?' Carol said.

'No,' he said. 'No.'

Carol covered the grooveless pulp of his knuckles.

'There's nowt I can do,' he said.

'Please give us back me son before Sefton gets out.'

'You know well as I do there's no getting round Jim.'

He wanted nowt to do with words. He was afraid of them and afraid of her and afraid to have to refuse her. Carol knew then there wasn't a chance he'd take her up on her offer while Jim was alive. He drew no satisfaction from seeing her beg.

Outside the clouds opened. The table polish went blinding. A few Ringway Airport pilots sipping halves and coffees rustled their papers. Then Mac remembered his and opened it back-to-front over their table. She lost his boxer's hand. Carol peered over at one pilot's uniform – a bad stain on the chest showing now in the clean sun. Mac looked with her. He looked at the pilots as if they were policemen.

She had too much power over Mac to use it.

He turned a page, tightening. Like he had a sneeze stuck there behind his nose:

'I've been checking on him, Carol, every day. He asks after you. You being his mam. The little man asks after his dad and all. He doesn't even know summat's up. Jim would *never* harm the lad. Carol, no one could.'

'Where do you tell him I am?'

'When the lad asks I say we're looking for you. He says *very good*. Then he asks if you're at Uncle Vern's. The other day he tried showing us where this Uncle Vern lives, but he'd forgot the way.'

Carol smiled, just glad to be listening. She gave Mac another place and another time, recalling what she had rehearsed. Then she left him with the paper. The Irishman waved.

Between aisles between books. Inside Portland stone and bricks as red as home. Under the bright cupola and its arcade arches. One two three four students milling. Microfiche *this way*. Half a dozen pensioners desked and huddled, coats on in late August. Directory pages turning like rips. Her Cuban heels sounding, then her gait a toppling rush almost a run almost tiptoeing out of her pointed shoes almost turning one ankle then the other. Onwards. Sounding. Vern green-pullovered at the photocharger. He straightened to nod her in the right direction and watch her go through into the children's library.

There he was: seven years old, her having missed a birthday, reading a book in neat silence at a small centre table. His hair weeks longer, combed. His legs were very still, his feet dangling with his right shoelace untied; it grazed the floor.

Minnie sitting, shapely, a painted hand resting on Carol's son's shoulder. Minnie's nose high and the eyes away and reading too: a shiny compact held like an examiner's stopwatch. Its glass turned her face into a jewel of twitching light.

Kelly finished the last page and looked for more words and then up at his mam and said nowt, only swung his feet.

'Get your coat on, love,' Carol said and when he looked to Minnie Carol bent to help.

But Minnie's hug caught her and Minnie's trap opened like a snake's. Her clothes reeked of *Park Drives*. She'd dyed her do a wine colour and stood inches taller than Carol that day. Fuller and finer. Looking younger while older. Wasp-figured in her mustard pencil skirt. Minnie's grip was bruising now, scalding; it moved to her elbow.

'Where's Mac?' Carol said, her voice dry; Minnie's skipped like glass breaking over solid floor:

'Jim's got the poor lump tied up on a job decking some bugger. Don't you worry. Jim don't know a thing.' Eyebrows up; teeth again. 'Kelly. Here she is, see. Here's your mam. And isn't she looking dead pretty for you?' Kelly was reading his book again from the start, his legs swinging beneath the table as Minnie kissed his crown. 'Show your pretty mam what we had for our dinner. Go on.' Kelly shut the flaked pages and pointed to the cover word *Moonshine*. 'Aye. We had a quick one in Turner's Vaults, didn't we, lovey?' Those eyes sinful and wise. 'Oh, he was *dead* good. A sip of Double Diamond and he had a kip in the snug, me gabbing away to me girlfriends on their lunch hour. Ay, Carol, did *you* know the Sinking Ship had shut? We had some nights in there, us, ay? Dancing away to Prince Buster, 'Al Capone'. *Chik-chika-chik-chika. . .* It was Jewish lightning, they reckon. Shame we'd not been for donkey's. . . God, you smell nice, or's that me? . . .And who's this? Well, well. You'll be Uncle Vern—' And Carol knew then that their meeting meant he couldn't work here another minute. Not now Minnie had seen him. What Minnie knew soon would Jim, soon would Sefton. 'Nice meeting you, love. Ooh, why, you're a first-class ticket, aren't you just! I'll bet a fiver yours is a face what's been on that University Challenge. Hope you take care of this one. She's not half been through the wars with that bastard husband of hers. Brute's been locked up God knows how many times. Mind you, she can get wild with the best of them, so you best watch it or you never know. Still. The poor cow deserves a softie like you to look after her while she's got some good years left on her. Just a shame you're not rich yet, ay? Right. Ta-ra then, kid. Remember what your Aunty Minnie's been learning you, won't you, lovey. There's a good lad. Carol, don't you dare say ta-ra. Now just mind how you go.'

NEDRA FELT THE TIGHTNESS in her middle sprout through her heart and old bones to her skull where the fright drove her mad. This was after seeing Mac come for Carol that Saturday, at a quarter to seven by the kitchen clock, whose hands had slowed the day to still after Linda's turn, so that she had heard the doorbell and found herself in-time again, the hands having jumped in one tick and moved, with the Devil, to a quarter to seven, where her kitchen was now the colour of crackling, in which for a clock-second and another she could smell and taste sulphur. Door-knocks followed the doorbell. The front door chained and shut by her own hand, not the clock's or the Devil's. She left her kitchen to open it – letting Mac in and the Devil out.

'Who's all that for?' Mac said, following her back through, seeing raw meat diced in bowls on the counter as she resumed chopping haystacks of veg: leeks and spuds.

Nedra stopped and raised her knife. 'D'you know summat – am not even sure now.'

Mac waited standing – all glum brawn like an old circus bear. '. . . Well then save us a plate, if you can.'

She said: 'You've come for *her* then, have you? Our Carol.'

'You won't miss her.'

'Won't I?'

'It's just for tonight,' he said, faking cheer. 'I'll bring her back to you.'

'And if she don't want bringing back? What if she's had enough of her lot and wants yours? What'll you do then?' Nedra sighed. 'You old fool.'

Then they heard Carol's step, above them.

'Mind how you go with her, Mac, won't you?'

'Right,' Carol said, ready in the doorway – fragrant and tuttied and scant-frocked. 'I'll be back late.'

'You off to town with him?' Nedra said.

'I am.'

'You going like that?'

'I am.' Carol was soap-scrubbed, gift-ribboned: looking cleaner and younger than she had in years. Tarted-up all modern, almost the spit of their Jan. Posed pigeon-toed and taller in her bridal heels, like new.

'. . .Aye, well. I shan't worry,' Nedra said to her knife. 'Ta-ra, love. Be good.'

Mac said ta-ra for Carol – for Carol to leave half-dressed and painted, with bright wet lipstick of a colour never mind shade so queer and new that Nedra didn't know its name. But then Carol shouted ta-ra herself from the hall and Nedra found herself knifeless and looming from the other end, a step out of the kitchen, stricken with hope. A hope that this would be it; that Carol would elope, like her other daughter, Eunice, and then all the hurt would be Nedra's alone to churn. But the thought resurfaced of Jan conceived in Carol's sin. But whether Jan was Sefton's too and not just born of his forgiveness, who could know? And what could not be known had no business being said. As Carol left with Mac it was as if the decades could be picked off like a final scab. All so that her daughterinlaw at forty-three might spend a night on the town and catch her death. He came for Carol in an oxblood tie, smart shoes; his hollow cheeks razored, his eyes blue – not clear, not young. He'd washed his car since the afternoon. Once they left she had hobbled to the frontroom window to see. Standing in the presence of none. Jan and Kelly out. Gene and Joey out, already forgetting their mam's trouble. Nedra was left impossibly alone for the first time in the house at weekend of an evening in the quiet. Without hectic distraction with only that baby above her and the tightness in her spreading. Without Linda behind the shared wall for comfort. With nobody to brew up for. No kiddies to chase in or out. None mithering to be mothered. Nowt to feed, wash or mend. Nedra felt no Dodds men's eyes but the Devil's. No saints' hands but the clock's.

Then she heard a cry –

but when she went upstairs numb with dread she found the black baby asleep, only it was too late; the cry was jailed inside her skull –

along with the tightness.

O Mary, Queen of Mercy, I have committed grievous sin in thought in word and deed

And with this she began to take on new shape and backed from the room and warped and wobbled at the top of the stairs, her landing a brown tunnel with only daylight from the frontdoor glass shining up and the door itself unseen but its light striking the carpet and cutting the stairs.

Then she heard the front door being tested and opened:

'Missus Dodds. . .? Nedra? Is they anybody in?'

While Nedra fussed, Father Culler said: 'Be a sin to waste the last drop on me hand.'

Over the sink she upped the finished brandy bottle onto cotton wool and sat with him at the table to unwrap her soaked teatowel and dab his torn hand.

'Bastard dog wants putting down. Must have rabies.' He chuckled this but his teeth were whistling as she turned his palm.

Her fingers, shaking. 'You'll need to get this seen to, Father.'

'You've had plenty practice over the years on flesh and garment, let's not forget.'

'Jim used to say I could've been a cutman at Belle Vue. I made me own recipes to stop swell and bleeding. Never had a neat stitch, mind. Plus, this is your writing hand.'

While his voice was warm, he was shaking with her. He curled her fingers with his other hand and patted them. 'Say it turns out not so well; I'll see that you're forgiven.'

'Don't, Father. You'll make me laugh.'

His still-thick hair went in silver waves, eccentric on a hot day, longer on top in a reverse tonsure and damp above his temples now with brandy-heat and suffering. 'Can remember Missus Stone telling us what a grand job you did hemming Susie-Ann's First Communion dress. How *is* that girl? She behaving herself?'

'We've not had Susie-Ann round today.'

He looked at her cold stove. 'And where's your Carol?'

'Out like the rest.'

He looked at her while the dog bite bled.

Nedra kept his elbow on the table like they were about to arm wrestle – his black sleeve rolled high. 'Father, why would he *go* for you? Just can't understand it. Snowy's never gone for anybody. Not from being a pup.'

Red water trickled down his forearm. 'That little lad set him on me.'

Nedra paused cleaning the bite. Then kept on.

'The mad dog only let go to chase its little master once he ran away.' Father Culler's ageing face became unkind.

'We'll get this sorted out, Father. I'm sorry. Gene'll bring him home before dark.'

He craned to read the clock for her.

'Father, I. . .'

'You wish to say a quick prayer for Linda? We knew that woman wasn't well.'

'She wasn't, no.'

'With her Joe inside – we can't be having two young tearaways, can we? And what with Gene Harvey thieving again, I'm told.'

'*Gene?* No.'

'While Linda gets herself right, Rose Hill might be best thing for her two – after *this*. No wonder Joey goes funny when you take him to church. Lad fears for his soul and he should.' And then Father flinched and sucked his teeth and said: 'Mind, Nedra. Mind.'

Nedra pressed more carefully. 'Little Joey's afraid, Father.'

'It's a blessing to find fear in today's young.'

'It's fear of *you*, Father. Isn't it? I mean, for Joey.'

He looked at her, without curiosity, as the clock ticked away his blood. He chuckled. 'That'll be the day.'

But Nedra knew.

Missus Dodds?

Yes, love?

How long is jail?

Depends how bad you've been, Joey.

Missus Dodds?

Yes, love?

How long is Hell?

Forever and ever, Joey.

Longer than jail?

Much longer. Much.

But Nedra knew. She would flood Hell with tears and sail them all up to Heaven. Their souls would dance on endless Manchester clouds.

Father Culler saw her cringing with him, but for her it was the thing that was and wasn't pain since she'd done nowt to Joey that could make his white staffie bite her.

'You've been suffering yourself,' he said.

'I'm getting on, Father.'

The wounds open and clean.

'Pain of conscience afflicts the damned,' he said to his savaged hand or to hers. 'Pain of body afflicts those unwise enough to enter old age.'

Nedra smiled as she rose suddenly and left him to fetch her sewing kit from upstairs; but when she came back in he saw her wearing her chocolate suede hat and her ginger anorak over her housedress and necklaces.

'I'm off to find our Joey,' she said, her knees holding, her heart free – with her sins fitting her square shape just right. 'You'll have to go elsewhere, Father, for your stitches and supper.'

IT WAS STILL LIGHT on Monton Street; its sunned bricks smooth, bloody; its strip of sky thinner and bluer than the one over Wythie. The neighbourhood was gridded and treeless, black and white, loud of a Saturday. Open doors, open windows, weekend music. Stuff Jan knew. From an entry corner she watched three taxis make drop-offs – each gone before the next arrived with another feller in a panel tracksuit over skivvies. They entered the last house; two came out quick – with their hair, their walks, like dressed-down punk rockers. One clocked Jan staring and crossed over. He had a bandy run.

'Ay, smiler.' Up close he passed into the entry after showing her his empty mouth. It smelled like Bully's blanket. He shrank into the distance and she looked until Loose Ends' 'Hangin' on a String' seeped across the road and turned her head.

Jan stepped out and knocked on the end terrace.

A white girl her own age with a coldsore and a crimped mane answered the door and showed her in. This girl had blinked slowly at her first. A bloke's ratty maroon jumper hid her hands, her shape, before Jan followed her chalk-stick legs sleepwalking up the stairs. The narrow dosshouse went tall. Old air choked with mildew, hash and curry. Slug trails glittered to a leak above where plaster and paper had curled into scraped butter. Through a hole Jan spied between floorboards: a bright inch. . . then eclipsed. She looked down in time to dodge a tipped Henry Hoover. His nose strangling the antique banisters like a python.

Speech-bubbled felt-tipped slogans and quotations followed them along the next flock wall between Care Bears and unicorns:

Here the girl stopped on the second small landing and pointed her to an open room. The girl and the house under the same spell: this weird dream-quiet, full of listening.

Jan peered into a cramped red office. 'You Rodney Westlake?'

'Come in, love.'

From inside she saw a long black-and-tan cowboy rifle propped against the radiator under the window. 'What's that for?'

'Any aggro.' The man stopped reading a salmon newspaper to glance at her, then the gun; then he smoothed the page on his desk. 'See, I don't do too well with me mitts.' He started the next column. 'It got used that thing for scaring birds off the airport runway. You know them pigeons what get stuck in the plane engines? Stops nice girls like you from going on their holidays. You see, that thing keeps the birds safe, the planes safe, the nice girls safe.' He squinted up again. 'You ever been on a plane, love?'

'Never.'

'I'm gunna go Concorde soon. Am saving up. And no fucking feathers'll stop *me*.'

His beard had colour but he had shoulder-length grey curls. Thin on top. Thin thatched arms with blurry tattoos. Braces and a string vest. He could've been forty or seventy. Extending his desk were turrets of half-squished cardboard boxes for foreign radio sets.

Behind her now Jan heard the other girl's tread. The girl stooped, came nearer, then froze. She had blistered lips, not a coldsore: 'Puss, puss. . . puss, puss. . .'

There was a squeak, maybe another floorboard.

'Is she all there?' Jan said.

'She used to be,' he said.

The girl blinked slowly and left.

The man thumbed a razorblade off the desk and scored-out a salmon square and put it to one side. Jan stood close, aware of the silence, reading upside down.

'They wanna do a Manchester edition of this,' he said, creasing the paper and putting it to one side. 'See, it's just London classifieds. Southern nutters tryna flog their southern shite. Your uncle Mac brung it up with him from London.'

Jan heard another squeak and crouched. A sleepy grey kitten wobbled across a folded blanket under the desk. A saucer and milk bottle to one side.

'Some skaghead give it us that puss-puss instead of cash. I'm too soft, me. I've always been soft. It's why the cheeky cunts call me *Madam*. But see I can't sell it round here, can I? Might pop an ad in the *M.E.N.*: *Give Wee Moggie The Good Life. No Time Wasters.*'

Jan scooped up the kitten.

'The girls wanna name it Duchess but I think it's a tom.'

Jan let it walk off her hands. Jan felt fingers in her hair, on the back of her neck. She stiffened but didn't flinch – just held the chrome-tube leg of his chair. 'D'you know me brother Kell?'

'Aye, I do, love. Your uncle's been bringing him round. But *me and you*'ve met before.'

'When?'

'You won't remember. Too young.'

'Me dad's funeral.'

'Well done. Can you remember?'

'No.'

'Plenty rum buggers what was after *your* daddy and granddad. Funny they all got pipped to the post by some kids driving home for Christmas pissed. Bet that's how your nana tells it, anyroad.'

Jan rose and shed his hand but it caught her waist and she looked to check if the door was still open and it was. Some bloke and another girl, crossing on the stairs, gone. 'Is me uncle *here*?' she said.

'He's out tonight, romancing. Wouldn't say who. Become quite the gentleman, has Mac. Mind you, he always had soul. Be what made him such a terror in his day. See, when he were working for Jim Dodds, he could go overboard, I mean, with his mitts, just so he'd have more to repent. Your dad were a bit like that. Worse at times. But, see, as big as Sefton was, he wasn't Big Mac.'

The window was shut – the street's music cut to a throb. Jan saw another taxi go, heard the kitten mewing, then life enter and leave other rooms: shoe steps and voices and skin and mattress springs and short-breaths behind walls.

Rodney touched her arse so lightly Jan had to pull away to be sure. Slowly she reversed to the door then shut it then came back. This time he didn't touch her at all, looking up at her harder instead, working her out. His face began to blur and she stared through the window again, its light not faint or even turning but better than the room's. She said: 'The neighbours never kick off?'

'We get cabs pulling up right through the week. We get allsorts, they come and go, wanting a wrap or a screw. You might have your grasses in Wythie but no one speaks to the dibble round here. You see, we hate *them* more than we hate each other. . . Now. What's it you're after?'

'Kelly.'

'You any better than him at maths, love?'

'Y'what?'

'If I get two fifty's worth of skag *laid on* and I keep fifty for me health, how much do I need to sell the two on for, not to recoup, but to double me dosh?'

'Enough to fly Concorde.'

He smiled. 'You know what your brother's getting mixed up in? That what you're here about?'

'I don't want our Kell robbing for you. This big job. This jewellers. Just tell him to fuck off next time he's round. He's shit anyway. He's not meant for it. I'm telling you. He'd wind up getting you all pinched.'

'That right?' Again he travelled her with care, her top half now, and with more interest, of which she was glad, since she was on. His movements clipped and exact. 'I said to Mac: Dodds men are bad luck.' Then Jan found herself weighing his left hand, inspecting a stump fingertip glazed smooth, nail-less and black. 'Your old man done this, you know, love. In the Silver Birch, after shall we call it a minor disagreement. Done it with Jim's lighter.'

He led her across the landing and opened a dusty blue boxroom with a camper bed on which the girl with blistered lips had curled asleep. Her fists against her knees. Right ear pressed into a skinned pillow. A topless bloke came out of the blind corner and sat at her feet, hunching over to toke from a glass pipe. He fogged the room lazily, stroking the girl foot to thigh. She didn't shift but her expressions phased, her face more awake in dreams than out. Jan saw them: read her passions, clear behind the clouds.

Rodney shut them in, ready to try another bed but Jan knew none was free. He laughed on her a little and his breath was sour but no more than most lads. He had her pressed against the graffitied flock wallpaper. When he turned her face to lick her cheek, it was then she saw him –

Kell, stood in the office doorway, aiming the rifle at them from his waist.

'Now, now,' Rodney said, seeing with her, their faces pressed together. Kell with the rifle still and still to move. 'That's *our kid*.'

'I'm telling you now, son. Don't get daft.'

Rodney left Jan at the wall and went to him and held the rifle with him and they didn't fight for it just held it between them two-handed and once they had it pointed high enough Rodney twisted and pushed and Kell having been twisted and pushed onto the landing he looked round to catch himself – grabbed for the banister rail – but Rodney twisted and pushed again and then the rifle was his and he kicked for Kell but Kell was already tumbling down the stairs. Her brother rounded the corner and the thud-thud moved the house. Brought some girls out of their rooms, to gawp at Jan, who was glued to the wall and trying to scream; those dopey girls posed there on the landing, beneath its swinging paper-globe lamp.

Rodney kept the rifle trained down the empty stairs. 'Speak now, Kelly Dodds of Wythenshawe, if you're still with us!'

Kell's groans and coughs came up the stairs.

When she heard them she shouted him but couldn't move off the wall.

Rodney looked at her then, his shoulders rounded. He seemed to be itching all over. 'It's not loaded.' He propped it in the corner, then he wiped his tattoos, wiping his arms like there were spiders climbing them. In outstaring him Jan freed her body inchmeal. He returned with the rifle to his office, muttering, 'Puss, puss. . . puss, puss. . .'

Zuley came home and found them on the top deck outside her Hulme flat. Jan saw she had her keys in her fist. A crop jacket blew open and her belted frock had fluttered along the Crescent's curve of dinted door after door – white stairwells spaced like knuckles jointing an endless finger. Kell wouldn't let her near. Jan tried to read them: wordless traffic between their features, their bodies. Zuley stared up at him until he turned and lent on the low concrete wall and dangled his fringe over the courtyard, the Crescents vast and hushed. Across Jan saw ring-rows of glittering windows winding like gold sand through ears of Blackpool shells. Jan saw below: a car battered to tin foil, a thirsty green, heaped binbags hugging pillars and trees. Empties skittling everywhere. She smelled bonfire on the breeze. There was another car, of black bones, and Jan closed her eyes and saw sheets of flame.

Zuley took her by the hand and led her inside.

And Kell followed.

Her place smelled like blown candles and Impulse body spray. The telly had been left on with the sound right up: *Tales of the Unexpected*'s end credits' girl was dancing in blood silhouette. The front room was plastic furniture, stacked records, a rainbow of drying clothes. Jan sat on a pink woolly mammoth rug glittering with cat hairs which itched her legs and palms. From it she unearthed one can of Lustrasilk and a lost spliff.

Kell perched, bruised and cracked, behind her on the settee arm, and stared down the hanging mirror. He tried to peel his T-shirt but the pain restricted him and his patience went before he got it over his elbows. Jan jumped up to help. A look kept her away. He heel-kicked the settee, split his T-shirt neck and Hulked off the rags. Jan went from wanting to cry to wanting to laugh. Burning liquid sloshed unspilt behind her face while he rolled his right shoulder, drew his left hand around his ribs and winced.

'Our kid.' Kell spoke to her in the mirror. 'Put some tunes on.'

'Wish I lived round here,' Jan said.

'You don't get to sleep much,' Zuley said bringing her a brew. 'Never know what you're missing.' The way she sniffed steam from the cup made it seem special. Like potion to fix everything. As good as her grin.

'What?' Jan said.

'Your hair. Looks dead nice like that. Wish I could towel-dry mine.'

Before she could say *But I love your hair*, or even just *Ta*, Zuley had passed her to give a cold can of Red Stripe to Kell which he tossed into the settee dip. Jan switched off the telly and reburied the spliff in the rug. Took her brew over to the records sandwiched in a wheelie cabinet with the player and speakers above.

'How bad's it look?' Kell said to Zuley –

who got behind him to kneel sideways on the seat cushion to explore him. To touch red black blue, first softly with her nails and then again, rolling the cold beer can over each colour.

Jan watched this ritual awhile, then pulled music, then held up the sleeves, making sure to cover the names. 'Oi, Kell, what's this?'

'Cymande, "The Message".'

'And this?'

'Skull Snaps.'

She played the next one first.

He nodded to it, soothed. '. . .Wait. Sandy Kerr, "Thug Rock".'

Jan cupped her brew with her back to them and just listened.

'We've danced to this in Legend,' Zuley said.

'Night we met.'

'Nice try, love. You met us in the Reno.'

'And I said to you then: don't get too romantic.'

Zuley opened the Red Stripe and drank. 'Am worried you've broke summat and you don't know it.'

'I know it.' And she gave him the can and he finished it in two.

'He fell down the stairs,' Jan said.

'Whose?'

'Uncle Mac's.'

Kell looked at her, wilted. 'Ask our kid why was she there.'

Zuley looked at him. 'Why were *you*? You stood me up!'

'. . .'

'Not cos you wanted this uncle and whoever to batter someone with you? Not to give you that dock-off gun he'd showed off to you the other day?'

Kell announced it: *'Patrick Somerville*. Teaching at Poundswick. His missus put his name in that book he give you.'

Jan twisted away again, saw the needle running out of record. 'I'm not telling you where he lives.'

'Don't you worry, our kid. I've put word out. We'll be on his door-step tomorrow.'

'You're being a right prick, Kell, you know that?' Zuley said.

'I know,' he said.

'How you getting Jan home?'

They talked at each other like this and Jan notched up the music and rummaged through more.

Polaroids slipped out of Terri Wells' 'I'll Be Around'.

A dozen showed them in this flat, in this room: against the wall, on the settee, over the rug. Taking turns with the camera.

disco-glitter eyeshade –
dancing legs parting
a frilly bra draped over her brother's ears, worn as headphones
a dark grinning cheek unscarred, blazing in the flash
dizzy angles made their bodies into mysteries
gave them fun-house proportions
the two of them stripped and shaped to each other
perfect somehow
for loving.
Jan left each Polaroid out to remind them.
Jan left, her brew untouched.

BEFORE THE FRENCH RESTAURANT, its hanging tasselled shades pouring dimmered light onto untranslated menus, where Carol and Mac would dine at the window table and both choose Tournedos Rossini (Carol choosing first) and Mac would point out for her over the road a King Street corner jewellers that he meant to rob the following week with her son and Rodney Westlake and God knew who else from the old days who could be found reasonably alive and local and out of Strangeways. Before this meal which was not unlike the Golden Garter specials, only dearer, the portions stingier, they went for a drink at the Midland. It was about to shut for a refurb. There she'd had him order her Buck's Fizz in a faded lounge of gilt edges and grand paintings. A pack of short businessmen, its youngest peacocked and lacquered, milled at the bar with six tall fragrant tarts in shoulder-padded frocks. Each gripped a plastic purse and a finished G & T, ready for a theatre show. Pinched toes and varicosed calves under fishnets; their weight shifting from hip to hip to ease boredom or pain. And all blinking attentively, clench-jawed, while the men prattled. Carol didn't recognise herself in these women at first with their wardrobes and hairdos. Her own do unbunned, misshaped and misstyled. In their presence she felt rusted and ancient and unfit to be out the house, amazed to be sitting neatly, sharing the same tired, magnificent room as these tired, magnificent girls; Mac content to drink Holsten Pils and watch her watch them, squinting at her across their booth with watery strain through that old speckled flesh like shaved granite. Handsome and stupid. A statue guardian too stubborn to fault and crumble. His was a fearful and dim devotion. That squint maddening in its tenderness – asking for her like the shattered mule asked for the rod.

'Another?' he said.

'Yeah, go on.'

Thank fuck she had on her daughter's perfume, a fake Fendi off Wythenshawe Market scenting her wrists and throat and pubic hair, the last squirt between her toes. Right before Mac had picked her up, Vern had appeared in the bathroom mirror beside her, wiry and pale, pretending to give himself a cut-throat shave with her toothbrush.

'Well?' she'd said.

Vern had parked her toothbrush behind his ear, taken Jan's shampoo bottle from between the slimed sink taps and pointed it at Carol like a tape recorder. 'Ms Lollobrigida. Vern Jenkins for *Vanity Fair*. Bogey claims that when it comes to sex appeal you make Marilyn Monroe look like Shirley Temple. Do you sympathise or would you like to press charges?' Then, in the mirror, Vern had backed up to admire her footwear and whistle 'Here Comes the Bride'.

She had kissed Vern ta-ra and breathed in his old-books smell, his useless cleverness and the rest: hopeless and daft, clinging to his forever-thirty years. She had let Vern's love sluice through their daughter's hair that spidered the clogged sink. His last joke delivered well. And her body's shadow, firmly reattached, following her again.

Vern had breathed her too, said she was smelling of spring woods. But an hour later she knew the cheap perfume hadn't taken, only curdled. Left a putrid rind across her pores. Carol knew this was a trick of light but couldn't help believing she smelled off. She only half-remembered what this was: *to care enough to care*. It was in her teeth and bottom ribs, a hunger-cramp, a pit of hope in her gut and between her legs.

And in the Midland were Mac's florid hands on the table for her to open and hold. His, like a retired boxer's or butcher's, swollen with talent, history and death. Carol wanted those true things inside her.

Trust his hands –

his squint.

The trendy tarts at the bar –

to resurrect her vanity.

Carol shredded a drink's serviette in her lap and wondered who could see her scalp sweat. That was until another tart arrived wearing Carol's lipstick shade; and as she joined the rest Carol smiled at her hard enough for her to notice and give a quick blank stare. In it was the hum of telepathy; an exchange of airs and sadness both women took to be funny.

'What's up?' Mac glanced round.

'Nowt' – Carol still smiling wide.

'You know her?' He looked again and a stocky ancient waiter in matching waistcoat and dickie bow brought Carol's first Buck's Fizz. Mac paid for each drink as it came. Like Sefton he seemed to carry no wallet just clipped banknotes. Mac produced them from a loose, taupe, double-breasted jacket; his gestures swift and careful and almost embarrassed which made the glary waiter more nervous – bowing his *thank you* after mouthing it.

When the waiter went Mac said to her: 'What my doing wrong?'

'No use asking me. Nedra's always said I make folk uncomfortable.'

Mac's hands closed huge as he carried them off the table to think about this, his squint sparkling. 'Aye, well, you can never tell what Carol Dodds's thinking.'

'If you wanna know just ask.'

'I know I'm best not knowing.'

Bloody ask and I'll tell you Mac I'm thinking about food about how I'm getting hungry but don't wanna eat and bloat up like a whale and have to take me kit off later and see meself through your eyes and I'm thinking how many glasses will allay me sad terror when you feel the weight I've put on as I take your lap and you compare me to what you saw and what you had more than eight years gone in your Minnie's bed with me husband Sefton hours' warm in his grave and I'm thinking what was I worth that night and what am I worth now to any man not least some shade of Dodds man and even though I'd had two kids by then and was never some ageless beauty like your Minnie and that even to a pining cuckold like you I wasn't worth a stolen fuck you having waited like a coward to fuck me only when I had twice been widowed with the first widowing of the heart and the second official but to me a footnote in a book nobody right-minded would ever read because let's not forget we're scum even to our own kin but let's not forget also that I had once been worth killing and burying a man over and it is this that has me thinking worth as in mine or female worth if you like isn't a currency that can be staked or disinherited like property or male pride and I'm thinking about whether you will want me after tonight which I know you will but what good is it to know until it's happened and I'm thinking maybe I'll get to keep me kit on although I don't deserve to but you might let me and if you don't it doesn't matter and if you do I will show you the lot just the same and I'm thinking about how I'll feel when you seep from me as my first living shag since, well, since you, and I'm thinking who I won't be tomorrow if you take me home empty of you instead of full because then I will be alone in a spring-cleaned ghostless house without answers for the living and without the dead to talk to and to talk for me and to heat and halve my half of the bed and I'm thinking how long Mac before I can taste your muck and the salt of its truth and have I remembered its taste wrong as brinier than Sefton's and Vern's now see I told you I was hungry and I'm thinking you have come back up North as pathetic and unmoored from reality as me and no matter what you think I never was no wife or mother I was just a whore princess and your Minnie a whore queen and as wicked as she was at least Minnie could not accept we were whores of men who would take our lives from us and live them for us in death like it were us women who had died and not them, and that has me thinking what might have been if you hadn't told her that we'd met at the Posthouse and what might have been if she hadn't brought Kelly to the library but you'd brung him instead as planned and what might your hand have done if it'd shaken Vern's that day and what did your hands do later after they buried him and have they forgotten where they buried him and tonight when you are buried in me and I beg you not to stop but to dig and dig till you remember and find him for me trapped under earth without flesh, my poor Vern having had his life stolen by us lot, will you tell me then where his broken bones lie?

Had Carol said some of this, or had she glanced instead at the woman with the matching shade and gone: 'See *her*? Like you she's thinking that I look *escaped*.'

Mac began to rotate to see the bar. He hadn't clocked that Carol was fishing.

Carol so wanted to see his hands. 'She's on the game, isn't she?'

Holding the table, he turned the rest of the way. 'They all are.'

'Any of them Rodney's?'

He shook his head. 'Too healthy.'

'Say hello to Rodney for us, won't you?'

'He's still got a scar your Sefton give him in the sixties.'

'What was that over? Your Minnie used to get her speed off him, didn't she?'

'Aye.'

'D'you know Rodney's youngest cousin was me first? Lee Westlake of Brownley Green. Used to go about in velvet and espadrilles. I was about our Jan's age. Took me to Rippleton Road when his mam went chip shop to fetch his tea. Put me in the washhouse and had me up against the slop stone. He couldn't get his drainpipes down they was that tight.'

'Dead now, Lee.'

'I'll never forget his face. Rodney though? Can just remember that reedy voice and them wandering mitts on Friday nights if he got you in a booth. Tried it on with me even after I got wed.'

'Then you know why Sefton scarred him.'

'I know it wasn't our Sefton, that. It was *you*.'

Mac held her in his squint, then finally he showed his hands.

She reached for and squeezed one and found out hers was clammy only by contrast and withdrew it. 'I need to go touch up me lippy.'

'You're fine,' he said, too tenderly for it to be true.

'Then I'll have another.'

He got her one; the twitchy waiter brought it; Mac seemed in no hurry to catch her up. 'We still scrub up well, don't we?'

'Even if you're getting on and I'm getting fat.'

Mac's cautious, rumbly laugh. 'We're not doing so bad.'

'Been losing me figure, I think, ever since I first got on the pill.'

'Sefton know you were on that?'

'Never asked, never had to lie to his mam.'

Mac let her giggle and drink.

Then she said: 'Remember the night your Minnie wet herself? We was watching the wrestling up at Belle Vue. D'you remember? Jim'd left Nedra at home like always but she didn't mind so much after Kelly was born since then she could be minding him. Anyway, Minnie got absolute blitzed and accused them Gorton lads at Beyer-Peacock of nicking her purse.'

'Her engagement ring.'

'That's right. She had you fighting one after another in the carpark. But then later we found it in Jim's Triumph. And this was dead funny to Minnie. It was like she was having a fit. She couldn't control it. Just laughed and laughed and then she pissed herself. I remember it running down her stockings. Ruined her fur. And she didn't care. She sat in his passenger seat pissing and cried laughing. Jim had to drag her out. Only time I ever saw him lose it with her. She had to hide from him behind you.'

'Minnie were pregnant again then.'

'What?'

'It always give her a weak bladder.'

'She lost them?'

'Each time.'

'Whose were they? D'you know? Was it Jim's?'

'Who cares? Not then. Not now.'

Carol was turning a lipsticked, empty glass: 'Aren't you good.'

Mac supped his lager; it'd gone flat. 'When we left. . . was there talk?'

'Gossip, you mean? Over Minnie and Jim?'

'About you and me.'

'You'd have to ask Nedra. Hope so. I'd gone deaf to all that by then. Ay, what time we on?' she said, collecting her bag off the seat.

'Booked the table for ha'past.'

Carol shuffled out the booth, graceless. 'Come on. We're late. Me stomach thinks me throat's cut. Finish that first. That's it. Big gulp.'

*

He lapped her in the French restaurant: sank four lagers and had half a bottle of red to himself. Carol was already drunk, her being so out of practice, and she liked the feeling of falling as much as she liked being out the house and if not free of ghosts then knowing that her ghosts were free from her. Seeing Mac trying to decode his first course (they'd chosen the same starter too, which turned out to be fish, not potato: 'Mind out for bones,' he'd winked) and seeing him this drunk and this old she recognised how easy it would really be to leave her life of sad perplexity and to love him; to shrug off all waking responsibilities she had foggily acquired, sustained or neglected and done so out of conceit or caprice; and she knew full well that tonight could damn her to satisfaction, could unmartyr her. She had no votive candle to burn, no true sacrifice to make. Her soul was worthless and as unlovable to the good and the living as her body. She belonged to monsters. She and Mac would be happy enough, together. To Carol this was true. But then she found her guilt raw again and from its meridian she could not feel herself let alone the guilt and this was the same mindless relief that she had known once before, on the Sunday in '69, when she had knelt to scrub Vern's blood off his doorstep. But as they ate and drank it was like she and Mac were dangling together over the Hellmouth and the fires below giving forth no light, just heat enough to free his hideous hands and her delicate feet from glaciation. Carol could cast him in but she would be lonely without her guilt. Without the lies and company of the lovesick gravedigger. All this shit came for the length of a thought quicker than a wine-gulp. Carol was dizzy now with the drink, when their second plates came identical.

'How's yours?' he said before she'd even taken a bite.

'Why?' she said. 'You wanna swap?'

'Aye. Yours is bigger.'

So, giggling they did.

'Must be costing you a bloody fortune to get us both merry in here.'

'Not that dear. Not after London.'

'What was London like?'

'Our Minnie took to it more than I did. We had us a flat in New Cross. Chaps I worked for, they had a club that did well. For a time. Same rubbish you get everywhere. Tell us about your baby grandson?'

'What's Kelly said?'

'Not even his name.'

Carol peered at the jewellers through the window. 'He was born in the house. He's never left the house. Neighbours know of course but nobody's grassed on us yet. Nedra's claiming that one.'

'How's she squaring it with her priest?'

'If Father starts asking questions Nedra's teeth start whistling and then she says it hurts too much to think about it. Then she'll feed him a second supper with a drop of that good stuff she hides under me sink.'

'Your Jan, though. Saw her briefly. Still a bloody kid herself. Not that you can always tell nowadays.'

'Sound like our Nedra.'

'How's your scran? Any good?'

'Dunno. Let me try yours. . . What d'you reckon?'

'Not too bad.'

'No,' she said. 'We've not done bad.'

'"Had Adam conquered the anguish of separation as a pure sacrifice of obedience to God, his reward would have been the pardon and reconciliation of Eve, together with her restoration to innocence." What do we reckon to that, love?'

'Sounds Mancunian.'

'Might just be how I read it.'

'Hmm.'

From the radiator Vern winged his book over Carol's bed. Its white pages fluttered like seraphim static in infinite motion with the book above her suspended without any sound or wind or shadow before descending quick and landing gently and open on her, drawing up her thighs.

Carol read the words again, to herself.

Vern said: 'To you that sounds Mancunian?'

Carol said: 'To me it sounds too sure of itself. So yeah.'

'Love you.'

'Come here and kiss me.'

'Sun's nearly up.'

'Then get a move on. Can leave this book out for our Nedra. We'll see what she makes of it.'

But always Vern's books flew away. . .

'Mac?' she said.

'What, Carol?'

'Who did we belong to? I get mixed up.'

She was matching his squint over the restaurant table. Both leaning in to catch whispers.

'Don't ask *me.*'

'Can't you remember?'

'Remember what?'

'And how many bloody jewellers you've robbed. . .'

They kept the table till closing after which Mac drove her drunk past Deansgate, past Castlefield, loosely following a Manchester of waterways and wreckage. He got them closer than roads and laws could: to the clogged black arteries which either fed or fled Pomona Strand. Here was their city's broken heart. It was a place invisible and unreachable to the waking and the living. To the winged worker-bees clubbing a kiss away. Town of a Friday night: dancing to the pulse of its mongrel blood. Unreal then to find a Manchester at its centre so quiet it was theirs. Mac parked up for confession. Food and fresh air sobered them somewhat. But at intervals Carol would burst into cackles at Minnie's engagement ring.

Its heavy rock weightless on her finger.

They walked linked along the Irwell towpath under a milk light from stretches of dying hooded lamps. Between them there was just Carol's lit cig to trust, like they were following a faerie into the city's untethered shadow, a shadow teeming and festering, alive and vacated, dank and sweet. In it and through it they could see but did not need to see. The water began to purl. It sent unnatural things past them – bobbing items exposed in absurd and bloated dimension, shared like dirty secrets.

'But why didn't you take your Kelly away then, that weekend we all went up Saddleworth Moor?'

'The bleeding moors.' Carol was sleepy and wet. Slurring: 'You buried him on the bleeding moors. It was your idea?'

'It was your *chance*. To take your Kelly and go somewhere.'

'That moon,' she said.

'Carol. . .? You cold? Want this?' – offering his jacket.

'Nedra told us she'd hated the cottage. . .' Mac was rubbing her gooseflesh anyway; he could cover most of her thigh with one hand; dozily she kept trying to strip off for him. '. . .She said your Minnie did some of the cooking.'

'Carol.'

'Where did you put him?'

'Can't remember now.'

'Then it doesn't matter.'

'. . .We came off the Isle of Skye road. Carried him to the old quarry. Above Alderman. Way off the track. Near where them big rocks join over the valley. Dug him a deep hole somewhere.'

In Jim's Triumph she had returned pregnant, with Vern folded in the boot, wearing a coal sack over his smashed head. She had brought young Kelly home only to be left there with him, with the front door unlocked like an insult. She had opened it onto her street, her overgrown privets, her neighbours' kids playing kurby with no coats on in October. They had looked at her in her faded polka-dot frock, asked her if Kelly was back, if he could play out. And she had smiled at them and told them yes he was, and yes he could, until came time for his dinner.

*

But when Mac rocked drunk on the towpath, preparing to recall his dinner, Carol, drunker, hurled herself blind at his size and felt next to no resistance – only heard the air fill the vacant space like a sea replacing a sunken continent. And alone she could return to his car ready to drive it to Vern's place of rest only she hadn't the keys and couldn't drive and so would sleep it off instead.

But when Carol looked she found Mac stood exactly where her hands and the lamplight had lost him. She had hyaline wings buzzing weightless on her back. And she was talking to him over the sound. About allsorts. Listing the things in this world that the two of them redeemed might still come to know. And together they could return to his car and sleep it off instead.

But when Carol woke in Mac's car, her seat tipped, she found him gone. She felt a surge of blood and scrabbled to catch the door handle and fell out in a tangle of limbs and undone clothes. She palmed chilly earth, wet grass stained yellow by the car's overhead bulb. Her old black cotton briefs were hooped tight round her left wrist and thumb. Her first thought was *Did he not watch me sleep*? Had any of her Dodds men ever stayed up watching her sleep? Carol shed what was left to shed to run. And when she reached the river she lowered herself in, sitting for a moment in the plants on the worn bank with her bare legs missing in the dingy water. Its temperature amazing. From there she stared out at the river judging how far from her he had got. Then she slipped into the Irwell and went under – even her arms which were pointed straight up. She had forgotten to close her mouth and she kicked to the surface and choked up the terrible water. When she was certain the cold wouldn't kill her she began to paddle further out. Mac was hidden, vertical, only a glittering crown of hair bobbing gently. She reached it and tore out some with her teeth. Then she emptied her chest to hug him, below. She was content sightless underwater and by touch she found his huge hand and held it like a child at Sharston Baths. The river had taken one of his shoes. She came up, drawing breath to the sound of crazed splashing behind her, off the bank, a bloody rescue. There was a light too and a big dog's spaced barks. Her eyes burned with icy grit and slime and when she touched him again he started to sink lower, having given her some peace in the end, having taken nowt but their meals to his grave.

LEE SULLIVAN, BARRY REED, Simon and Ronald Ashworth, all of Fellside Road, all skinny St Jude Junior School lads whom Nedra knew, having fetched and fed them, and more than once out of charity, just as she'd fetched and fed their mams and dads back when they too could be found laid like beached seals for games played across the bubbled tarmacs that marooned these flat-roof estate pubs.

This was a good hour before night with May's Saturday sun bloody. It bled the vast empty carpark into a lake of fire with the Red Beret its centre island. Nedra stuck to the long shadows of the short brick walls but felt her feet burning.

'Iya, Missus Dodds,' Lee went.

They had a ragged porridge-coloured blanket on which they'd pitched a ring of plastic soldiers and robots.

'Lee, have you seen Joey Harvey?'

'Little Joey can't play with us,' Simon went.

'He nicks the marbles,' Ronald went.

'He hides them round your house,' Barry went.

'I'll put *you* lot in the mad house if you keep this up. Now, have none of yous seen little Joey Harvey since teatime?'

They squinted up at her, propped on their elbows, their fists bursting with marbles. 'No, Missus Dodds. . .' they said.

Her brass necklaces had gone quiet when she stopped to ask after him and she began to worry them just to hear them, as if to convince herself she was still moving, towards Joey.

'. . .No, but we seen his dog, didn't we?' Marbles flushed onto the blanket but as they scattered Simon cupped and herded them in one motion and hid them under his gliding hand. 'We fed it Golden Wonders and then he ran into the pub. And then they put him out and give him a drink of water, and then he run off down there. . .'

All four pointing into the sun till she looked.

'Keep away from that dog, you hear me?' Her walking stick's shadow striped their backs. 'God bless.'

To enter the pub Nedra parted a great wedge of lasses cackling under its covered porch. Painted like, smelling like, drinking like the Devil's daughters – as did her Jan and now her Carol too. Their colourful brassieres: peeking out of electric blouses and shiny wrong-sized frocks. Workshy buxom Sabrinas, the lot, giving her slitted glares of amusement. Abdicated mams; defeated wives; the fickle unwed; faithless elders and keen apprentices; some circuitously blood-related but most complexly estranged from hopeless husbands not-quite replaced or divorced; almost all Sharston Industrial Estate girls at one time or another; all keyed up for incitement. Assuming Nedra's arrival a harbinger of scandal they intuited a stir. Nedra knew each face, it weathered by age or sin or trial or ruin or just the slow daily quarry slide of garden disappointments. Nedra knew the names of the child-less whom she rarely directly encountered. Nedra knew who'd been sacked from the cake factory when and after Carol was there.

'Evening, love,' they said, their red cheeks high and red mouths lines.

They followed her in quick.

Inside Nedra was greeted by wet coughs and chatter and lazy whorls of smoke. She waited for summat to happen while cooking in her hat and coat. For older men, tashed and stooled, to put down their drinks and tilt with their good ears. For older women to hold their elbows, letting their fag ash grow. For history to suffocate the stale-sweet air and make them kneel to it with her. But in her local Nedra felt obscene and forgotten. Like the victim of a life-long joke or conspiracy – one that mattered no more and had been abandoned before its punchline or exposure. Nedra could not keep the past in proportion or the present at bay and there she began nodding at them sadly and slowly.

As she nudged forward then crossed the bar none made way. But a fat pony-tailed barman about forty-odd mirrored her coming, and asked: 'What can we get you, love?'

She tried to de-age his features to work out his name or his street but couldn't. He held the bartop, stamped his hand in drinkspill, leaning over to hear her but no words came. A wet gold sovereign ring instead of a wedding band. It reminded her of Father Culler's signet, which he'd always remove before Mass so as not to upset the prelates.

Nedra swivelled carefully and looked. The myrtle seats, the red Victorian carpet, the walls with dead footballers framed. Pints foaming over distorting glass. Ice cubes and mouths and blinking game machines. Such separate things got up to move about, then join up, smudging into queer patterns. It was like she had opened a wardrobe and freed a giant stripy moth – its wings batting on her face.

These punters were foreign to her. Even ones she thought she knew, and she thought knew her, were strangers.

'Her youngest lad's not come home,' she told them.

'Who's this?' the barman said.

She turned again. 'Little Joey. We need to be out if we're gunna find him before dark.'

'His mam's in here?'

'Noooo. They took Linda away.'

'Oh, I see. That's a shame.' He served three fussy drinks to two gormless fellers and took pound coins from them and tossed their coins into music by cupping and uncupping his fist. He said: 'Right, love. Where was we? How about a drink a water for now? Have a sit down there.'

'I've not set foot in a pub since my Jim and my Sefton was taken.'

'Well, there's another shame, love.'

'Good customers, they was, my Dodds men. Once upon a time. They made sure they wasn't no trouble round here, and if they was trouble then it got sorted quick.'

'Oh aye?'

'You must tell them all now to come out and look for little Joey.'

'Tell who?'

'All *them*.'

'Ee-ah, love. Have a drink of water. Can have summat else on me if you're feeling better after that.'

'They don't know me, do they?'

'Should they?' But he looked past her and then stood taller, broader, and went: 'Bev Willows, did you forget you're barred?'

'That were *last* week. Oi, I know her. That's Missus Dodds.'

'Well, can you see to her and I'll see about letting you drink in here next week?'

'*You* can't wait that long to see me. Don't tell lies.'

'How the bloody hell does *she* know someone like you?'

'I'm here,' Nedra said. 'You don't have to talk like I'm not.'

Bev Willows crushed next to her in a sleeveless frock: 'What's the matter, love? Won't he serve you either?' – a voice blasting her and pumping smoke. Nedra's hair moved. Bev, a shameless slattern about Carol's age, cow-lashed, pancake complexion worse in this stained light. A lapsed Catholic and recurrent homewrecker who had chased after Linda's husband years ago, no doubt after his big win at Belle Vue. That was before Joey was even thought of, before Gene could crawl. But Nedra remembered. It had all come out.

'Little Joey Harvey's gone missing,' she said.

'Right.' Bev dropped her lit fag in somebody's drink. 'Come on, old girl. Let's have a look.' She led her back onto the carpark, the lingering sun a burst yolk and the sky still blood.

Nedra watched Bev watching the kiddies play.

'Pink as piglets and twice as wiffy. Mind, our Alice and your Jan were like that. Still bloody thick as thieves, aren't they? How's Jan doing with her babba, anyway?'

From her ginger anorak Nedra unslipped the photo she'd taken of Joey, lined up smart at the privets with the rest of her flock, for the Pope's visit. She showed it to Bev, careful not to crease it. 'He's six so a bit bigger now but not much.'

'Faces on this lot. Bunch of smacked arses.'

'They'd just seen Linda getting upset.'

'Linda Harvey? Sounds about right.' Bev glanced up and whistled like a bloke with her ringless fingers.

Nedra hunched at the sound.

Lee, Barry, Simon and Ronald came over.

With the photo: 'You know who this little lad is here?'

They nodded.

'Well go tell every kid round here Missus Dodds wants him. And when you find him tell him he's not in for it, but *you* will be if you don't bring him back. First one to come back with him gets a quid.'

'Show us the quid,' they said.

'Cheeky buggers. Get going!'

Nedra called after them: 'But make sure you're in before dark. I'll be round tomorrow to ask your mams. And if you see Gene, you tell him to get home and all.'

'Yes, Missus Dodds!' they said. And were gone.

Bev laughed and linked her and they crossed Simonsway to try Painswick Park. Both women sturdy – shaped and scaled almost the same but with very different walks.

'Has Joey ever run off before?'

'His brother has. Once.'

'What happened?'

'I found him.'

News that Joey was missing had already reached the park but nobody had seen him or knew where he could be.

As they arrived Kevin and Roger were leaving with a frog in a bucket.

'Oi, leave her in the pond,' Bev told them. 'It's where she lives.'

They turned to Nedra for final word, then raced to the pond edge and tipped the bucket together.

Kevin told them Gene had gone to Rodger's Park to see if Joey was hiding there.

'What about Susie-Ann?' Nedra asked.

'She's in,' Kevin said.

'Good.'

'Her mam's not letting her out now. Since she cut all her hair off.'

Bev scoffed. 'Who's this? Who's her mam. . .?'

But they kept on.

Nedra began to twitter her prayers.

Bev's touch: kind, scalding. 'Don't be worried, love. He'll be right. you'll see. Think you can walk it or do you wanna get home and wait?'

'I'm gunna go have a look.'

'Aye. We'll do that. No harm in looking, is there? Ay, how's your Carol? Never see her now.'

'Carol's in town tonight.'

'Don't tell us she's finally found herself a feller?'

' . . .'

'Good on her. God help him.'

'Our Sefton's long gone.'

'Never knew Sefton. Remember your Jim, though.'

'You didn't know our Jim. You weren't old enough.'

'Too bloody right I weren't! I were *fourteen, yeah? March fourteenth, nineteen-fifty-seven.* I can remember it dead well cos it were the day that plane missed Ringway and crashed on Shadow Moss Road. Landed right on a house over there. You remember? Killed a wife and tot.'

'I knew her,' Nedra said.

'Me mam did and all. He was a bad bugger, your Jim. I wasn't the only one he had his way with, you know?'

'. . .I've stopped going visiting their graves. I've been too ashamed.'

'Listen, love. Me husband was a bastard too. Got more kids now. Lives down south. Doing well and all. Heard he bought his new missus a car. *And I still love him.* Pray to Our Lady we never see him again. Cos I know I'd only forgive him.'

O Mother of Perpetual Help

'What do they say about me these days?'

'Who?' Nedra said.

'Oh, the Knickers of Virtue, Mother Mary and the Holy Caboose? I used to go Mass with some of your lot, you know? Before I had our Alice. I were wed up at the one in Edgeley. What's it called. . . *Our Lady and the Apostles.*'

'They say that you like a drink.'

'That all?'

'That you bring fellers home and don't care whose. That they feel for your Alice.'

'Can tell them our Alice gets looked after, and she gets taught more wisdom than their daughters put together. I'd sooner she be *trouble* than troubled, if you get me drift. Ay, are they all still knitting cardis for Father Culler? *I'm* the best seamstress round here, me. No, I am. Owt you ever want altering – just give us a ring, love. Now, there's an idea. Could stitch them all nooses, couldn't we, for Lent?'

'What's the bloody matter with you?'

'Just imagine what they say about your lot? Birth not been registered? They'll shop you for that, you know. Can't hide it in the house forever.'

'Go back to the pub. I'll find Joey meself.'

'Oi, I know they all call me round here. *Fat slag. Sucks right down to the priest's collar*. They've gotta blame someone for their lot, haven't they? It's flattering to think at forty-two I'm still summat to worry about. But listen. You wanna know what they have to say about Missus Dodds?'

'Go on.'

'They say nowt, love. No bugger round here knows you. They don't remember. That's why you're lucky.'

Trees curtained proud homes and junk gardens from one to next. Rodger's Park presided; the breeze dropped after bringing to her its wild scent. She turned her weighted neck. Through fence bars foamed cow parsley and milkmaids and floating crosshatches of evening insects.

Park-side on Firbank Road was without voices and traffic. Nedra tried not to see this as an augury – telling herself it was not unnatural when in the deserted street they passed suckered arrows and a plastic sword; hula-hoops and a torn football like a peeled satsuma. Skriking magpies began to travel the trees that greened the red houses, reporting their coming. Wings casting brief shadows on the cracked pavement. A white longish feather floated down and kissed a broken flagstone that waited raised before them and Nedra reached this flagstone a step first and it see-sawed loose. But she didn't trip.

Bev Willows tightened their link, her expression pinched now and held forward avoiding hers.

They heard summat ahead.

Nedra's stick fell away. It clacked on the pavement like another discarded toy. She led now, shuffling along at a good clip.

In the middle of the road, they were. A circle of young kiddies. Crushed up and faced in. They stood squirming and pushing and Nedra's eyes sought little Joey Harvey among them since her eyes could recognise these moving heads: shorn skulls and bowl cuts and twin pigtails. Nedra could name each one in his or her handmedown swaps but needed to wait another split-second for some heads to turn. She could extract the right cry or salty playing-out smell that she caught ripe and from above, when soaping Joey's tiny hands at the sink, him unable to withstand the tickles of her nailbrush.

'Get out of it,' Nedra told them. 'Let's see.'

Their sweaty heads spun to her. The group was Joeyless and not speaking not breathing not picking noses, scabs or coldsores. Nedra saw them all ageing as quickly as they parted for her.

His white staffie lay with its chin on the road. Against tarmac the fur shone bright and smooth. There was no blood she could see but the muscled domes of its limbs were too still for sleep. Only its brow was wrinkled; the eyes under rucks of skin and fur-tuff like button-less threads. 'Look, Missus Dodds. Look. Snowy's dead.'

'Joey's not dead,' she twittered at the children and Bev shushed her gently.

'There's the moon!' said Sally Morrison, a dungareed girl without top teeth, craning and twisting to show it her bleeding elbows.

Between the Heavenlit trees the streetlamps came on like altar candles as the rest of the kiddies stood around, church-quiet, illu-mined, stumped by drab mysteries: perhaps aware of their obscure intimations and unable to shake them or make any use or sense of them.

Soon the fidgeting bug spread – once each clocked they'd been snuck up on by the dark.

Nedra turned away from her flock to cuff her vision clear and dry. She saw flying insects assume Our Lady's glow. A quickening struck her. It ran her heavy old bones and lightened them. It hit her middle. Nedra felt unsteady for a moment only and in no danger of pain. Though Bev Willows rushed to hug her. Bev's arms were not *through* hers but *around*, supporting her.

'Steady, love. Steady.'

'. . .Can't breathe.'

'Is it your chest?'

'No; it's bloody you!'

She saw Bev the Incorrigible: a giving, wayward, smutty, sobered-up woman, afraid to smile at her. Bev let go.

But the children lingered –

itching to scatter

waiting for her word.

Nedra gave it and they took off in all directions to fly their streets on true feathered wings that carried them home in a few blurred beats.

'What's his name again?'

'Joey.'

'No, the other one. His brother.'

'Gene.'

Bev called out for him while Nedra plugged her ears.

It took one try for Gene to call back.

In near dark, spit glistened enough on Bev's teeth to show she was smiling at her now.

They stopped and waited in the long field grass that prickled their calves, Bev's without tights, in what felt like no-place, edged in by great dimming tree trunks and fern meadow. A dense weave that bobbed and twitched with foraging sprites.

Sprinting Gene found her.

He leaned back to halt before he ran through her. It happened too fast for her to panic that he wouldn't stop in time.

He was panting a little, his shoulders moving up and down. His polo smelled rank hot. He was Jan's age and heads taller than both women but had only begun filling out and in the gloom he seemed less grown, more precious to her. She saw him better here than in her kitchen. Here: without looks to read into or stages to ignore. It was like she'd cut him out of a picture that her mind had taken, of a young man costumed in his dad's Man City shirt – cadging a meal at her table and never leaving a crumb on his plate, to sit there invisible almost in her full house, stealing glances at Jan with a hankie balled inside his pocket sleeve in case of nosebleeds. But Nedra had to glue this cut-out of a young man and fold him into natural dark to see the lad he still was.

Together they searched under a final sky. It could deceive them. Tint and un-detail all they could see so that the small park expanded with the night. Right above their heads tiny bats flitted in drunk silhouette. Nedra grew afraid but when Bev noticed her fear, Bev warned the bats like husbands – not to get tangled in her hair.

'Joey. Joey!'

'JOEY!'

'He's here,' Nedra said. 'Have a listen.'

They leaned into the nervous quiet and heard him shift over crackly twigs.

'This your den and that, love?' Bev said.

'. . .'

'Wouldn't happen to have any ciggies in there, would you?'

'. . .No,' Joey said ruefully.

Bev laughed and its boom woke things in the trees and sent them scurrying. Bits of stick and bark rained and Nedra held her hat.

'Can you reach down there?' she asked Bev.

'Can I fuck; no. I'd never get up again, me.'

Nedra shut one eye and then gripped one knee to bend down and peer into the deep narrow furrow roofed with skinned branches that let the moon in. There was a soily beard of exposed roots; green lush bracken of fading lambent.

'Out you come,' she said.

Gene pinned the branches to help Joey crawl out.

Nedra put him on her hip. He had no more weight to him than when he was four. His arms, his legs were gritty and cold. Their hollowness unbearable. He wanted feeding up till she didn't dare lift him.

'Ay, where's your specs?' Nedra said.

'They broke,' Joey said, and she could hear tears mulching his voice.

'We'll get them fettled, love.'

'You're best taking him to mine.' Bev's fingers: combing soil out of his hair.

'Why?' said Gene.

'I'm only the next street. Plus, I've got me a pack of Lamberts in the back of a drawer. Unless our Alice has took them.'

'He's hungry,' Nedra said. 'You got food in?'

'Have you not seen size of this arse?'

'Where do you wanna go, mate?' Gene asked him.

'I've a dog, you know?' Bev said.

'Have you?' Joey said.

'Aye. He's a staffie. And he eats arses.'

Joey giggled, in spite of the tears.

Nedra jogged him higher on her hip, leaving the park with the twilight gone. 'Take no notice, Joey.'

'Well, what d'you eat?' Bev said.

'Go on,' Nedra said. 'Tell Missus Willows what you eat.'

'Butties.'

Bev touched his head. 'You'll be alright eating your butties at our house – so long as you're sitting.'

Nedra said to him: 'You'll manage that now, no bother. Won't you, love?'

Joey pressed his arms around her, pressed his face into her coat. She held him close and closer so he didn't bounce with her step.

SEE, JAN KNEW THINGS.

How to climb the ashbins to use the side drain-brackets to reach the top window to squeeze headlong into Kell's room or what was. How to accept that he had moved out a year ago and returned only to pay them four days' visit and move on. How to save him (for now) from Strangeways (again) before he left her (behind). How to save him from that room, too, his old room, having given it away somehow, maybe partly to keep him gone. How now she'd be stuck, unliving, with two mad mothers who could only grow madder and sadder and fatter without him. How to end up the same: growing out and in, not up. Learning how to overburden the dead with love.

But Jan knew how many dead men they needed. How many living. Not just how many for *her* house, but for next door's too, and for their street, and for the next and the next – counting up for all of Wythenshawe's daughters beached between Southern Cemetery and Styal Women's Prison.

See, Jan knew things after bussing it home solo from town under no penance. Sitting bottom-deck, middle-bench, by herself of a Saturday night, her temple to the window – its cold vibrations making her skull hum – her reflection in it like wet sand. Admiring herself so forlorn, so sullied. Till the bus swerved for summat and divided her from the glass. Then she saw a smeared face whole with teased petal hair bobbing like an evil flower. Jan was escaping town just as town began to buzz. From the streets she'd seen a hymenoptera of

Manchester clubbers descend as one noise. Arrive on defiant wings. Piss-tinted, bow-shaped wings. Each buzzing set drawn to, drawing from, the same blood-rap. The night whispered it to her at first, then played it louder as more wings joined it while she trudged to Oxford Road from Hulme Crescents to catch her bus – only unfolding her arms to stop it before it missed her, and only then remembering she'd no spends left or clipper card rides. But when the bus stopped, just for her, outside Rotters, she got on and let the pale old whiskered driver look at her through his Mike Read goggle-specs. Then without looking he nodded her on but she stayed there seconds, waiting in stubborn hazy disbelief as if trying to summon abuse from one of them. Because every encounter demanded grief – grief-giving, grief-taking – even if right then she was fit for neither. But the doors clapped shut and the bus pulled away before she was ready, and Jan caught herself and swung to her seat without really taking in the other riders. A half-dozen shapes foreign and female, sitting separate and silent. Not one dickhead lad got on to mither her. A posse dressed like DeBarge, but with lours and brawl scars, got on at Withington. They skenned her together – chins north, nostrils flaring – then went and sat upstairs. They could smell she was on. Jan sniffed her wrist. Her perfume had blunted but she was still good for it. She still smelled like a brothel as her Nana Dodds would say if ever Jan had to slip out through the kitchen to collect her shoes from under the table after the kiddies had gone home. *Like a bloody brothel. . . Jan Dodds, your dad would've shown you the door! / He don't have to, Nana; I've seen it.* That night Jan had smelled the inside of a brothel. She sniffed her wrist again. She didn't.

See, Jan knew things. Even if she knew them as loneliness unshared. She knew them with a clarity that would be clouded and confabulated by time and talk and was wise enough not to tell herself she knew them. She knew them only as summat inside her that had neither chance of nor purpose in making the journey into words. And before the bus got her home this knowing had made her tired and gluey; voided her like a sick bug that had you spewing long after there was nowt left to bring up. She had filled Kell's old room with summat big enough to keep him out and tiny enough to take up the whole house.

The window looked open a crack, maybe the width of a draught; it was tough to tell from below in the dark. It felt like robbing her own house. Both feet off the ground – a buzz of fear rid her head of owt else. But the higher she climbed the less afraid she got until the knowing began to return, first to her guts and toes; her jelly thighs and ticking temples; her shoulderblades winged but too weak to fly her to the sill.

With the backdoor bolted and the front deadlocked, Jan had known full well no one was there before hissing her invective into the letterbox. Call it speaking ill of the dead since there was more chance of her mam and nana having snuffed it than having bobbed out.

Mid-climb, a toe's purchase on the drainpipe bracket, her hair in her eyes from the first-storey wind, Jan took a moment to conjure her mam stiff and blue in that spring-shot bed; her nana keeled over with the hob on – a burn stain scarring the bottom of an empty pan. Jan had it like summat off *Tales of the Unexpected*, which she'd caught the end of in Zuley's flat. Cursed antiques and clueless husbands trying to off these posh clever bints. Always naff by the end, the final twist, even if it gave her dreams.

She longed for someone to see her hanging starfish from the drainpipe to the window, and she imagined him. A clueless husband.

So, she started singing Terri Wells' 'I'll Be Around', her voice feathery and cute, to make her wish true:

Ooooh noooo. . .

'I'll give you summat to sing about, girl.'

The next-door voice came from under her – not the Harveys' side, but the Galvins'. Jan left a gap between her notes and heard Mr Galvin panting drunk behind the partition fence. The breeze went. She tried looking. Not even a figure. But his fag smoke reached her like pigeon post:

'What the bleeding hell you up to, girl?'

. . .Baaaabyyy. . .

'Can see all that and Heaven too from down here, you know?' He shone a torch at her. Jan blinked at it blinded and screamed and held on and kept singing to stave off fear.

'. . .'

'What you been out doing, ay? Messing about with wog lads, I bet.'

' . . .'

'If the wife saw this she'd have a mind to ring dibble.'

' . . .'

Jan knew Mrs Galvin had left him nine month after he got laid off from the Kellogg's plant. After he'd been barred from the Happy Man for spending his temper with his giro, which cost Mrs Galvin her credit at the newsagents. Jan had heard Nana Dodds and Linda Harvey gossip about paschal candles going missing from church when it looked like the Galvins couldn't pay the bills. Jan had also heard round school that Mr Galvin had a daughter from his previous missus. The daughter lived somewhere hot like Spain or Italy. She was summat: an actress or singer. Her picture had been in a magazine. . .

Jan belted Terri at him now, and all the while she felt him looking up her, choking on her, listening.

His torch went out. Other lights came on. Jan sang to her street. She knuckled the bricks trying to hook and widen the window gap; then she trapped the strings of her wrist on the inner sill, clasping most of her weight. The outersill splintered. She climbed in before it broke off, pulling the curtain down with her. As she fell in headlong she shinned the radiator and it gonged. She stayed prayer-knelt with her face a crushed can in the warm carpet, with her soiled skirt flipped over her waist.

The thing was there with her, skriking in the gloom.

Jan pushed off the carpet and swinging hair tunnelled around her face. She was in too much pain to decide where it hurt. And she was confused by the delicate patter of black blood. She cupped her wet chin and explored the hole her tooth had pierced in her lower lip. Then she laughed on the floor so hard it couldn't escape. Laughter fluttered round her ribcage, pecking at her heart. It tired her of course, and she was hurting, bone and muscle, but at least afterwards she felt stoned. And had the sun-faded moon-grey carpet looking like the time Alice had sneezed on the bathroom mirror while brushing her teeth. Jan plugged her gob with a stinking flannel from a floor-stack of hand-medown rags and quilts and bibs and nappies and baby-grows that gulped the room. Then Jan got up to turn on the light and admire her art.

Her laugh had stopped the thing skriking.

Jan leaned over the cot but the stench made her pull back. The thing rolled its eyes to study her with its arms already out, signing for her in tight circles – skin stretched over bunflesh.

Jan pulled out her flannel dyed and wringing.

Jan baptised it he –

as her blood fell a kiss

and bruises began to swell over her forehead, on her wrist and legs.

She gathered him up funny in his cot-blanket, then took him downstairs to find him a name.

ACKNOWLEDGEMENTS

Oxblood was not a swift or easy book to write. It swallowed almost eight years of my life. I am grateful it found a sympathetic, clear-sighted and super-suasory literary agent in Isobel Dixon. Cheers, also, to my editor, Allegra Le Fanu, whose bravery and quality of attention further strengthened the book and its chances of finding a few readers. Thanks to Sarah Ruddick, Charlotte Norman and Elisabeth Denison for their patience and diligence, and everyone else at Bloomsbury, especially Greg Heinimann and Terry Lee.

Cheers to my missus, Alex Ivey, for everything; our daughter; and my Mancunian mates and family, particularly my parents for supplying me with stories and their proud mongrel blood. A special thanks must go to *Oxblood*'s earliest readers – especially Georgie Codd, Laura Joyce, Tom Avery and Andrew Cowan – for their encouragement; my Norwich mates and colleagues, especially Nathan Ashman and Henry Sutton; Laurie Kirkham, for being able to see around blind corners and through netted windows into the hearts of the Dodds women (and explaining my book to me); Arts Council England, for awarding me a grant in support of *Oxblood*; and the student cohorts on the UEA Crime Fiction MA, who gamely suffered more than half a decade of annual pub readings from an '*Oxblood*-in-progress'.

In loving memory of Edna Benn of Wythenshawe, and her third son, Ronald.

A NOTE ON THE TYPE

The text of this book is set in Minion, a digital typeface designed by Robert Slimbach in 1990 for Adobe Systems. The name comes from the traditional naming system for type sizes, in which minion is between nonpareil and brevier. It is inspired by late Renaissance-era type.